Janet Lynn, Beware yet of darkness. enjoy the story. Wade Lij...

MW01689032

VAMPIRE ROADTRIP

DOREEN SERRANO
WADE LIJEWSKI

Copyright © 2011 by Doreen Serrano and Wade Lijewski
ISBN: 978-0-9841074-6-9
0-9841074-6-0

Published by JimSam Inc.
P.O. Box 265
Lobelville, TN 37097

www.JimSamInc.com

All rights reserved. No part of this book may be reproduced or transmitted in any form or by any means, both known and unknown electronic or mechanical, including photocopying, recording, or by any information storage and retrieval system, without express written permission from the Publisher, with the exception of brief quotes used in connection with reviews written specially for any written, audio or visual media.

This book is a work of fiction. So many of the names, characters, places, and incidents are products of the authors' imaginations or are used fictitiously and are not to be construed as real. Any resemblance to actual events, locations, organizations, or persons, living or dead, is entirely coincidental – except where the people being made part of this book are aware they have been included and they have gladly given permission for that inclusion.

1st printing 2011
Printed in U.S.A.

Editing by Kristen Lijewski
Cover design by Jeff Couturier
Photograph of Doreen Serrano by Michael Norris

Dedication

To my loving wife Kristen and my children Vinnie, Piper, and Memphis, who inspire me each and every day.

I'd also like to thank my parents, Tom and Marlene Lijewski; *all* family members and friends, including but not limited to: Eight Ball Grifter (John Mizga, Matt Theodoroff, and Dylan Ratzsch); the Deans (Morgan May Moallemian and Eric Hardy); Doug and Leslie Ditto; Sam Ditto; Jacob Ditto; and every band and every person who has contributed to life's experience.

~ Wade Lijewski

- Mom and Tom for remaining my baseline for morality.
- The sisters who complete my Circle: Colleen and Julie, whose roles in this lifetime have given me the strength, power, and courage I would not have had as only one.
- My son, Michael, for proving to me that I've done something right in this world.
- My son, Alex, whose story ideas and creativity can be seen throughout every page of this book.
- To Rob, my One and Only Devil Forever – for bringing me back to life and showing me that some risks, no matter the outcome, are worth it.
- And to my Dad, who taught me to love thunderstorms, to find the positive in a negative world and to always trust myself despite all else. No matter where you may be in the Universe at any given moment, you will always be with me because your real home is in my Soul.

~ Doreen Serrano

Chapter I

Central Park had always been Dominic's favorite place to reflect. It was where he went when he needed to get away from the pack and when he needed to remember the man he once was. He appreciated his place in the family and he took his role as leader seriously but there were parts of Dominic none of them knew; he wanted to keep it that way. Memories of his mortality were still branded in his brain, giving him hope. Immortality had been a generous gift but no one had warned him of the true price. There had been no manual to which to refer and no frequently asked questions website to introduce him to life without a soul.

Dominic had wanted it all. It had always seemed a cruel joke from God, the greatest prankster of all, that human life expectancy wouldn't allow him to even make a dent in his ambitions. The time and youth allotted to humans were a teaser – a cheap appetizer thrown on their table as a reminder of what they could never really have. Because of the fleeting qualities, time and youth could never quite fill the needs of the mortals, so they were always left hungry and wanting for more. Suppressing his appetite as a vampire had been far more satisfying than quenching his thirsts as a human had been.

Dominic had always seen the universe as being filled with an infinite amount of flavors and he wanted to taste them all. He wanted to be an icon in the entertainment industry. He had longed for an important career that meant something, one that made an important mark on the world. He had yearned for a normal, quiet life with a wife and children and a beautiful home of his own. He had wanted to save the world. Suffering from frustration at his five meager senses and his short life span, he had always searched for ways to extend his time. In the end, he knew that was the reason that he hadn't resisted the bite that turned him.

Walking through the dark fog that seemed to envelop the entire park, Dominic remembered the hungry fangs and how they had penetrated his most prominent vein. Rather than defending himself and trying to protect his vulnerable throat, he had tipped his head back to expose it further. Every day for the last twenty years, he had wondered if the acceptance of his turning had been his most unforgivable act of all in the eyes of his first maker. Dropping himself onto the closest bench, he rested his back against the hard wood and narrowed his ice blue eyes as the fog surrounded him.

The simple gesture worked as an on switch that activated his night vision, one of the many gifts given him upon the change. It allowed him to see all of the things that, as a human, he was unable to see; he shook his head slowly, snickering at the irony of it all. The gifts that seemed so special to him in the beginning gradually lost their novelty over the years especially after the realization that his existence had been far better when he couldn't see the world for what it was. Dominic had come to realize humans were fortunate indeed for their inability to see the universe in all of its ugliness and torment.

He was antsy but couldn't quite figure out from where it was coming. Rising from the bench, he continued his walk through the park as memories from that night played out in his head over and over again. The bite, though painful and terrifying, had begun the metamorphosis that he could neither fight, nor resist. He remembered the blackness that had taken over and how it had been followed by a deep fear that he had been stricken with blindness and paralysis for the rest of his days. Pulling his jacket tighter against his body, he tried to shake away the memories as he concentrated instead on the sounds of the park – squirrels scurrying to their trees as nuts fell from their filled jaws; debris as it was pulled along by the wind until a stronger gust swallowed it entirely; discarded cans scraping across the gravel; humans giggling in the distance.

He enjoyed the noises and wanted nothing more than to bask in their presence but was not strong enough to fight the memories when they demanded his attention. Reluctantly, he found himself tuning out the sounds from his present as he was transported to that moment of his past, which he couldn't make himself forget, no matter how hard he tried. He had awakened from his death to a burning passion he had never before known with the realization that his new existence had no end and the discovery that he could hear the thoughts of those who passed him on the street.... It hadn't taken long to find his new life had certain advantages over his human life. He had been blessed with a different kind of awareness, one he thought he wanted until he actually possessed it. God's once questionable existence became undisputed knowledge so there was no longer the requisite that he rely on blind faith. Sadly, he had come to realize that faith was necessary to the continuance of his spirit; without it his soul was painfully malnourished and impossible to sustain.

Dominic had been pulled into some inner circle of understanding, becoming privy to God's design for the universe and His penchant for soul play. He learned that reincarnations were designed to accommodate the humans' continued existence and he had reeled from the truth of their existence. God's plan had been well thought out and perfectly executed; Dominic felt a certain privilege to have been blessed with the knowledge. It wasn't until years after his turning that Dominic fully understood what it meant for him.

When time no longer mattered and loss of life was no longer a possibility, appreciation was a gift of the past. Because of their knowledge of a beginning and an end, the humans lived with constant gratitude they didn't even realize they possessed. Upon his discovery that happiness actually thrived upon the limitations of the human experience, Dominic had finally been forced to admit to himself that his gifts had actually been curses. He had fallen into despair upon learning the painful truth; by throwing his gift of mortality back into God's face, he had committed the worst of all possible sins. He knew he had been deemed the villain in the Good Book of the believers and it was an agonizing conflict for him.

His only choice had been to find some way to continue without falling victim to the debilitating resentment that had overtaken him. He had refused to allow the darkness to take him entirely because he knew once he surrendered himself to it, he would be sacrificing the last vestiges of his humanity. He had forced himself to welcome the new awareness and to view it as a gift but had to work hard not to share it with the wickedness that repeatedly whispered out his name, lest he allow himself to become the monster that the bite had intended.

He had found ways to utilize his amplified senses and his bestowed abilities of mind-speak and thought reading only for the good of man, refusing steadfastly to share his abilities with the darkness that beckoned him. It was a difficult, almost painful balance to maintain but there was never another choice for him. Dominic had vowed to destroy himself before allowing innocent blood to stain his hands. He would do what was necessary to survive but would not do so at the expense of the humans who were truly pure of heart.

With the help of the music that had always guided him and the ability to feed off only the evildoers, he had been able to survive in his new role for the past twenty years. His family had been handpicked from a pool of other like-minded vampires who believed as he did. Existence hadn't been easy for any of them because the balance had to be maintained at all times and it was not easy to keep. He had learned to live with the painful irony that his new life could never be as enjoyable as his old one because the promise of a forever ruined it for him.

Dominic slowed his pace at the first signs of need. His cravings had become stronger and more powerful than they had been in the past and he began to worry that his plan had a flaw he hadn't foreseen. There was a new desperation attached to his hunger that had begun to cause an imbalance within and he knew what would happen if he tried to ignore it. Never wanting to reach the point where the need took over, he and his pack had devised a schedule to include the routine thievery of human souls.

Killing wasn't truly a necessity as it was not the mortals' life source that filled the void. It was the taste of their souls and their essence that sustained Dominic and his pack, drawing through small increments of blood. However, deep-seated greed and gluttony teased them to drink long after the need had passed and his pack had discovered it foolish to believe they could stop after only a few drops. It was who they were, what they had become, and after learning the hard way that they were incapable of stopping themselves once the feeding had begun, they had put into play a new course of action that would keep them alive without forcing them to succumb to the darkness.

Dominic's knees began to weaken and his palms were saturated with nervous sweat as he flinched against an ache. Suppressing his instincts was uncomfortable and it stirred up an eerie sensation inside to which he referred as his 'dark passenger.' Having recently started justifying to himself that it might be acceptable to harm an innocent here and there, Dominic had begun to face the reality he had hoped would never come. The evil he had ingested had begun to turn on him. If he did not find another way, and soon, a choice would have to be made – continued survival as a monster or the sacrifice of his own existence altogether.

He knew the answer was somehow related to music – the one force that had not lost its power and that still held the ability to tame the savage beasts within that worked so hard to take over. It had been another of God's gifts that the humans had not come to fully realize and it had the power to inspire untapped abilities in both species. It was their catharsis and their anchor and Dominic knew if he could figure out how to use it to its fullest potential, it was quite possibly their salvation.

His hunger needed to be satisfied immediately and Dominic sniffed the air like a dog. His blue eyes shone as they darted around in every direction in search of something, anything that might hold him over until he'd arrived as his intended destination. A nearby squirrel scrunched its nose rhythmically as it analyzed the acorn in its paws and Dominic's eyes narrowed as he manipulated its thought waves. Commanding the rodent to stay put, he crept up slowly behind it and readied his built-in arsenal: his nails and his teeth.

The squirrel became alerted to his presence right before Dominic's mini blades pierced its side with brutal force. With his sharpened nails, he pulled the small, meaty snack to his mouth like a shish-ka-bob and tried to feel grateful for the two bites the tiny creature offered. Still hungry, he continued to trudge along, depressed that the excitement had been so short-lived. Breathing a sigh of relief after turning the corner, he made his way to the end of Central Park and gazed upon the apartment complex before him. Looking at the address that stared back at him, he felt the excited palpitations that always preceded a kill.

Dominic jumped over the low gate that enclosed the courtyard of the complex and followed the short path that led to the side of the building, remaining hidden in the shadows the whole way there. Passing a first floor window, he looked in and saw the woman – the wife, the victim of domestic violence and the mother who was too afraid of her own punishment to protect her child. She had a black eye and swollen cheeks that were stained with tears. As she leaned over the oven to put a meat-loaf inside, Dominic accidentally tripped over an empty beer can and it ricocheted off the nearby gate. He ducked down just in time for her to turn his way and remained below window level the rest of his way around the corner. Part of him wanted to kill her for her cowardice but it was the part that Dominic refused to nourish yet.

The next window belonged to the nine-year-old boy he had seen in the newspaper. His room was painted two different shades of blue, as though the painter had changed his mind halfway through. Model airplanes hung from invisible string in each of the corners and their display boasted endless hours of time and concentration. The window was opened a crack and a dim light escaped from the closet, making the boy visible in an otherwise darkened room.

Dressed in Spiderman pajamas, he sat Indian style on the floor with his head rested back against the wall. His thumb was lost inside his mouth and he sucked away at it with desperation, as though he had reverted to his infant years when life had been safer. He seemed oblivious to the world around him and the sight made Dominic hate the father who had forced him into such a pathetic state of regression. He fantasized also about making dessert of the judge who had sent the boy back home as well as the social workers who slept peacefully in their own beds. When he tapped lightly on the glass, the boy showed no response so Dominic continued on to the next window in search of dinner and justice in one sitting. The hairs standing up on the back of his neck told him he had found his prey and he remained as quiet as possible as he peeked inside.

"You."

The angry whisper inside of his head only added to the rage he already felt rising within. He pulled his head out of view and held it firmly against the wall as he worked to reel in the emotions before they could cause him to make a mistake.

"Charles Mahoney."

Dominic spit the words out like they were a bad taste. He had seen the monster's name and face in an article at the previous day's 'first wake' and there had been no doubt in his mind where he would go to dine. A school janitor, Charles Mahoney had been accused of molesting eleven boys between classes and during after school activities. Though he had lost his job and had his son removed from his custody, something had gone awry in the state's case and because of their errors, the boy was returned to a father who was willing to hurt him and a mother who was unwilling, or unable, to put herself in harm's way to protect him.

Lounging comfortably on his rumpled bed, the pervert faced Dominic with closed eyes. He napped peacefully while his wife despaired over meatloaf in the kitchen and his son sat catatonic in the next bedroom, ruined in all the ways that mattered. Charles Mahoney deserved a slow and painful exit from the world and Dominic felt no guilt for ridding the world of the sleazy pedophile. He did harbor some concern, however, that the man's wickedness would infect him upon the bite and that by absorbing the monster, he himself would become monstrous.

Dominic tried to embrace his role as Bible antagonist as he pulled open the window and squeezed himself in quietly beneath the glass without disturbing light or sound. He tried not to gag on the heavy stench of beer, smoke and sweat that assaulted him and he had to stop himself more than once from pouncing on the man without fanfare. Charles Mahoney deserved to experience the same fear and pain that he had brought down upon his family.

The bedroom was cluttered with empty beer cans while a pack's worth of butts overflowed from an ashtray next to him. Dominic looked with disgust at the child molester, propped up comfortably against the pillows, snoring soundly; he made a beeline for the sleeping sloth, too excited to draw out the moment any longer. Dominic pressed a hand tightly over the man's mouth and utilized enough force to keep him pinned to his pillow despite the struggle. Filled with satisfaction, he watched in delight as the pedophile's eyes flew open in shock and he greeted him with a blade-toothed smile. He saw the plea, the fear... the submission in his eyes and felt a sense of justice in the tingling of his own fingertips.

Dominic cocked his head to the side and studied Charles Mahoney with interest as he listened to the screams inside the man's head. He could feel the desperation in his victim's incessant squirming but he felt not an ounce of pity for his terror. God had gifted Charles with humanity and he had made of himself a monster. For that alone he deserved to die.

"How terrifying this must be for you," Dominic said gently, shaking his head with feigned sympathy. "I mean, to realize that hell has come for you personally."

Charles screamed into his hand and the vibration tickled Dominic's palm, causing him to laugh louder and press down harder. Tipping his head to the right, he cherished the taunting for all it was worth as it recharged his energy and made him feel alive again. Though he enjoyed the rush completely and would have loved to continue it all night, he was mindful about the child and woman so close by. They didn't deserve any more trauma.

His original plan had not been to kill the man in his own home but instead to lure him out into the streets and hunt him down, a game he and his pack enjoyed playing on special occasions. Dominic had deemed the molester worthy of such a treat but the only opportunity that presented itself was in the here and now so he took it. Aware that he did not have the luxury of time, he pulled his hand from the man's mouth and drew a shush finger to his lips. From the horrified expression on the face of his prey, Dominic knew his transformation must have taken over completely and that Charles was no longer looking into the eyes of an intruder but instead, staring into the eyes of the creature the intruder had become.

"Sssshh," he whispered soothingly. "You don't want to scare your family, do you, Charles?"

Charles shook his head back and forth. His ragged clothing and unshaven face made him seem older and more fragile than he really was but he didn't put up as much of a fight as Dominic expected. It seemed as though he somehow knew that resistance would be futile.

"What do you want?" he cried. "I have money!"

"Do I look like I want money?" Dominic laughed.

Charles tried to make him comfortable with a smile but it came as more of a grimace. Lacking an appropriate amount of teeth and sincerity, Dominic found it disturbing on a strange level.

"Well then, what do you want?"

"Your remorse."

"Okay, okay! You got it!," Charles surrendered. "But what am I remorseful for?"

"You see?" Dominic asked, shaking his head in disappointment. "It doesn't work that way, Charles. You cannot vow remorse for something when you don't even know what that something is. Kind of defeats the purpose, you know what I mean?"

"I'm sure whatever you think I've done is good enough reason!" he groveled.

Dominic laughed heartily.

"It's that easy, huh?" he asked. "It's that easy to accept that you've done something heinous enough to warrant this kind of punishment?"

Before letting him answer, Dominic clamped a hand over the molester's mouth again but this time, he used the silence to do more than just frighten him. With the long, thin blade that was once a right pinky nail, he sliced along the crooked crease above the man's eyebrows and it created a glistening line of blood from one side of his forehead to the other. Along with another muffled scream came a generous rush of tears and more fruitless struggling.

"What's the matter?" Dominic asked with sarcasm. "Did that hurt?"

Charles nodded violently as he tried to speak through the hand silencing him. Although Dominic heard the prayers inside of Charles' head and knew exactly what he was saying, he was having too much fun playing along.

"What?" Dominic asked, cupping an ear with his free hand. "I can't hear you."

He was rewarded with more tears and more muffled screams to which he simply rolled his eyes and covered a yawn. Plucking a piece of hair from the pedophile's head, he pulled it into his line of vision and started examining it, just for fun.

"I'll make you a deal," he said to his victim.

Charles nodded and blinked repeatedly as the tears ran off his cheeks and onto his neck.

"I'll take my hand off and let you speak if you promise not to call attention to yourself," Dominic bargained. "You wouldn't want to chance bringing harm to your family now, would you?"

The man shook his head to signify his obedience and Dominic fulfilled his promise to remove his hand. Glaring down into the cowardly eyes, he fought the urge to literally wipe the mouth right off Mahoney's face but out loud, he praised him.

"Good boy," he encouraged, rising to his full height. Knowing the pedophile would be unable to uphold his end of the deal, he walked over to the bedroom door and locked it.

Just one more night, Dominic thought. *One more night of horror and then perhaps your young boy will have a chance at life; despite his unfortunate role as the devil's spawn.*

"What are you doing?" Charles called out.

"Ssssh," Dominic scolded. "You're not following the rules."

"I'm sorry," he apologized sheepishly.

Pulling a lighter from his jacket pocket, Dominic lit the cigarette that he had stashed behind his ear and then threw a smile and a wink to his restless host.

"What are you doing?" Charles asked again, his voice shaking with the pending tears. From murmurs of apologies to unrestrained sobs, the sight and sound made Dominic sick. He found it insulting to them both that the vile man die with such a lack of dignity and he watched with amusement as the pervert discreetly eyed the rifle perched against the closet wall.

"You wanna go for it?" Dominic taunted. "Think you can make it?"

Charles stared back, silent but open-mouthed.

"What are you?" he finally asked.

In quiet response, Dominic flipped down the light switch on the wall beside him and waited for his eyes to adjust to the darkness. He didn't turn on his night vision because he wanted everything about the moment to be natural and authentic. An aromatherapy candle, though failing miserably in its task to combat the stench, flickered softly from the dresser, setting the right mood and intimacy he desired for his part in ending a life. He walked back to the bed and eased himself into the seat beside Charles

"What are YOU?" he finally answered, disgust interwoven in each word. "That's the real question."

"N-no," Charles started to stutter and point.

He looked on in horror at Dominic's growing fangs and stared at the drool that dripped from them and the eyes that shone back from the darkness. Eyeing the sharpened blades that had replaced his nails and taking note of the rage that had replaced civility, he continued.

"I m-mean... you're a monster; a real monster."

"I'm not the monster, Charles," Dominic defended. "You're the monster!"

With incisors that reached his chin and lips that had been pulled into a ferocious snarl, Dominic walked quickly toward him and punched a bladed fist directly into Charles' stomach. Still inside of him, he leaned over his face and smiled as he took a long drag of his cigarette with his free hand. After blowing out a stream of smoke, he put out the remainder of the butt on Charles' forehead and stared with interest into his dilating pupils. He had always enjoyed staring into their eyes and watching as their pointless lives drifted past him on their way to hell.

Charles opened his mouth and made a weak attempt to scream but nothing came out, the agony of disembowelment apparently too painful to allow creation of any sound. Dominic twisted the hand that was still jammed inside the molester and watched closely as the sporadic writhing and wriggling began to cease. He could smell the fear that still clung to Charles' life source as it looked for a new home to invade.

It had always been the seconds just before and just after a kill that had been the most intense for Dominic. There was a silence in those moments so filled with screaming significance that it was almost deafening. Dominic pulled his hand out of Charles' abdomen and shook the blood off his nails and onto the corpse. He lowered his mouth to the thick, red nectar that had drawn him there to begin with but felt a blanket of disgust cover him. He despised having to feed off such filth but had no other choice but to drink in the dirty and undeserving criminal who had brought nothing but harm to those he was supposed to take care of.

As the last drop of life evacuated Charles' body, Dominic could hear the nervous thoughts from the boy on the other side of the wall. He seemed to somehow know that a life-changing event had just touched him. Dominic hoped his anxiety would turn to a sense of freedom that the man who had abused him would no longer have the power to do it again. He could not tell if the boy had heard the muzzled screams or if his father's ghost had somehow passed him by as he sat on his cold and lonely spot on the floor of his bedroom. Before exiting the home and hearing the high-pitched screams in his wake, Dominic bowed his head against the thin wall that separated them.

"That one was for you, kid," he whispered.

Sirens wailed from the distance and Dominic saw a crowd had gathered at the next corner. Making his way toward them, he smelled the smoke and descended the curb to head for the growing audience. Distracted, he didn't hear the oncoming ambulance that seemed to appear from out of nowhere and he jumped out of the way, his right boot landing in a dirty puddle. Cursing silently, he crossed the road to find out what was going on.

By the time he made it to the corner, the crowd had multiplied and the smoldering fire had become visible. Though contained by firefighters at the scene, the damage had evidently already been done. Dominic heard the murmurs of grief and shock that rippled through the crowd and learned from their chatter of the tragedy that had occurred. The humans were mourning a firefighter who had died of smoke inhalation after having saved a mother and her baby from what would have been an agonizing death. From his angle at the corner, Dominic watched their bowed heads and, from their collective thoughts, listened to their silent prayers. Though the hero had been a stranger to most of them, they cried for his family and for his loss, their faces aimed downward and unmoving. He couldn't yet see the fallen firefighter but knew he must be lying on the ground amidst the human circle.

Dominic walked toward them slowly, wishing he had arrived earlier when he may have been able to help, feeling self-pity for his inability to make a difference. He passed the crowd quietly but allowed himself a sideways glance, just in time to see paramedics lift a white sheet over the man's pale and lifeless face. As though theme music had been provided by some unseen universal orchestra, he heard a hypnotic melody that made him want to put a hand to his forehead in salute. An emotion-provoking version of "Amazing Grace" played through bagpipes somewhere in the shadows to his left and Dominic could picture the musicians in their signature skirts, their instruments producing a beautiful melody that seemed befitting for the departure of a man who had selflessly dedicated his life to making the world a better place.

It should have been me.

He continued walking as he headed toward a more desolate area of the massive park but found himself unable to resist glancing over his shoulder just one more time. Noticing the sheet covered everything but for soot-covered boots, Dominic wondered if the man had a wife who would have to rush out in the middle of the night to identify him. He tried to utilize his abilities to see who the fireman had left behind but found he was unable to read the thoughts of the dead man whose soul and energy had already been transferred to places unknown. Dominic envied him his end, wishing he too could meet the day where his own soul would travel to its next intended destination.

Female voices pulled him from his reverie and he looked up in time to see three pretty young women were about to pass him. Their clothes said they had just gotten off work at the local strip joint at the south side of the park and their loud laughter and staggering walks said they had decided not to wait to get home before cracking open the liquor. They teased one another playfully as they poked fun at the evening's customers but Dominic heard the truth of their realities whispered in their thoughts. They were neither content nor happy and he had to force himself to turn away from them, feigning a lack of interest.

He knew from experience that many of them harbored deep insecurities stemming from unresolved childhood abuse. They had always been one of his greatest weaknesses and would always have the power to draw him back in if he allowed. Only after a long succession of relationships with women of the pole did Dominic finally realize the truth of his attraction toward them. The gorgeous women with the unmet little girl needs had more than once become entangled in his savior complex and the result had been frustrating and painful. Never certain whether he had chosen them for who they were or who he wanted them to be, his penchant for dancers had turned to resentment on their part and exhaustion on his. Dominic had long before made the decision to resolve all future problems with them by making the commitment to stay out of strip clubs for the rest of all eternity. He passed the women without making eye contact. His powers were strong but had always seemed to weaken in the presence of high heels, the stage, and their silhouettes as they danced in the fog. Dominic refused to look their way. He would take no chances.

"When she moves and she sways she becomes my one desire….," he sang to himself quietly as he headed home to his pack.

Chapter II

The wind blew in Raina's eyes but she didn't flinch against it. She welcomed the chilling breeze as much as she welcomed the rain, the thunder, and the lightning. Something about a wilder sky and a restless climate helped her embrace her favorite combination of feelings – invigoration and peace. The whirling winds made her feel as though the universe was trying to communicate with her in the most tangible way it could and she stood still at the doorway with her face tilted upward to enjoy it. Smiling at the sight of the swaying trees and the leaves that flew freely through the air, she pretended nature was playing a game of hide and go seek with the passing breeze.

The sun had retired only minutes before Raina stepped out onto the porch with a fat mug of steaming coffee in her left hand and five thick newspapers clutched in her right. It was her evening ritual that always began at seven p.m. and only ended after each of her pack mates had chosen their night's dinner from the delectable pages of the *New York Times*. The stories within provided the sustenance they would need to recharge their fleeing souls for another twenty-four hours. Raina was always the first to awaken to prepare their meals. She was the nurturer of their family and she played many important roles to the men she loved. To all four, she was a mother, a sister, and a daughter. To two of them, she was a wife and a lover.

Breathing in the scent of the coming rain, she willed herself to let go of her anxieties and inhale the freedom and independence that came attached to her time alone. Her sheer, blood red nightgown reached the cement, which felt cold and unforgiving beneath her bare feet. Walking toward their large round breakfast table, she giggled as the wind played with the lacy bottom hem of her silk gown and when the breeze transformed into another powerful gust, she laughed out loud as it blew her gown high above her waist. Instead of pulling it back down, she dropped the coffee and newspapers onto the glass and allowed the soft fabric to slap playfully at her face. Reaching her arms up toward the sky as she silently dared the universe to throw another gust her way, she dropped her head backwards with her eyes closed, and stood still in her position until the wind surrendered itself entirely and she was satisfied that she had won the mystical game. The short, precious thirty minutes she had by herself would come to an end once her family opened their eyes and she intended to enjoy every delicious moment of it.

Raina sat down on the chair reserved for her and looked out at the four empty seats before her. Tossing a newspaper toward each of them, she looked around thoughtfully at the dimming sky and willed her spirits to remain high. Trying her best to not focus on the disappointment of her losses, she watched as the last hint of light disappeared into darkness. It worried her pack that she rose sooner than she should but Raina felt the risk was worth the few moments of sun she allowed herself. Though she knew she was playing with literal fire, it helped her to stay positive in the face of constant darkness and worked to relieve the self-pity that threatened to bring her down.

Her days were spent in reluctant slumber and the forced late risings were the most painful reminder of the light she could never have again. The ability to bask in the sun's rays was one of many of God's gifts that had been stolen from her and she often had to remind herself not to ruminate in the 'what ifs' or the 'remember whens,' lest the whispers from the darkness gain power. Taking a slow and careful sip of her steaming black coffee, she enjoyed the burn as it ran down her throat and recoiled slightly from the creeping onslaught of tears and sadness that begged to take over.

Raina pulled one of the newspapers into her line of vision and opened it automatically to the local crime section. The part of her that didn't want to draw in the violence and the debauchery lost out to the part that reminded her of its necessity. A brutal rape had occurred the night before, just two blocks from their home, and Raina scowled as she read the gory details of the violation. Her soft starry gaze turned into an angry glare as she stared with hatred at the picture of the attacker. The snapshot had been taken just minutes after his violent destruction of a young, pretty girl who attended the local university and Raina knew instinctively that he was the one.

"I can't wait to wipe that smile off your face."

His hair was a mess and he sported a black eye and a purple cheek, courtesy of the New York Police Department, but it was his half smile that turned the rapist's destiny around in the blink of an eye. His slick grin begged for karma to dole out its justice earlier than human law planned, in the form of a fire-haired enchantress who despised rapists above all other scum combined. She flicked at his picture with an angry finger and penetrated his image with intense loathing in the hopes that her lethal intentions would somehow be transmitted to him, wherever he was at that moment.

"I'm coming for you," smiling at her own thoughts of sweet retribution. *"How unfortunate for you that you made bail."*

Finished exposing herself to human suffering, she dropped the offending newspaper back onto the table and eased back into the plastic chair as the rim of her coffee mug rose to her lips once more. Though she knew it was still too hot to sip, she couldn't help herself. Allowing the scorching black liquid to lend itself to each of her taste buds, she welcomed the burn in her throat and felt alive when the searing sip landed inside her stomach. The pain woke her up more than the caffeine did and she sat up high in her chair, alert and prepared for the night ahead.

The door sounded behind her and footsteps marked the arrival of one of her pack. She felt sure it was Dominic who approached from behind as he had no doubt awakened before her to secure their small fortress for another evening. To all of them, he was their fearless leader and their beloved friend but to Raina, he was also the heartbreak of her past, the conflict of her present, and the shadow of her future. She hated the fact that she still looked as forward to his arrival at first wake as she had each previous night for the past twenty years.

"Good morning."

He greeted her in the soothing familiar voice that she knew so well and in it, she could still hear the intimate memories from their past together. His tone always started out softer than the one he would be forced to adopt upon Leo's rising.

"Morning," she threw back nonchalantly, hoping to appear as unaffected as possible. It was a difficult feat to disguise anything when dealing with one who had the power to read minds. Raina knew that if he so desired, he could uncover the truth of her continued feelings for him and thereby defeat her greatest defense of hiding her truest emotions.

"Did you order yet? Gonna treat yourself to an appetizer tonight?" he asked, sliding lithely into the seat to her left.

"Nope," she answered. "Went straight to the entrées and decided on one that should fill me up quite nicely."

"Started without us again, huh?" he asked, disappointed. "Rapist?"

"Yep!"

"Be careful," he warned.

Raina tried to hide her smile at his protectiveness but was powerless to control the tug at the corners of her lips.

"Do you want me to go with you?" he asked.

"No thanks," she answered, as she did every time he asked.

It was difficult adjusting to her new role in his life after having known him the way she had. There was always a sense of awkwardness as she fantasized about grabbing his cheeks and planting a long kiss on his mouth but she didn't dare act on her compulsions. Nervous that he had snuck into her mind, Raina envisioned shutting her internal doors to his possible intrusion.

Dominic picked up the paper before his seat, pulling it out of its plastic sleeve. The Metro section was always his first choice as its heinous features and unacceptable crimes were given the highest media attention. The winning perpetrator would win a date with the leader of a five-man vampire pack who staunchly refused to feed off the innocent. His eyes fell upon the picture of a young bride who had been murdered by her new husband. He envisioned the man's fate; Dominic was happy to oblige. He could almost hear the young groom's agonizing screams as they were cut short at the realization of what was happening to him. Thoughts of the blood spilling from the man's torn throat sent a tingling sensation to Dominic's fingertips and he dropped the newspaper back onto the table with a sideways glance toward Raina. He noticed she seemed lost in the wind and worry invaded his heart as it always did where she was concerned.

He knew how she loved the stormy weather and didn't want to pull her from the peaceful place so, instead of initiating conversation, he simply stared at her profile without words. He still loved her and probably always would but had made the decision he thought best for all of them. Dominic told himself he shouldn't have to justify his decisions to himself each and every evening but it's exactly what he found himself doing as he admired her far-off gaze and wondered which internal demon would become the first to tear the smile off her face. He would never violate her private thoughts, no matter how much he sometimes wanted to, but didn't feel the need to share that with her. He didn't see the harm in allowing her to believe in his willingness to utilize his powers because it kept her in check when rebellious thoughts prompted her to justify breaking rules.

Dominic looked up at the trees towering menacingly over their modest two-story house and allowed himself to accept the feeling of being smaller than something. His life demanded constant control of self and others and sometimes it felt nice to tread in less intimidating waters. Glancing back at Raina, he noticed her shiver and knew from experience that she was falling victim to her dark thoughts. Still, he envied her ability to feel the chill from the breeze, a gift he had somehow lost upon his turning and the one he missed most of all.

Their atmosphere turned tense and the change that interrupted both of their thoughts could only mean one thing. Leo had arrived. Though he didn't speak and remained completely apart from any social interaction, his presence succeeded in pulling them both out of their contemplations. The angriest of their pack, Leo was known for trying to compensate for his short stature with his abundance of rage and strife. With a loud flop, he plopped himself into the chair to Dominic's left, his incisors already reaching halfway down his chin in anticipation of the feeding foreplay. His complete lack of social grace blocked his ability to recognize his rudeness and Raina looked to Dominic with an exasperated eye roll.

Pulling his newspaper roughly out of its plastic covering, Leo grunted. His entrance was never a cheerful one and his essence was always so tightly entombed in perpetual rage that it was impossible to not experience the negativity along with him whenever he entered their cipher.

"You sure you're not still sleepy?" Raina taunted. "No need to spread your disease and devastation before its time, is there?"

"No need to commit yourself to just one man or embrace sanity, is there, Jezebel?" came his quick and brutal reply.

"Unnecessary and pissing me off," Dominic warned them both.

"She started it," whined Leo.

"I don't care, I'm finishing it," Dominic said. "Got it?"

Leo pulled the newspaper in front of his face and blocked them both out of his view as way of an answer. Never one to allow disrespect to permeate the sanctity of their group, Dominic leaned forward and pulled back at the corner of the paper until he was satisfied he had Leo's undivided attention.

"Got it?" Dominic asked again, his piercing eyes warning against anything other than obedient acknowledgement.

"Got it," Leo answered. His incisors drew back into their roots like a dog pulling his tail between his legs.

"Anything look appetizing yet?" Dominic asked, hoping to start a friendly banter and to change the direction of their conversation.

"Let's see," began Leo's rant. "There are three new baby killers, two con artists preying on old people's retirements, and a rapist who likes little boys on tonight's special."

When he turned the page with a loud and obnoxious crinkle, his smile disappeared entirely. Though neither of them asked what he was looking at, both anxiously awaited a burst of angry explanation.

"Jesus, what is it?" Raina asked, jumping up from her chair.

Finding a spot behind him, she leaned over his shoulder to share his line of vision, ignoring his complete and utter disapproval of her intrusion. She saw the snapshot of a petite blonde woman who had been photographed as she received an award for her work with inner city children. The woman bore an uncanny resemblance to the wife that Leo had left behind and Raina cringed at the sudden sense of foreboding. The last time Leo spotted a look-a-like of his beloved wife, he lost what little control he had left and made a mistake that had led authorities to their door.

Raina shot a glance toward Dominic and in it, he saw the plea for intervention. Rising from his seat, he pulled his and Leo's empty mugs into one hand and rose from his chair.

"Refill?" he asked Raina as he made his way behind Leo to see what held his attention so completely. When he saw the woman, he knew immediately that his friend needed a firm reminder and a dose of tough love.

"We don't dine on the innocent, Leo," he advised firmly. "Just turn the page and look for the crime of your choosing."

"Okay," Leo whispered hoarsely.

"Even when the urge is strong, we don't surrender to it," Dominic continued. "It's not her, Leo. It's just a woman who looks like her. Collette is fifty years old now."

"I know."

"If she's in tomorrow's paper for anything other than her good deeds, I'm going to have to kill you. Do you understand this?"

"Yes," Leo choked out sorely.

Barely able to pull his eyes away from her beautiful face, he memorized the address of the recreational center where she worked and turned the page.

Dominic slapped his rolled paper onto Leo's head playfully and headed back to the kitchen for refills. As he approached the doorway, he saw a massive shadow fill it so entirely that it blocked all of the light from the kitchen. The sight of Jarek threw him into a defensive posture that made both his gums and fingertips itch.

"Morning," Dominic greeted him through clenched teeth.

"Morning," Jarek answered in a tone just as strained.

They passed each other as they headed in opposite directions and as Dominic made his way toward the coffee pot, Jarek slipped into the chair to Raina's right. Leaning in, he dropped a kiss onto her lips as his eyes darted toward the kitchen window. He would give Raina her public display of affection but would not allow it to linger. Their blossoming relationship was no secret to anyone in the house but it was in all of their best interest that they keep the affection to a minimum when Dominic was around.

"Good morning, darling," he greeted her.

Raina smiled at the excited tingles that she always felt when he was close. Her love for Jarek had evolved over the past year and the novelty of their new affair hadn't yet worn off for her.

"Hi, handsome," she said with a wink, her own gaze flickering toward the silhouette at the kitchen window as she sought out disapproving eyes.

Christoph paraded onto the porch with as much light and positivity as Leo's dark and negative entrance had provided. Cascading toward them with his usual upbeat attitude in tow, his presence worked to combat the tension that had begun to infect their circle. Raina smiled and turned her face upward for a kiss. She wasn't certain how he always managed to stay so positive when it was he who was burdened most of all, but she appreciated it nonetheless.

He called out a sincere good morning to each of them, including Leo who glared back at him with a frown. Picking up the newspaper intended for him, he laid it out carefully on the table and opened it to the more lighthearted sections. Christoph would not begin with the local crime or the high profile headlines and would not choose his meal until he had exhausted all of the entertainment the paper had to offer. He never considered dinner until he'd read his pack mates their horoscopes, whether they were interested in hearing them or not, or until he had finished chuckling over the comics. When finally satisfied with his intake of amusement, he would dive into the sports page long after dusk had passed and long after the coffee had turned sour from too much time in the pot. Only when he had prepared himself emotionally would he finally open to the Classifieds and choose his evening meal.

His pack never complained about the eccentric habit because they knew that he experienced the perilous stories far differently than they did. His empathic abilities forced him to feel the pain personally and, at times, it was unbearable for him. Even Leo sympathized, although he would never admit it out loud. Through the simple touch of hand to ink, Christoph would experience the sweltering heat of local fires and the angry slice of blades as they pierced flesh. He would feel the grief and despair of the father who had just received a police call that his daughter would never again walk through the door because of her brutal murder the night before. One of the strongest of all known empaths, he believed that his power came with purpose and value but it pained them to see the toll it took on him.

Though he tried to hide it, the anguish was evident in his eyes and it saddened Raina most of all. Christoph was her cherished friend, her protective brother, and her disapproving father all at once. It was his ability to feel and think from the inside of every situation that helped him to fill all of the roles she had lost upon her turning. She would share his burden if given the opportunity but that was impossible; it was his alone and he had no choice but suffer the curses the universe had assigned to him.

Christoph finally placed his right hand onto the Classified pages and quietly absorbed the requests for employment, the search for new relationships, and the invitations to yard sales through his other antennae of awareness. He didn't need to read the nearby obvious news stories of tragedy as the rest of the pack did because he could discern the wicked from the pure through their personal ads. The crease in his forehead and the straightening of his mouth always told them when he had happened upon something that they could not see.

As Raina looked on with worry, she hoped for her best friend that none of the ads or news articles were heinous enough to send another jolt of shock through his system or cause him to clutch at his abdomen in shared grief. She felt her eyebrows rise with concern but tried to hide the gesture the best she could, refusing to share her anxieties and cause him further turmoil.

"You okay?" she asked gently.

He nodded and offered her a tired smile.

"What is it, honey?" she prodded softly.

Christoph sighed deeply.

"Their evil is infecting me," he admitted beneath a bowed head that shook back and forth.

Raina placed her thin hand over his long, worn fingers and locked her eyes onto his.

"I know," she comforted. "But we have no other choice."

"Maybe we do," he whispered back quickly.

Her eyebrows shot up again and she glanced around the table to see if anyone else were paying attention to their conversation. When no other eyes met hers, she looked back at him with a question mark penned onto her forehead.

"What's up?" she whispered back.

Looking around at the pack, Christoph considered sharing his thoughts right then and there but something stopped him. He knew that he feared bringing it to the table because he still wasn't certain himself that the idea he'd been playing with would even work. He had always known their plan for survival wouldn't last forever but had hoped it would last longer than a couple of measly decades.

"Answer me," she pressed.

"Not now."

"Why?"

"I'm not ready to discuss it yet."

Christoph leaned forward, paying no mind to the fact that his hand still touched the newspaper carelessly. He never allowed his flesh to have unsupervised contact with any of the printed material because it was a dangerous move for him as an empath, a dire threat to his system should he make contact with evil, unaware and unprepared.

Without warning, his body began to spasm in seizure and each of his pack mates jumped up from the table, wordless and terrified. His chest heaved and his breathing became dangerously labored but his pack turned fear into action without hesitation. Dominic grabbed him from behind and pulled him from his chair as Jarek leaned in to throw Christoph's hand off the ad it still touched. Raina leapt up to stand before him, grabbed both sides of his face, and forced him to stare into her eyes as Leo kept a watchful eye on the entire scene, ready to step in should it become necessary. The seizure ended almost as fast as it began and only when it was over did they reclaim their seats and glare at Leo silently.

"What?" he asked. "I would've helped if it got worse. Geez!"

Christoph dropped his face into his hands but remained silent. The seizures were always the biggest reminder of the moment he had been thrust from the only life he'd known into a new universe that lacked rhyme or reason. It had been a gradual discovery to find he still walked the same planet and that he was still housed in the same body as he had been before the bite. It was an even more bizarre discovery to find that, even though his soul had been hijacked by his maker, he would continue to struggle with the same thoughts and feelings that he had in his human form.

The pack shared certain powers, a blanket gift to each of them upon their initiation into the world of the immortals. They could jump heights that a human couldn't reach with a catapult and they could see through the darkness. They had the ability to reach speeds greater than that of a racecar but it only worked for short distances. Their powers didn't always come at will but instead had to be earned through either intense emotion or serious concentration. Their bodies still experienced pain but it was only remembered pain that came from the simple awareness of their injuries rather than from a neurological standpoint. Their inability to reconcile to themselves that they were no longer human led to phantom aches much like the diabetic who required narcotics for an amputated leg. The more aged the vampire, the less one suffered from human limitations but their pack was still young and still new to an otherwise long-lived species.

Garlic was a constant staple in their cabinet and they could no more fly than their next door neighbors, but reflections were indeed a thing of their past. Their vices worked much the same way as their pain did; past pleasures were so embedded in their memories and their perceptions that they were almost as powerful as realities. Magnified even more by their specific gifts and their amplified senses, the desires of their flesh had actually become stronger rather than weaker.

Christoph's first craving for blood had been so overwhelming that he had gone delirious with need and by meal's end, an entire wing at the local animal shelter was decapitated, found the next morning. He had never gotten past the carnage of that first night but it wasn't until his need for human blood became overpowering that he went in search of others like himself. Happening upon Dominic, still in his human form as he played his guitar at a nightclub, Christoph had known right away that Dominic was destined to play an important role in his life. Though still uncertain what had drawn him to the show that night, he had watched Dominic's death and rebirth from start to finish, empathizing with him for his loss of spirit but never regretting that it had happened.

Throughout the years, they had created their family out of the rare and like-minded vampires they had met along the way. Dominic, Raina, Leo, Jarek, himself... all initiated through a vow of dedication to one another and a vow of protection to their pack. They had created a melting pot of their special abilities and lived out their days together in their tall, gray, split level house in the outskirts of New York City.

Their common goal was continued existence without the harming of innocents. Since vampiric law dictated they live as groups, they had pretended for twenty years to worship the darkness while quietly continuing their search for light and sharing the fantasy they would one day reunite with their souls. They didn't believe, as did the rest, in their species as a whole above the needs of the individual. Agreeing that Dominic would take lead of their pack, they had devoted their lives to one another as they hunted the night streets in search of the blood of only the wicked.

Christoph needed another night to think it over before bringing his idea to light; he decided to wait until their next 'first wake' to bring it up. He circled his finger back to the article that had led to his seizure and he poked his finger at the blurb accusingly. A husband, having decided that his wife was unfaithful, had followed her to a storage unit and poured gasoline all over her body before igniting it. Christoph made a mental note to visit him tonight and decided that he would enjoy the visit immensely. Spent from the excitement of their pre-meal, Dominic was the first to stand up. With hands folded together, he looked down at the table and smiled at his pack.

"All right, boys and girl, up and at 'em!" he cajoled, clapping his hands together once. "We've got another long night ahead of us!"

Chapter III

Christoph wanted forgiveness. He needed to purge himself of his own sins as well as those of the humans he'd absorbed but couldn't just fall to his knees and confess as could the mortals. Unlike the humans, for him there was no great entity to offer him the exoneration he so desperately needed, so he considered himself cursed in the worst possible way. His endless search for absolution had been fruitless and he had come close to giving up hope for the mercy he so desperately needed.

He wanted to shake the humans senseless when he saw them disregard the God they were so lucky to have access to. All they had to do was fold their hands, call out His name, and sincerely apologize for their wrongdoings. They weren't required to become celibate or to sacrifice their children or to even modify their lifestyles to a great degree, yet they still resisted. All they had to do was ask and He forgave. Christoph missed many things about his mortality but the opportunity for redemption was one of the things he missed most. His greatest loss, though, had been the ability to look up at the sky and to glare into the rays of the sun, a gift that, as a human, he had not appreciated the way he should have.

Sitting on a chair in the corner of his room, he looked around at the few items that belonged to him. Aside from his coffin, the seat he was perched upon was the only piece of furniture he owned and Christoph liked it that way. 'The lesser, the better' he had always declared to his pack and they all seemed to know that his minimalist attitude came from the overwhelming emotions that bogged him down day in and day out. He hadn't always been cursed with the empathic powers. He had, in fact, served more years as a vampire than he had ever disclosed to his family but the burdensome abilities were not bestowed upon him until about fifty years before. The powers were a punishment from his maker who refused to understand his unwillingness to surrender to the darkness.

Christoph had foolishly believed he could turn the curse into a gift and had vowed to use the ability to care for the humans rather than watch it go to waste or drive him to madness. But over two decades later, he found himself – more often than not – kneeling on the floor with hands clasped in prayer as he thrust them toward an unforgiving God, begging to know what he had done to deserve such torment.

Walking toward his small closet and opening the door, he stared at the hangers that carried his black jackets and black pants, each garment entombed securely in a large plastic body bag. The floor beneath them was decorated with several pairs of expensive leather shoes and Christoph kicked them to the side as he walked in to sit down in the corner. Pulling the door closed from the inside, he welcomed the darkness and settled into it as a human might settle into a warm bubble bath. It was his thinking spot and where he often made his most difficult decisions.

Christoph had convinced himself that he could use his empathy for the good of mankind, relieving the humans of their pain if only for the moment necessary to reconsider suicide or to make a better decision. Though he often trudged back home in the early morning hours, heavy from the burdens of others and near-blinded from the horrors he had witnessed day in and day out, he continued to thank a silent God for his gift of healing. With dignity and grace, he would wait until he was alone each night to raise a tear-stained face toward the dusky sky and pray for the souls that were still worth saving. Christoph's greatest gift as a human was his ability to make lemonade of the lemons life seemed intent on throwing at him and it was that gift to which he had held tightly upon his turning.

The problem was that he no longer felt capable of holding onto the same hopeful and optimistic attitude. When life threw lemons anymore, Christoph was tempted to throw them back and he knew that eventually, innocents were bound to get caught in the crossfire. The years of borrowed pain had begun to take their toll on him and his desperate need to rid himself of his empathic abilities was what had given birth to the idea of a roadtrip.

"If only I could shed myself of their emotions and their agonies. If only I could watch the sun rise one more time. If only..."

His life had turned into an endless cycle of 'what ifs' and his heart felt heavier each day because of it. Christoph pulled his knees inward and rested his chin on top of them. Though the inside of the closet was pitch black, he still felt charred by the phony light in which he was forced to live. It was only in the midst of total darkness that he could find reprieve from the pain and so he had sealed up the cracks that ran down through the closet's hinges as well as the small opening beneath the door. Though the possibility of light penetrating his space was impossible, he reached a hand out repeatedly to run his fingers along the sealants to ensure its strict adhesion.

"Tonight, I will tell them my plan," he said out loud, though no one was there to hear his self-made pact.

He had decided to present the idea to his pack because he hoped they would decide to join him. Christoph knew he possessed the courage to travel to Louisiana or to any other place in the universe for that matter. It wasn't geography or travel that scared him, nor was it the unknown or fear of the humans that prevented him from jumping into the driver's seat and heading south on a mission. It was the solo part that made him uneasy. Christoph never felt the clarity and the texture of his pain as much as he did when he was alone for too long and because of it, he had learned to depend on those closest to him.

His pack's survival tactics had weakened because the wicked they ingested had begun luring them into the darkness even more than feeding off the innocent would have. He knew it was only a matter of time before they all succumbed to the whispers that called out to them and there was only one person who had the power and the ability to give them what they needed.

Christoph had always planned to seek out the headmaster; for many years, he had carried a wish that it now was time to pursue. After careful consideration, he had decided Lucius could become the saving grace for his family as well. He wanted to look up at the sky and to glare against the rays of the sun. He wanted to shed himself of the empathy that threatened to overwhelm him. Most of all, he wanted something else, something that he could not accomplish without the assistance of the head vampire and he had finally admitted to himself that the time to ask had come to call upon him. As one, it was a risky venture that would most likely end in capture by another pack. As a group, there was a better chance of making it there alive and unharmed. Christoph had no idea what the reception would be should they reach their destination safely but he knew they had run out of options and that the time had come, once and for all, to seek out help from the only one who could give it.

He planned to bring it up over coffee and the shared newspapers at their next meeting and his heart palpitated with anxiety over the possible responses of his pack. He had almost told them at first wake but had chickened out because of his seizure. The next time, he would follow through.

Christoph rose from his crouch, opened the closet door, and stepped back into his bare bedroom. Walking down the hallway and passing the bathroom, he saw that Raina stood before the mirror applying her make-up yet again. Instinct forced his attention to her reflection, or at least where her reflection should have been but rather than seeing a copy of her beautiful features or her long red locks, he saw only the towel rack that was perched on the wall behind her. He knew that, as much as he wanted to find peace and light, she wished for the chance to look at herself just one more time.

With a mascara wand to her lashes, he watched as she pulled it slowly upward as she stared longingly into a mirror that provided no source of measurement for her cosmetics. Though he could never quite figure out her obsession with the constant applications, he refused to question it. They all had secrets hidden away in the deepest recesses of their minds and no matter how long they lived together or how close they became, there were certain things they would never be able to explain to one another.

He leaned his back against the doorjamb and smiled. "What's up, beautiful?"

"Argh!" she screamed playfully. "I hate these colors!"

Gesturing toward the vanity beneath her, he saw that it carried numerous lipsticks, foundations and eye shadows that reached from one end of the dresser to the other.

"Are you kidding?" he praised. "You're gorgeous!"

"Thanks," she smiled softly. "Are you hungry? Do you want me to make you something?"

"No, thanks."

Glancing down at his watch, he realized that midnight was still two hours away. Their next communion wasn't until twelve o'clock; pre-flight served as their second meeting of each day and one where they shared the specific details of the night's schedules.

"Do you think you'll be finished in here soon?" he asked gently.

Raina looked into the mirror for an answer but no one looked back at her. She didn't know how well her make–up had come out because she couldn't see herself, a truth from which she could find no escape. Instead of complaining, she turned her attention from the useless glass in disgust and finally met his eyes.

"I'm done," she smiled, shaking off the bad vibe as quickly as it had come upon her. Her smile widened and she tilted her head to the side while batting her lashes at him.

"Why? Do you need the bathroom or are you ready to tell us what's on your mind?"

"The latter," he replied. "I'm ready."

Raina narrowed her eyes suspiciously.

"Are you alright, Chris?"

"I'm fine," he lied. "I'm great, actually."

"Does your plan happen to involve getting us out of this hell hole for a little while?"

"Quite a while, in fact," he answered, nodding.

"Then I'm in!"

Christoph laughed.

"But you don't even know what it is yet."

"It doesn't matter," she conceded, hands by her sides and standing up straighter with sudden conviction. "I like it already."

"I appreciate the vote of confidence but when I do explain, I really want for you to give it a lot of thought, okay?"

"Fine!" she relented, sticking her tongue out at him.

Christoph understood why she had agreed so quickly and so blindly. It was the answer of someone who felt she had nothing left to lose.

"See you at pre-flight?" he asked.

"I'll be there with bells on!" she answered excitedly before turning away and resuming her incessant face painting, despite the mirror's refusal to reward her with any results.

He walked away knowing she would spend the next two hours before her invisible image, longing for the days when she could look into a mirror and see her own eyes staring back at her. He wished he could wrap up a magical mirror for her, one that would show her all the beauty she refused to see in herself. If he could, he would wrap it up with a big huge bow and leave it at her doorstep, but it was a gift that he didn't have the power to give her; it was a power that lay in the hands of only one powerful vampire – Lucius.

Christoph walked away from the bathroom and ventured further down the long upstairs hallway. The house had belonged to them for years and it had become a safe haven for all of them. Nestled comfortably in the cul-de-sac of their suburban New York City neighborhood, it intrigued passersby with its many windows and its Goth-like designs etched into the bars that covered them. Peeking out the window and down onto the street below, he noticed a group of young neighborhood kids looking back up at him.

They had often used the pack's house and lives for their entertainment. The bolder and more courageous of them would gather out front to hold streetside séances and long distance exorcisms. The following morning, they would meet up at school to tell the other children about the amazing feats of courage they had displayed in their fearless battles with a vampire pack and though no such battle was ever really waged, Christoph enjoyed playing along whenever he could.

He looked down onto the group of naive faces that stared up at him and threw out the most terrifying expression he could muster. Though the windows were closed, he could hear their shrieks and cries for their mothers. Christoph snickered to himself as he watched them take off down the road, their speed doubled from terror.

"Scaring the kids again?"

Christoph turned around to face Jarek, who had one towel around his waist and another hanging around his neck. Having obviously been lifting weights, he looked to be headed for the bathroom and, no doubt, in search of a shower.

"Just playing along," Christoph blushed, neither offended by the children's' curiosity nor insulted by their ignorance. He understood their confusion and their fears as he still felt that himself.

"The tots should consider themselves lucky," Jarek said, stopping for a quick chat.

Their meeting of the eyes showed Leo reflected off both sets of dark pupils. The last time their Napoleonic friend walked by the same window and noticed the bevy of young thrill seekers, he didn't react well. When an eleven-year-old neighborhood boy was rushed to the hospital with a long cheek gash from a fast flying Ouija peg, police had begun paying as much attention to their house and their lives as the nosy kids had.

As Jarek continued toward the bathroom, Christoph felt a pang of jealousy from elsewhere in the house and he knew it was Dominic's heart he had tapped into.

"Wait," he called out to Jarek's fleeing back. "Where are you going?"

"Prayer group," his muscular friend answered on a grin.

"Raina's in there."

"And?" Jarek smiled.

"And… be careful, my friend," Christoph warned. "He's very unhappy with you lately."

Jarek's smile fell away as he lowered his gaze to the floor.

"I haven't broken any pack rules, old boy."

"Maybe not," Christoph answered softly. "But you have broken some friendship ones."

Staring back quietly for a long moment, Jarek turned away again and continued down the hall. He always discouraged conversation about issues he felt were nobody else's business and most often simply ignored uncomfortable situations when they arose. Christoph watched as Jarek nudged open the bathroom door and he saw the smile that spread across his friend's profile.

"Hey, darling," he heard him greet Raina, before he walked inside and answered Christoph with the click of the bathroom door lock.

Glancing around for signs of Dominic, Christoph wondered how he would deal with it should a real fight ever erupt between his friends. He loved them both and would give his life for every last one of them including Leo, although he'd never admit it out loud.

He walked slowly down the long spiral staircase and heard the television blaring from the living room. Leo was obviously up and Christoph hoped to tiptoe quietly by the room without alerting the unpleasant little prick to his presence but something stopped him and told him to join Leo in the den. Cautiously, he opened the door that separated them and then poked his head inside to check out the emotional temperature in the room.

Dominic entered simultaneously from a door on the opposite side of the room. He gripped a glass of Jack Daniels and coke in his pale right hand; his light hair was in its perpetually neat style with nary a strand out of place. His sideburns were drawn upward with his smile and Christoph decided that it was a smile that could disarm the wicked and diffuse a war. Each time he found himself in Dominic's presence, he considered himself both lucky and honored.

He appreciated his leader's humility and judgment above all else. Though his power was great, he never made them feel lesser for their subservient roles but rather accepted their flaws, protected their secrets, and calmed their fears. Christoph was more anxious about Dominic's reaction than anyone else's.

"Hey, Dom," Christoph greeted him cheerfully.

"Hey," Dominic returned. "Feeling a little better?"

"Much."

Sensing the tension when Jarek suddenly walked into the room wearing only a towel around his waist, Christoph noticed Dominic withdrew eye contact quickly. He longed for the days when the two of them would drink to the new night together. It made him wonder if the female gender had the ability to destroy the male bond in every species.

As if on cue, Raina walked in and it was that moment that Christoph decided to finally share the idea of his plan. Trying to decide how best to take control of the moment, he addressed them weakly and with less confidence than he had hoped.

"Do you ever feel like you need to just get out of here?" he began.

"Ha!" Leo shot back. "Do I ever not?"

"What a coincidence," Jarek threw back. "We wish you'd just get out of here too."

Leo's response was a heartfelt up-shoot of his short middle finger and Dominic remained quiet, answering with nothing more than a raised eyebrow.

"Let me reword that," Christoph tried again, glancing at Raina for support. She returned his smile and he couldn't help but envision a halo on one side of her head and a horn growing from the other. Dominic turned away from them as he walked toward his organized rack of old albums. All of them knew he would reach for Johnny Cash as that was the album their leader selected first in times of stress. Ignoring Christoph's feeble attempts at the important conversation, they each continued doing their own thing.

"Uh, hello?" Christoph sang out before clearing his throat and eyeing the group more firmly.

Raina floated past him and levitated closer to the sofa where Leo sat. Flicking him in the forehead without provocation, he grabbed her wrist roughly, causing both Jarek and Dominic to advance on him without hesitation.

"I want to pack up the hearse, drive to Louisiana, and call a meeting with Lucius!" Christoph finally yelled.

They each stopped what they were doing and stared back at him as though he had grown a second face but it was Leo who finally broke the long, uncomfortable silence.

"What the hell?"

Crossing his arms and forcing a taller posture and a firmer stance, Christoph tried to appear more masculine than he felt. Too late to turn back, he forged on bravely.

"I said I want to go on a roadtrip."

Chapter IV

Leo was infuriated. He couldn't stand Christoph or his stupid ideas and refused to even entertain the newest one with any modicum of seriousness.

"Let's go on a roadtrip," he muttered sarcastically to himself. *"What a moron."*

On the way to pull his Murphy bed from the wall it was encased behind, Leo kicked angrily at a can on his floor and then stopped to listen to the sound it made as it ricocheted off the wall. He loved all sounds related to chaos, ruckus, and disaster, though the sound of breaking glass was one of his favorites. However, he had promised Dominic there would be no more of it inside the house, especially since the unfortunate accident with the nosy kid.

"I'll bet they're not so curious anymore," he directed toward the unresponsive can that stopped to rest under the windowsill.

Leo had warned the intrusive youngsters the day before the incident that curiosity had already killed their cat but they had pursued their macabre investigations anyway. What, did they think he was joking? Should he have produced their dead feline to enhance his point?

He shook his head and continued his angry gait toward the wall. He wasn't as tired as he was overcome by the instinct to hibernate and the ability to close his eyes to the putrid world in which he was forced to live for all eternity. Bedtime was always Leo's favorite part of every day.

Standing before the tuck-a-way bed that was housed behind his bare and dirty wall, he used a long nail to pull the release switch and then stepped back to listen to the sound it made as it hit the floor. Knowing the nightly crash annoyed his pack to no end, Leo appreciated the loud clatter that much more. He could just picture them sitting together in the downstairs den, settling down to their glasses of wine while hiding comfortably behind their ridiculous thoughts when the sudden crash from above destroyed all hope of serenity. If Leo couldn't enjoy a sense of peace, he decided nobody else would either.

He sat on the soiled mattress and glanced around each of the four walls without expression. The only one in the house without a coffin, he had decided on a more discrete way to enjoy the suffocation and restrictive darkness required for sleep, finding it in the nifty hidden bed. Each morning, he folded himself into the wall, entombing himself entirely as he blocked out every last reminder of his useless existence.

Although it beckoned, Leo wasn't entirely ready for sleep yet. The instinct to shut down was increasing but it hadn't yet surpassed the power of his inner turmoil. He didn't want to think any more about the roadtrip but he couldn't help himself. To hell with their need for an answer by morning; he lived by no one's schedule but his own. It was far from some sympathetic sense of duty that thoughts of the roadtrip were inspiring his momentary insomnia. It was something else that Leo didn't want to admit to himself.

Excitement and a nagging sense of hope violated his brain functioning and though Leo would never admit it to his pack, there was something he wanted more desperately than the rest of them could ever want anything. A deep yearning for revenge pumped up his aorta and he tried to stuff it back in. The sheer possibility that Lucius might actually help him find and destroy his maker made him feel alive and warm inside but he resisted its magnetic draw because of his self-made promise to never again rely on hope.

The television, mounted high on the wall and catty corner from his bed, turned on suddenly. Leo had it rigged to an automatic timer that powered up the tube each hour before daybreak. Though their windows were securely tinted and could effectively protect them even without their coffins and their Murphy beds, no member of the pack liked to remain awake during daylight hours. Their inability to open the door and walk out into the daylight was a reality they chose to ignore and they could so successfully only through sleep.

Leo lay back on the lumpy mattress and stared at the ceiling thoughtfully. Three roaches glared down at him and he fought the urge to smash them to a pulpy mass. Their scrawny little antennae sickened him and the shine of their dirty brown coats made him want to vomit. Even though Leo believed that their species had no valid reason for existing, their presence on this night made him feel less lonely.

His pack thought he was an asshole and he didn't care or, at least he didn't let them know he did. He didn't want to give them the satisfaction and definitely didn't want to expose any weakness that could be used against him. He turned over onto his side and let his eyes caress each bit of garbage that he'd gleefully strewn all over his sticky floor. It was no wonder the bugs had chosen his room in which to live. Leo pushed away the disturbing thought that he intentionally left trash lying around in a subconscious bid for their company.

"You're better company than them anyway," he told the bugs.

Images of each of his pack mates penetrated his thoughts and Leo allowed himself to inspect each vision that presented itself. He loved them all but would rather be drowned in holy water than admit it out loud. He had long before decided against the use of sweet words and acts of kindness as they only led to rejection and humiliation. Leo had no tolerance for either.

Admitting that forcing sleep was futile, he finally got up from his bed and headed toward the dilapidated dresser by his window. Opening the top drawer and pulling out the framed picture sitting atop his dirty underwear, Leo stared longingly at the man in the photo before gently tucking it under his arm. The photograph was the only thing Leo treated with the care it deserved.

He opened the second dresser drawer and pushed aside the sweaters that he hadn't washed in months. Though he could smell the musty odor upon its opening, he inhaled deeply. Leo had long stopped caring about his appearance or hygiene. His hand rifled through the clothing until he felt a curved handle and when he did, he smiled as he pulled the sharp blade from the tunic where it was nestled. He had always enjoyed knives and this one had once belonged to Jarek. Technically, it still did but Leo had no intention of returning it just as he'd had no intention of asking to borrow it.

He slammed the drawer shut and walked back to his bed with a more confident stride. Having looked at the picture, he felt rejuvenated. Resting his head back against the pillow, he did so with a smile instead of his trademark scowl. Leo looked up at the roaches with a grin and he licked his lips.

The man from the photo still stared back at him within his mind, his eyes filled with hope for a future he had never before cared about. He had only just been gifted with a wife and an unborn son when the attack had occurred and Leo felt the familiar resentment and rage begin to race through his veins. Collette had accepted him unconditionally and had managed to tear down the walls that he had always used to shield himself from the rest of the world.

The man's eyes penetrated Leo's every thought. For death to have found him, taken him, and then abandon him had been like suffering the Tortures of the Damned. Leo had never let go of the anger and vengeance he felt toward the maker who took everything away from him. He had never stopped reliving the night he had closed up his small shop and headed for his car, the feeling of excitement for what awaited at home fueling his movements. He would never forget the sting of the bite and the helplessness he'd experienced upon realizing he could never again return home, could never again see her.

The bitterness had consumed him and he had begun to rely on nothing but rage to propel him into each moment thereafter. Leo hated his maker with an intensity that wouldn't diminish and had never really believed he might get the chance to one day uncover his true identity. He wanted to find him and tear him to shreds. All the talk of a roadtrip had begun to create havoc within. Leo felt a sense of hope he hadn't experienced for many years.

He pulled the picture up from his side and rested it on his chest. He didn't need to look at it again to remember the hopeful eyes because he could still feel the man someplace deep inside of him. If he had the human's gift of reflection, he would stand before a mirror to assess what he had become but a knock at the door disrupted his stream of thoughts. The simmering excitement over his decision made him jump.

"What?" he barked at the unknown visitor as he aimed Jarek's knife at the roach. With care and precision, Leo squinted one eye and drew back at the small family congregating above his head.

"It's me," Christoph said, his voice muffled through the closed door.

"What do you want?"

"Just checking to see if you've thought about the trip any further?" he inquired hopefully.

"I've thought about it," Leo growled.

Christoph was silent. He was afraid to hear the refusal and watch his dreams float away because he knew in the end he would never leave the little rat behind.

Leo continued to aim the knife at the roaches with accuracy no human could ever possess and with a quick flip of the wrist, he shot the blade forward. He smiled as he watched it gouge through the biggest roach of the bunch and his smile widened more when the knife pierced the ceiling and hung suspended from its wobbly anchor. Fantasies of revenge filled him with passion and renewed purpose and the sudden motivation pulled him into a sitting position. Dangling his short legs over the side of the bed, he waited before indulging Christoph with an answer. Only after satisfying himself that he had tortured him through his long silence did he speak.

"I'll go," he said simply.

"What?" came the surprised reply.

"What are you, deaf?" he asked. "I said I'll go. I'll go on your roadtrip and I'll follow your damn yellow brick road."

On the other side of the door, Christoph smiled. And inside Leo's bedroom, hard as he fought it, the small statured, largely angered vampire felt a sense hope that he simply couldn't deny.

"Good one Leo… maybe we'll even come across a few munchkins along the way, huh? I mean, no offense."

Unaffected by the reference to his stature, Leo shot a stern glare toward the closed door.

"None taken, asshole! Now you wanna get the hell away from my door and leave me alone!"

Christoph turned away with a smile as he headed for Jarek's room as well as another answer.

Chapter V

Jarek paced the floors of his bedroom, clenching and unclenching his fists. He had never experienced heartbreak as a human and he didn't intend to start as an immortal but the truth was, he couldn't get her out of his mind. There was no question about whether he wanted to join his pack on the roadtrip or not; the answer was a given. Fearless and always up for an adventure, he relished the idea of heading to New Orleans to seek out the almighty Lucius for some quality one on one time.

He had never been able to adapt to the idea of living as a pack despite the warm feelings he had for his family, and could think of no better way to extricate himself from his forced union than to seek out the headmaster himself. His desire to remain solo had nothing to do with his love for his family but everything to do with his innate need for independence and freedom. He felt a surge of relief at the possibility that he could one day live alone again and answer to nobody but himself. It was the one thing he missed the most about his human days and the one dream he had held tightly to every single day since his turning eighteen years before.

Jarek felt no dismay or fear over the possible dangers ahead. He knew there would be resistance along the way but confrontation and the threat of battle appeared on his list of pros rather than cons. He was beginning to experience a surge of hope that he might finally get his wish after all and receive a blessing from the League that forbid vampiric individuality and disentangle himself forever. Nothing would stop him from accompanying his pack on its mission. Jarek vowed to ensure the safety of his family before saying goodbye to them and walking away from the world that kept him bound.

His only issue of contention had to do with Raina and the consequences to their relationship. Jarek loved her, there was no doubt about it, but League laws prohibited them from coupling. The rules dictated that all females belong to their pack, and therefore, to every male within that pack. He knew that even if Lucius gifted him with the ability to travel afar and remain on his own, it was much less likely Raina would be allowed to go with him. He understood Dominic's struggle when having made the choice of leadership over the woman he loved but knew he would have chosen differently. He would have found a way to make it work, even if it meant running for the rest of their days.

Whenever images of their separation intruded upon his thoughts, he felt an ache in his heart unlike he had ever known. Jarek had never felt the sting of a painful separation because he had never before known real love. As a human, he had been married for many years but had never experienced the agony and ecstasy that were attached to his feelings for Raina. The jealousy, the insecurity and the euphoria had exposed him to emotions he hadn't known existed. Though he had been dutiful and loyal to Victoria, he had never been able to offer her the love that she had wanted and deserved; had never before been victim to the illogical passions he had only heard about. His marriage had been of such little significance that he hadn't even sought out his widow to bid her a final farewell after his rebirth.

Jarek had never been bothered by his loose and selfish lifestyle. A loner since birth, he had figured it was his destiny to find fulfillment in the material gifts the world had to offer. He loved money, he cherished weapons and he coveted his whiskey and other vices. Mostly, he overindulged on women but had loved them only as a species and never one as a lifelong mate. Both as a human and in his new world, he appreciated their delicious offerings and had made a habit of feigning a level of love that he didn't really have. Jarek had been the master of charm and had acquired many females but he saw them as nothing more than trinkets along the way. Known afar for his wild escapades and his whorish lifestyle, he sensed a form of karma the night he fell upon Raina's doorstep. She twisted him from the inside out and, because of it, had now become a liability to the opportunity that had finally presented itself.

Noticing the bedroom door was still cracked open, he walked over and kicked it shut. On edge and annoyed, he had grown tired of sharing a home with others. A man needed his own territory and the time had come to turn it all around, but he would do it the right way. Keeping his cool and maintaining control had always come second nature to him and the love he had come to feel for his pack had taught him to calm the demons that always itched to come out and play.

It had taken him awhile to adapt to honoring another member of his own dominant species but Dominic had made it easy, earning Jarek's respect. Jarek was grateful for Dominic's friendship and loyalty. If he had been pulled into another pack with another leader, there was little chance he would have survived and most likely would have been punished severely the first time he challenged authority or asserted his own ideas.

Dominic had always allowed them the individuality and privacy that other leaders forbid, so the obedience and devotion Jarek gave back was of his own free will, rather than a demand. He had agreed to honor him as a leader because they shared the same views and perceptions. Dominic had not succumbed to the darkness and had not allowed any of his pack to do so either. He knew deep down that, had he himself been chosen as leader, the pack would surely have been in trouble because of his weakness in the face of temptation and seduction.

Jarek kicked his shoes off by the closet door, not wanting to drag in any dirt that might damage his expensive Italian carpet. He took good care of his possessions and had collected as many things as he could since his turning. As he paced his room, images of Raina's face overrode all other thoughts and shaking his head to expel them didn't work. Her energy was contagious and the liveliness he felt around her made him regret that they hadn't met as humans. She was the epitome of every male fantasy and had the remarkable ability to crawl inside a man's mind and make herself comfortable. Her willingness to try anything and her skills of adaption were remarkable; she was a chameleon. She could siphon a man's insecurities with a kiss and restore his courage with a caress. He knew that the longer she existed as a vampire, the more powerful her abilities to enchant would become and he was both proud of her for it and envious of the others who would want her for themselves.

He had respected her role as Dominic's partner but it was she who sought him out upon the break up. Vulnerable, hurt, and rejected, she had come to him in search of comfort and Jarek was a weak man where women were concerned. The fact that she no longer belonged to Dominic was subsequently of no consequence to the rest of the pack and the tensions their union had caused had begun to weaken them from the inside out.

Jarek walked past the small mini-fridge in the corner of his room but thought better of it and doubled back. He opened the door and enjoyed the freezing mass that streamed through his fingers as he curled them around the bottle. There was no need to look inside as his whiskey always sat in the same spot, refilled religiously by a generous girlfriend who loved to take care of him whenever he chose to allow it. Forgoing a shot glass, he held the bottle to his lips and with a deep tilt of the head, drank with the kind of thirst that could only be quenched with liquor.

"Thanks, darling," he said out loud.

Jarek offered the universe his daily appreciation that he was still able to enjoy the same vices that had always fulfilled his needs. Had he been forced into celibacy or ordered to sacrifice his self-medicating methods, he would surely have chosen death.

He closed the refrigerator door and opened the bottom drawer of his dresser. Almost as meticulous about his belongings as he was his person, Jarek kept everything in pristine condition. He believed in having the greatest things life had to offer and knew he would remain undeserving if he didn't take care of his possessions. Gently pushing aside a neat pile of folded black t-shirts, he grabbed the small baggie hidden beneath them, pulled a fat joint to his nose, and inhaled its pungent scent.

"Nice."

Jarek lit it up, drew the smoke into his lungs deeply, and enjoyed the numbing effect it had on all of his senses before walking over to his coffin and perching himself on its edge. Momentarily neglecting his drug for his drink, he took a long refreshing sip of the whiskey and fell into thoughts of the trip and of an ending to his life of forced subservience. He thought of the ability to enjoy all of the perks of his vampirism without the control of the league. He thought about Raina.

When she looked at him, he knew she saw in his eyes the soul he had lost, still surviving inside of him somewhere. And when he looked at her, he could see the reflection of the man he once was – the passion, the independence, the power and all the things he missed so desperately. It was her power. Humans and vampires alike could look into her eyes and find themselves in her stare, a painful irony for a woman who was forever blocked from her own reflection.

Jarek closed his eyes to envision her with even more texture and clarity – her soft touch and her sweet kisses. There was passion in everything she did; it was impossible not to absorb her energy when she was close to him. He thought it courageous of her that she didn't try to protect or restrain her abilities but, instead, shared them with eagerness. He thought about how she saw signs in everything and made each moment an adventure, no matter how mundane. Yet, despite her old soul, her wisdom and the massive desire she incited in all those around her, she was still just a little girl inside. Her unwillingness to accept certain maturities or to set appropriate boundaries made her someone who needed constant protection.

He needed to be liberated from the pack but he needed also to take her with him. Jarek didn't know what he would do if forced to choose and didn't want to think about it so he took another hit and another swig, pushing all thoughts out of his mind. Running a hand across his wet lips, he decided not to wait to start packing. He would leave for New Orleans within an hour if he could and would ask Lucius to free him from his enslavement and from the vampire community. All he knew was that, if asked to choose between his freedom and his love for her, he would not react well.

Chapter VI

Raina felt the paranoia creep in again so she crawled into her coffin and pulled her knees up to her chest. Looking around at her bedroom, she wondered if anything were out of place, though she would have no real way of knowing because her life and bedroom were always in total chaos. The opposite of an obsessive compulsive cleaner, she intentionally put things in her own way and drove herself to madness; it was an unfortunate habit for as long as she could remember.

She hated the lack of structure and acute disorganization in which she lived but had found ways to make it work for her. Raina learned to thrive under the pressure of her wayward lifestyle but wouldn't have recommended it to her worst enemy. Having never allowed peace in her life, she wouldn't know serenity if it smacked her in the face; it was a practice she was finding more difficult to accept as time went on.

The television in the corner crackled and it made her jump. Always set at a low volume to provide the requisite background noise, its sudden disruption with static told her she wasn't alone. A breeze passed her ear with both purpose and direction but it wasn't an uncomfortable sensation. On the contrary, the knowledge that another presence was close made her feel less lonely and she relaxed deeper against the hard inner wall of her coffin. She allowed a small smile to escape her drawn, tired face and waited on pins and needles for the greeting from the other side. Never certain what form he would take, Raina always became most excited in the moments before he spoke.

Sam had a sense of humor she had never encountered in either human or vampire. He had first appeared to her when she was a little girl in desperate need of a friend and though he couldn't intervene in her physical world, Raina credited him with having saved her life on more than one occasion. He had supported and empowered her throughout her most difficult moments and had been the only one who could find his way past the thick wall she had erected.

Because of his strong resemblance to Sam Elliot, Raina had dubbed him Sam and had found in him a best friend and a trusted confidante. When she had tried to introduce him to her human family, they hadn't been amused. Unaware ghosts were invisible, Raina hadn't understood why her family was so frustrated by him and eventually learned to just pretend he didn't exist when they were around. Though her pack couldn't see him either, their reaction had been kinder than her real family's and they embraced his essence whenever she announced his presence in the room.

Raina pulled her knees in closer to her body and used them as a pillow. Sensing the humor of Sam's presence, she giggled out loud. He always chose one of three personalities and she looked forward to seeing whom he came as this time. Her heart raced with the possibilities and when she could no longer take the anticipation, she spoke first.

"Some crazy people develop multiple personalities," she laughed. "I have you."

She heard the chair leg scrape the floor by the window and saw the shadow of a woman, though she couldn't discern which woman it was. Sam obviously hadn't come as himself and that left only one of two choices.

"Lucy?" she called out.

"Hello, crazy lady," sang the reply.

Raina squinted into the darkness but still couldn't make out any facial features. Disguised as Lucille Ball, Sam loved to pretend she was married to Satan and was visiting from hell. Though unsure why he had decided upon the copper-topped funny lady, she guessed it was more for her own benefit than for his. Somehow, he knew that she would be able to relate to her goofy troublemaking character from the 'I Love Lucy' show and as usual, he had been right.

Raina pulled a cigarette out of the box she had stashed in her coffin and lit it despite the no smoking rule in the house. Knowing it would annoy him, she blew a long stream of smoke directly toward the unmoving shadow.

"Put that out," Lucy scolded.

"Why?"

"It's bad for you."

"Huh! Said the Chesterfield girl. . . ."

"So?"

"So?" Raina continued. "Didn't you die of lung cancer or something?"

"I didn't!"

"What then?" teased Raina. "Not drugs?"

"Nah," Lucy answered. "Never was very interested in that stuff. I had enough trouble."

"Then how did you kick the bucket exactly?"

"Aneurysm," Lucy answered. "And thanks for your sensitivity."

"That's it?" Raina asked incredulously. "You smoked your whole life and then died of an aneurysm?"

"Don't discount the smoking, crazy lady," she said.

"You wanna stop calling me that?"

Lucy ignored her.

"It almost got me; would have if not for the heart problems and the aneurysm. But it did take my husband away from me."

The shadow moved forward and Raina could finally see her clearly. The bright red bun perched on top of her head said that she had come in character. Even her personalities had personalities.

"I'm sorry for that," Raina said sincerely.

"Thank you."

"Knowing my luck, I'll probably get some terrible combination of diseases. Like Tourette's and Bell's Palsy or something."

Lucy laughed the hearty laugh that Raina had always loved.

"That would be an unfortunate combination indeed," Lucy replied. "How's the man situation?"

"Crazy and confusing as always."

"The best love affairs always are."

"I'm not laughing as much as I used to, that's for sure," complained Raina.

"Life isn't always funny."

"That's kinda weird coming from the queen of comedy."

"I was queen of the Bs too but you don't reference that," Lucy countered. "Sometimes you just don't know what's really going on beneath the surface."

"You were queen of the what?"

"Queen of the Bs?" she reiterated, as though Raina should have known what she was talking about. "B-rated movies?"

"Ohhh, okay," Raina patronized. "Huh?"

"We're not all just one of anything, Raina. There are lots of different parts to each of us that we should embrace."

"What're you saying?"

"You want to go on this roadtrip, don't you?"

Raina didn't even bother to ask Sam how he knew about the trip. She never took for granted that he wasn't there just because she couldn't see him. She turned her face away so that the eye contact was broken and, not wanting to commit to answer head on, spoke out of only one side of her mouth.

"Maybe."

"Why?" asked Lucy. "What do you want from Lucius?"

Raina re-established the eye contact but lost her smile.

"You know what I want"

"Humor me. Say it out loud for the both of us."

Raina shook her head back and forth.

"I can't."

"You can."

Raina's head shaking became more pronounced.

"No."

"What will you ask for, Raina?"

She slid further down into the coffin and hid the blush behind her hands.

"Mortality?" Raina finally asked.

"Are you asking or telling me?" Lucy asked, annoyed.

"Mortality," Raina corrected. "Sorry."

"Don't apologize," redirected Lucy. "Don't ever apologize for wanting fulfillment."

"I know most people would want what I have here but…," she trailed off, "I'm not one of them."

"You think most people would want this?" Lucy laughed, looking around and shaking her head. "You're even crazier than I thought."

"Really?"

Raina was surprised. She had assumed that the gift of immortality was one that would gratify most people. To find that she might have been wrong all along filled her with a strange sense of hope she didn't understand.

"Not even Mr. Ball would want to be stuck in this war zone forever," Lucy smiled. "It's why he built our getaway down south."

"You're hilarious," Raina laughed.

"Queen of comedy, don't forget it," joked Lucy.

"I'm so glad you came tonight."

"Me too," Lucy smiled as she slowly evaporated back into nothingness. "It was getting hot at my house."

Even when Raina could no longer see or feel her, she could still hear her voice, small, distant, and bidding her a farewell in the same sing-song tone she had greeted her with. "Bye, crazy lady."

The static that had continued to crackle from the television throughout their conversation stopped suddenly and David Letterman took its place. He was listing the ten funniest street names in the country and his studio audience was laughing hysterically. A knock sounded at the door and Raina jumped.

Wondering what would happen if she didn't answer, she remained very quiet and very still. The rap came again, louder and more persistent than the first one and her stare toward the door widened.

"Who is it?" she asked quickly.

"It's just me," Christoph half spoke, half whispered.

"Oh, sorry," she answered with relief. "Coming."

Raina scurried to the door and opened it with a worn grin. With no females to turn to in times of trouble, Christoph had always satisfied her periodic needs for estrogen. He possessed such an equal balance of masculinity and femininity that she didn't feel cheated. Taking a couple steps backwards, she welcomed him in with a sweeping and welcoming arm gesture. Christoph looked around and circled back to look in her eyes.

"Whatcha doin'?" he asked.

"Nothing," she lied. "Just thinking."

He stuck only his head in and used it to shoot glances at all four corners of her room.

"You alone?"

"Sam just left," she admitted.

"Aaahh," he smiled. "Have a good talk?"

"Yes."

Christoph crossed his arms and leaned against the open door jamb.

"You guys didn't happen to discuss the roadtrip, did you?"

"It came up."

Though he was smiling, Raina could see the concern that seemed permanently etched into the creases by his eyes.

"And?" he asked slowly.

"Did you really think I'd ever say no?"

Relief inserted itself into his eyes and his mouth and even his skin somehow. Raina reached up to touch his cheek.

"Even if I didn't want to go for myself, I would have still gone for you," she answered as she hugged him tightly.

Chapter VII

The day for departure had finally arrived and no member of the pack was more excited than Christoph. The moment he had anticipated for seven agonizing days had finally arrived and though he felt as if he might jump right out of his skin, he felt an unexpected sense of comfort in thoughts of the days ahead. Never expecting he would be accompanied on such an important journey, it was even more surprising he would be traveling with a family that he not only created for himself but had, surprisingly, grown to love.

Looking down into his shiny, polished coffin, Christoph took in the contents that lay before him. Articles of clothing he had meticulously folded were about to find a new home in his hard, vintage blue, plastic suitcase. Opening his luggage to finish packing, he felt a stab of shame for not having treated it with more care. The lining inside had seen better days, becoming worn and tattered from his years of travel. Each side of the interior had an elastic bordered cloth pocket and he planned to use both to stow away the small, homemade weapons he predicted they would need along the way.

At times, passing sensations of doubt would stiffen him and force him to stand frozen right in the middle of an undergarment roll or a crease inspection. Christoph wasn't just anxious over his own fate but also for the potential trouble the roadtrip could cause his family. Fortunately, his jumping nerves gravitated more toward excitement than fear and he smiled as he closed the lid and secured the rusty golden latch. Hurriedly, he rushed down the stairs and out through the front door to seek his pride and joy, the chariot that would whisk them off to their destination.

Parked out of sight of nosy neighbors, Christoph's cherished 1961 black Cadillac hearse had remained hidden inconspicuously behind their home. It boasted custom green ghost flames, which he had always been fond of but he couldn't wait to see the expressions of the passing drivers when they saw them in it. He wasn't bothered in the least that the exterior paint was imperfect or that the interior upholstery was worn. He was just plain excited at the hearse's inclusion in such a significant adventure and he chuckled to himself at thoughts of chauffeuring himself and his pack of vampires across the country in such a fitting vehicle.

Christoph rarely had the opportunity to drive it as they had all agreed during one disheartening first wake that its presence in their driveway drew too much attention to their secret. Finally getting the chance to drive it again was akin to being reunited with a favorite toy from childhood. As a subliminal shout out to his clan, he jangled the keys in his right hand the way a human might shake a bag of dog food for a wayward puppy. Placing his luggage on the cement beside the car, he ran his hand down its sleek lines and reminisced about the past adventures he and his chariot had shared together. More than aware that he was quite early and that the others were not yet ready, he grinned as he loaded up the back and the trunk. Deciding there was no law against an early start he jumped behind the steering wheel of his cherished vehicle and waited patiently for his pack's arrival.

The feeling that he had left something important behind tugged at Christoph's comfort level, so he reluctantly pulled himself back out of the driver's seat and darted back up the stairs to his bedroom. Slamming the door behind him, he entered his closet and stood on the tips of his toes to reach the top shelf as boxes of random photographs and unknown paperwork fell onto his head before spilling onto the rug.

Spying an old, leather-covered box, he grabbed it and paused for a moment before unclipping the two latches and opening the lid. The box creaked slowly and Christoph carefully peered inside to admire its contents. Nestled protectively on a foam bed was the wooden crossbow he had carefully handcrafted but not looked at in many years. Next to it, in their own separate foam enclosure, were the silver arrows he had constructed to go with it. He didn't dare let his pack see he was bringing the weapon, especially not after the way they had mocked his invention the first time he had showed it to them.

Glancing at the wall in contemplation, he finally slammed the lid shut, clicked the cover latches until they locked, and ran back down to the hearse with the crossbow and silver arrows clutched tightly under his arm. He placed the carrying case in the back corner of the hearse and attempted to hide its existence by positioning his suitcase in front of it. Slamming the rear door shut and taking his place back in the driver's seat, he nervously thumbed the steering wheel to the up-beat tempo of his heart and wondered with trepidation if each pack mate would keep the promise to join him.

Upstairs, in the back bedroom where his pack had banished him, Leo kicked and cursed his way through a half-hearted packing routine. His movements appeared to have no rhyme or reason as he did more pacing and stomping around than any semblance of productive planning. His incentive simmered on the back burner and the only thought that drove him was the one that warned him to meet his pack at the car before they left him there. Struggling with thoughts of backing out of the crazy venture, Leo stopped circling the room and looked down at the floor.

"Hell," he mumbled. *"I ain't got nothin' better to do."*

As the day of their departure approached, Leo had spent many hours contemplating all of the ways he could make the trip unbearable for his pack. One idea that sent him into fits of hysterics, which he would always refuse to explain, was to avoid any further showers or hygiene tasks so that he could fill the car with his intolerable stench. Though many other amusing sabotage techniques sprang to mind, Leo had not acted on any of them in the end. Half-heartedly throwing random shirts, pants, socks, and underwear into a duffle bag, he would occasionally lift an item to give it a good whiff. More often than not, Leo was pleased to discover his clothes would surely emanate an odor that was offensive to them all. He zipped his bag with more force than necessary and sat down on his wooden chair with his head resting in his hands. Knowing his procrastination had become obvious, he expected a knock at the door and a whining plea for him to hurry. As if on cue, a brief rap sounded as the door and Dominic stepped in without waiting for his invitation.

"You ready?" he asked him.

"I guess," Leo replied slowly before pausig. "You sure you want me goin' with you guys? It's been said that I'm not the most pleasant guy to be around, especially for long periods of time..."

"Look, man," Dominic interrupted, "you're not gettin' out of this one. We've all agreed to deal with the misery of being stuck in a car with you for several days because your place is with us. You're going!"

Leo looked up into Dominic's eyes and noticed an expression of seriousness that he didn't understand but appreciated nonetheless.

"You're sure?" Leo tried again, trying to give his friend an easy out if he wanted it. "Maybe you want someone to stay here to, you know... look after the place."

"No, sir," Dominic answered firmly and without hesitation. "I want you with us, so let's go. That's an order."

"All right," Leo relented. "I'll be down in a few"

"No, I'm not coming back up after you, Leo," Dominic warned. "I'm tired of climbing these stairs."

Realizing Dominic's visit was really just an excuse to make him feel included and necessary, Leo offered a slight smile that had rarely been witnessed by anyone else in the universe and he followed Dominic's extended arm toward the door. As Leo shuffled down the stairs to join the pack, Dominic headed to his own room to gather his belongings.

Always the planner, he had already been packed for a week, having started immediately after their decision to go on the roadtrip. Though he had packed enough clothing to last the length of their journey, he did not pack anything for the drive back because something inside told him there would be no return trip. He sensed in the deepest and darkest recesses of his mind that the outcome of their meeting with Lucius would not end well for all of them. Though he was typically confident in a positive outcome, his bright side had turned dark given the unknown circumstances.

Dominic patted the top of his luggage before walking past it toward the corner of the room. His guitar lie propped against the two intersecting walls and he picked it up carefully, held it horizontally waist height and ran a finger down its smooth side, smearing new lines into the dust and grime. While other musicians took pride in the constant cleaning and coddling of their guitars, Dominic had appreciated the wear and tear because it was a representation of its use. He felt pride at the stains of the sweat droplets that still remained intact because each one of them reminded him of his glory days performing on stage. Though unnecessary for the trip, it called out to him and he fought the urge to bring it along.

"Not this time, my friend," Dominic answered gently, consoling the inanimate object before placing it back in the darkened corner.

He had made it halfway through the room on his way out the door when he felt a strong sensation that he had forgotten something important. It was a feeling he was accustomed to and one he experienced each time he left his room, left the house, or left any other location, for that matter. Dominic patted his pockets to check for his valuables and everything seemed to be in its place. His wallet, his keys, his ChapStick… his sanity; but even though his checklist seemed complete, the nagging sensation that something was missing grated on his nerves. Instead of mulling it over further, he snatched up his luggage and forced himself into the hallway and down the staircase, glancing back at his sanctuary one more time on his way down. Upon entering the kitchen, he caught a glimpse of Jarek reaching for the front doorknob.

"Got everything?" Dominic asked him.

"Everything I need," answered Jarek, giving a quick tug of his jacket. Evidently, he planned to travel light and with only the items he had tucked away inside various pockets.

"Seriously?" Dominic asked. "That's it?"

With a smirk, Jarek lifted up a small backpack.

"And this too…"

Dominic returned the knowing grin and followed him out to the car where Christoph and Leo studiously avoided each other. They were lingering around the hearse in nervous anticipation but not bickering, insulting, or acknowledging one another in any way. They both seemed lost in their own worlds as though neither was even aware of the other's presence. Dominic noticed how full the hearse already appeared and instinctively looked in Christoph's direction.

"Brought a little extra baggage, did we?" he asked, amused.

Fidgeting at the inquiry, Christoph tried to prevent a guilty expression from reaching his eyes or a conscious thought from entering his mind.

"What?" he asked innocently.

"A little overly cautious bringing such a device, don't ya think?" Dominic asked.

"What did he bring?" Leo asked. "What is it, Dom?"

"Yeah, what are you hiding?" Jarek chimed in.

"Wait!" exclaimed Leo. "I think I know!"

Recalling a conversation years before where Christoph had bragged about a stupendous invention he created should they ever take to the road, Leo knew immediately what he was trying to disguise behind the luggage.

"Please," Leo teased. "Tell me it's not that stupid crossbow."

Though he tried to stifle it, even Jarek couldn't prevent the snort of laughter that escaped him.

"Wait!" he jumped in. "Did you bring the silver-tipped arrows too?"

A rumble of barely suppressed laughter traveled from one traveler to the next, affecting even Dominic. Refusing to give any of them the dignity of a response, Christoph ignored their mocking and kept his focus straight ahead.

Sensing his sensitive friend's need for solidarity, Dominic stopped laughing, snapped for the others to follow suit, and gave Christoph a light punch to the arm.

"If you say so, my friend," he comforted. "If you say so."

Raina stood alone in her room, surrounded by thoughts that mingled with the darkness around her. Knowing that music was the only medicine that would work for such an occasion, she moved slowly toward her stereo intent on filling the void where her soul used to be and pressed the play button.

Click. A wave of relief rushed over her at the familiar sound. Music had always played a significant role in her life and she welcomed the eerie sounds that streamed out even more than she would welcome an embrace at that moment. A sense of relaxation and escape began to caress each of her nerves as she forced herself to tune out any noise unrelated to the dark melody. She needed the music to transport her to a place of reassurance and comfort and to provide her the strength she needed to take the first step toward embarking on the journey of a lifetime.

Raina acknowledged the magnitude of such a quest and while she did not know the specific dangers that lie ahead, she knew there was great risk attached to their trip. It was unheard of to seek out the headmaster and those who even made mention of the idea succeeded in placing themselves at great risk from the League.

"Why are we doing this?' she mumbled to herself.

Drawing a hairbrush through her locks in long, flowing strokes, she meticulously placed each thick strand into the style that made her feel most beautiful. Of course, she had no way of knowing how it looked since no reflection stared back from any of the mirrors that surrounded her room.

The music began to work its magic and she felt the onset of her inner strength trying to take hold, providing her with a much-needed burst of energy to finalize her preparations. Glancing one last time into her golden handheld mirror, she applied her fourth coat of lipstick since the onset of the song and then hid it in her bra for quick access. Tossing her hairbrush into her purse and stuffing a compact in the other cup, she decided she was just about ready. The cosmetics were essential to her and she would keep them close to her at all times.

In a sudden flash, troublesome thoughts began to penetrate her relaxed state and she knew it was because the time had come to leave their safe haven. Questions and doubt raced through her mind, her veins, and her borrowed blood as the uncertainty of their future taunted her. Annoyance crept even deeper into her nervous system as her soothing music was interrupted by the sound of guitars pulsating from the driveway; her pack's discrete way of telling her to hurry up. She felt a jolt of frustration followed by some aggressive opinions about her traveling companions, but though the stress mounted, she did not resist it because it was accompanied by an increase of empowerment.

"I am doing this for me," she said out loud. *"And no one else."*

From the street, she could hear the rumbling of the engine and a honk of the horn but she ignored it and instead concentrated on the song, vowing not to leave her room until the last note had played.

"She's going out on the town and she's dressed to kill."

Singing along with the lyrics that blasted from her speakers, Raina slammed both hands onto the armoire in front of the mirror and thrust her face toward the glass with her nose slightly touching it. Narrowing her eyes in anger, she tried her hardest to will some kind of image to appear as she searched in vain for an outline or a hue or a shadow but was gifted with nothing in return.

Raina jumped and almost fell backwards when a flash of Joan Crawford's face appeared, an intense and penetrating look in her eyes. Sam had arrived under the guise of his other alter ego and had apparently decided to use her mirror as his venue.

"That's not funny," she said angrily, trying to blink the image.

Her efforts were in vain; he was not going anywhere until he'd had his say. The cold, hard eyes continued the stare down so she began shaking the mirror back and forth. It only caused Joan to laugh and the sound was unsettling; almost scary. Raina had wanted for Sam to visit on the day of her departure but had hoped he would come as either Lucy or himself as they were much more uplifting than Joan's cryptic, accusatory drop-ins.

"What?!" Raina yelled.

"Tsk tsk," Joan chided. "What kind of welcome is that, darling?"

"Your eyes are dark and chilling," Raina complained. "They drain me of all peace."

"They're Bette Davis eyes, darling," Joan cackled in her witchlike manner.

"Please, leave me alone right now," Raina pleaded. "This is an important day for me."

"Of course it is. Why do you think I'm here?"

"To destroy my serenity or convince me to do something terrible, I'm sure," Raina answered.

"You're funny, little girl," Joan patronized. "I would support your trip if you weren't going to ask for something so incredibly stupid."

"Why is my desire for mortality so stupid?" Raina asked, hurt.

"To throw away such a gift... it's shameful," Joan scolded. "When you don't listen to my advice, do you ever notice all the trouble you get yourself into? You ignored me about your men and look what happened?"

"You told me to cheat and to lie to the two men I love! Your advice only gets me into trouble!"

"One is a tear-drinker turned on by your crying," Joan defended. "The other abandoned you to lead a pack of misfits. I don't understand your loyalty to either of them!"

"Well, you don't need to! This is my life... my decision. Now, go away!"

"All I'm saying is... block out your feelings and simply remain in control."

"No!" Raina countered. "I'm tired of that and I'm not doing it anymore. Even if I don't see Lucius and even if he doesn't grant my wish, I don't want this life anymore. I want to feel and I want to love and eventually... I want to die."

Raina considered letting out a short scream to punctuate her angry statement but reminded herself that it was the reaction Joan was looking for, so she stayed quiet and let her head fall backward to break the intense eye contact. Her next question was meant for Joan but aimed at the ceiling.

"Why are you always trying to talk me into doing bad things?"

"What?" she heard from the mirror. "I resent that."

"No, I mean it. I think you really enjoy watching me make a fool of myself."

Joan cackled again.

"Maybe a little," she admitted. "Don't blame me! You're quite entertaining."

Raina met Joan's eyes once more and answered by pulling the lipstick back out of her bra and throwing it at the trouble-making entity.

"You know, for such a tortured soul, you sure are funny," Joan laughed. "I'm just saying darling, be careful what you wish for…."

Raina shook her head back and forth and then looked back into the mirror, grateful to see Joan's image start to dissipate. Appreciation turned to anger when the hard eyes reappeared just as quickly and her uninvited guest threw one last unsolicited piece of advice her way.

"You're about to make the worst mistake of your life, darling," Joan warned. "Just don't blame me when it all comes tumbling down on you."

Raina snatched the mirror from its spot and smashed it against the top of the armoire, shattering it and leaving two tiny indentations in the sides of the golden frame. She grabbed her purse and her travel bag and headed for the bedroom door. Passing her coffin, she tossed the mirror frame with its broken glass shards over her shoulder and heard it land in front of her coffin.

Chapter VIII

Several hours had passed while traveling. The lights of the passing buildings and sounds of the fellow vehicles on the road had been a welcomed sensory experience for the pack in the early stages of their travels, but the excitement had quickly worn thin. Their legs were becoming restless and jittery and their minds were falling into memories of past experiences, of current random thoughts linked to boredom, and of the wonderment of what waited ahead. Sensing their uneasiness, Dominic made an announcement.

"Hey! Truck stop just ahead... I need some coffee for my soul."

They chuckled but it was more a half-hearted collective laugh, some from sense of need to respond to their leader and the others in appreciation for his humor and obvious love of coffee.

"One truck stop, comin' up," responded Christoph.

"Your eyes look a bit worn as well, sir," Dominic nudged their driver.

"I'm good."

As he spoke, the car veered to the right, grazing the rumble strips before the ditch, filling the hearse with a deep, low warning of pending danger.

"Right," said Dominic. "Pull it over."

The car cruised through the winds of the exit ramp to the entrance of the oversized truck stop that offered travelers all they could ever need. The large sign out front announced that they were visiting the Tiki Truck Stop, which alluded to the possibility of a retro beach theme, but in reality appeared more industrial. As the car slowed, Jarek's eyes widened with the vision of a chrome shop whose sign notated the availability of custom knives.

"You know where you can find me!" he announced, bolting out of the rear passenger door before anyone in the pack could discuss group plans.

In such a rural area, Dominic was not concerned with them splitting up individually to pursue their own interests. The quaint little diner with the invitation to a twenty-four hour breakfast was the only place of interest to him at the moment though he knew they wouldn't all be joining him.

"A little self-indulgence may be good for everyone," he thought.

He was also aware that their immediate location still offered him the ability to sense the activities of all his surroundings. This was also the rare opportunity for a mini-vacation that, while short-lived, would seem more like a month-long retreat compared to the daily routines and activities they endured.

"Go have fun, but be back at the car in a half hour," he warned.

Dominic made his way through the gift shop and convenience store refreshment area toward the entrance of the diner. With a Mountain Dew in one hand and two large bags of Pizza Pretzel Combos pressed against his chest in the other, Leo turned the aisle and bumped directly into him, causing a few Combos to spill from the top of the bag he had already opened prior to checkout.

"Shit, Dom!" he mumbled with a mouth full of Combo goodness before he shuffled off to the counter. Dominic laughed internally at the sight of him running around and filling his hands with whatever junk food he felt would satisfy his needs.

From the corner of his eye, Dominic saw Christoph fumbling around in his pockets and counting quarters in front of the door that led to the shower stalls. Just beyond him were the glass windows that separated the main gift shop from the chrome shop. Through the panes, he could see Raina attempting to talk to Jarek, though his focus was clearly on the selection of knives before him.

"Apparently, I'm alone for breakfast," he whispered as he made his way to an empty table.

A young waitress approached and her nametag indicated she was Shirley, but her mixture of Gothic and Emo tattoos suggested she was likely known to others by another name. Possibly Raven or Miss Understood. She was alert, but her overall appearance left the impression that she had just clocked in to work, having come directly from the club following last call. Dominic could smell her perfume masking the hint of a recent cigarette and second-hand alcohol, while techno trance music waves permeated from her being. She started writing on her order tab before even looking at her customer.

"Hello. My name is Shirley. I'll be your...," she paused as she eyed Dominic with menu in hand.

"Hey, cool outfit. Did you just come from The Castle too?"

He glanced down at his leather pants and tugged on his black trench coat. Her thoughts of a fog-filled laser light dance room revealed she was not acknowledging him as a true vampire but rather referring to the name of the venue that accommodated the local Goth scene.

With a smirk, and still touching the collar of his coat, Dominic replied.

"Me? No... was gonna try to make it there tonight, but no such luck."

Shrugging it off, she inquired, "Then what can I get for ya?"

"Coffee... black... and the Old Timer's Breakfast, please."

The menu's description of his selection excited him as it offered the full array of breakfast delectables he had always enjoyed: two eggs over medium, two pieces of toast, hash brown casserole, grits, two pancakes, and a biscuit with sausage gravy.

"Comin' right up!" she exclaimed with a newfound energy as she hurried off to the kitchen.

The moment of isolation gave Dominic a much-needed moment to reflect on the details of their journey. Normally, he would be strategically calculating every step of the way, but exhaustion from the drive had set in and his penchant for planning was replaced with intrigue as to the events that could unfold along the way.

"Be comfortable with the fact that you can't foresee the future," he told himself.

He had often tried to convince himself that the mystery of lands unknown was a good thing and that he should enjoy the experience for what it was... but uncertainty made him anxious and he knew he had to keep reminding himself of what he wanted to feel rather than what he did feel.

Spinning a spoon between his fingers, Dominic sensed the pending arrival of two of his companions. Making their way around various tables and booths, Jarek and Raina walked side by side. The brown paper bag clutched in Jarek's hand undoubtedly contained the recent purchase to add to his collection. The two slid across the vinyl seat of the booth and while Jarek placed the bag on the table next to the condiments, Raina reached into her purse to find her lipstick. The waitress appeared briefly to fill three coffee mugs before quickly darting off again.

"How we doin'?" Dominic asked.

Excitement in his eyes, Jarek answered first.

"Dom, you gotta check this out."

From the bag, he pulled out a new mother of pearl handled custom knife, which boasted an engraved Celtic cross at the base of the blade. Raising an eyebrow in interest, Dominic asked the first question that came to mind.

"How much you got wrapped up into that one?"

"Four hundred bucks, out the door," he answered, sliding it back into its paper container and placing it down by his side. Their club-loving waitress returned and placed several plates of food before Dominic.

"Get you anything?" she asked his new companions.

"Just the coffee," Jarek declared.

"And a piece of toast with just butter and blackberry jelly," requested Raina.

"You got it," Shirley replied, as her personal cell phone rang a stripped down version of a familiar song by Depeche Mode.

"So now what?" asked Raina.

Mixing the eggs with his hash brown casserole, Dominic looked up at her and answered, "All in due time my dear..."

Raina had always been attracted to the mysterious side of Dominic, but at times found it to be a source of frustration as well. Mostly, it worked to spark her interest in the days to come. Dominic always had big plans, was always involved in several big projects at once, and always shared with her just enough information to ignite her excitement as to the possibilities of the future. Following several insignificant side conversations, their late night breakfast concluded and Dominic left enough money on the table to cover their bill and enough of a tip to allow their youthful waitress to enjoy herself at tomorrow night's club scene.

"I'll go get Christoph and Leo," Raina offered, and without waiting for permission took off out the door.

"Hurry up," Dominic called after her. "And be good!"

"Yeah," Jarek agreed. "Be good!"

Raina's search for her pack mates ended as soon as she passed an antique jewelry store. Doubling back, she decided it couldn't hurt to just walk in and look around for a minute or two. Admiring the jewels and gems that glistened from their cases, she instinctively clutched at the amber hanging from a thin chain around her neck. A memory played itself out against her wishes and she could still feel Jarek's hands as he clasped the chain gently at her neck. Ignoring the lump that began forming in her throat, she slammed the door shut on the memory before it turned into an uncomfortable feeling and moved quickly onto the next case.

Her eyes gravitated toward the price tags on the onyx and the silver and the blue topaz and she seriously considered enchanting the clerk long enough to snag a stone from its display. The emergence of her criminal mind meant that Joan was probably close by though Raina sincerely hoped that was not the case. Caressing the glass with her fingers, she lowered herself to the floor to peer in at a lower rack and just as her eye fell on an amethyst ring sparkling atop a ring rack, Raina felt a puff of hot breath and heard a whisper in her right ear.

"It's your birthstone, darling. Take it."

Rising quickly to her height, Raina prayed the change of position would rid her of Joan's unwanted intrusion. Snapping her head toward the opposite direction, she found herself looking directly into a make-up mirror and realized with growing anxiety that there would be no easy escape. The reflection staring back donned a red bun, a piteous grin, and a slow and disappointed shake of the head.

"Don't do it, crazy lady."

Wanting to scream at both of them for their public appearances, Raina instead kept her mouth closed. If her pale skin, blood red hair, and dark apparel hadn't already placed the other customers on guard, a loud argument with herself most certainly would. She headed toward the shop exit as fast as possible, and half walked, half ran down the sidewalk. Her only plan was to blend into the busy streets and if lucky, lose her annoying entities before they found a way to get her into trouble.

As she passed the different shops, Raina looked through the storefronts and stared longingly at the humans as they tended to their different needs and desires. From haircuts designed to enhance an appearance to ice cream cones meant to appease a sweet tooth, she felt a pang of envy for their simple, mundane lives. Daring a quick glance behind her, Raina realized that Joan and Lucy had continued to pursue her quietly through the winding streets of the plaza and instinctively, she picked up her speed. They gained on her and when she checked again, she realized that Lucy flanked her left side and Joan flanked her right. Their placement reminded her of the perpetual devil and angel that took residence upon every human's shoulders, their influences of good and evil working hard to convince her of the merits on each side.

"Listen to me, Raina," Lucy pleaded in her trademark, smoky rasp. *"Don't ignore your conscience or you chance losing it forever."*

"Pay no attention to her!" Joan countered loudly. *"Follow your instinct and take what you want! You are no longer human and need not continue to follow the rules of the mortals!"*

Both of her unwanted visitors maintained an even pace with Raina's speed walk.

"You know who you are," Lucy reminded her. *"Don't turn on yourself or your roadtrip will be for nothing. Stealing, cheating, lying... they will become your downfall and you know it."*

"Come on, Raina! Think of the powers you're capable of," Joan pushed. *"You are a natural enchantress and because of it, your potential has always been greater than most! Think of how much stronger your abilities could become if you just allowed yourself to make your own rules."*

"She's enchanting enough on her own without the power of darkness! She doesn't need..."

"Give me a break!" Joan cut Lucy off. *"Power over humans and useless men and low level vampires means nothing!"*

Directing her attention toward Raina again, Joan continued. *"Think of the power you could have if you were able to enchant the masses and manipulate the pack leaders! It could be limitless!"*

Turning back to Lucy, Joan continued. *"Do you honestly believe she wants to reclaim the misery and pain she knew as a human?"* she asked angrily. *"Mortality offered her nothing but loss and grief whereas immortality can provide her with the sweetest and most abundant of all pleasures while asking for nothing in return!"*

Joan tugged playfully at a lock of Raina's hair that had begun to fall free from its loose ponytail.

"Nothing in return?" Lucy laughed without humor. Reaching around Raina, she slapped Joan's hand away and delivered her next words in a raspy whisper. *"Nothing but your soul, crazy lady."*

"Her soul, hah!" Joan responded as she squeezed herself between Raina and Lucy. *"What good is a soul? It's as fleeting and useless as the body! Besides, it's already gone..."*

"Then why is she risking her life to get it back, you wicked creature?" Lucy responded angrily as she moved to the other side of her mistress and slipped her hand into Raina's. *"You've held on this long. Don't give up now, not when you've come so close to finding it again."*

Raina continued to walk forward, still refusing to acknowledge either one of them. She stopped short at the next window and realized it was the diner she had left the men at. Jarek was holding his new knife high above his head in admiration and Dominic was laughing at something he had said. She sped up before they saw her walking aimlessly and finally broke her silence, speaking in a voice filled with longing.

"He loves knives," Raina said more to herself than to her stalkers.

"Of course he does," Lucy answered sarcastically. *"He's a lunatic and lunatics love sharp objects."*

"He's no lunatic," Joan defended. *"I find him quite charming."*

"You would," Lucy snapped.

"Don't let him see you watching," Joan advised.

"Why?" Raina asked.

"You never let a man know how much you love him," Joan answered. *"Especially a man like your Jarek."*

"You're a fool, Joan," Lucy chastised.

"No, silly heart. You're the fairytale spinner who will lead her to trouble much worse than I ever would," Joan winked knowingly. *"Men like Jarek will turn a woman's love into a weapon sharper than that knife he's holding. She needs our protection, not our lies or our false reassurances. Why don't you just get out of here and come back when she needs help shopping?"*

Raina didn't respond to either argument. She was too disturbed that her ghosts not only insisted upon visiting her but that they were arguing with one another. If ever there were an asylum for the immortal, she imagined she would become the first patient. The fact that both of them had shown up at the same time sent her concern spiraling even further. If it were in fact Sam who had been the sly portrayer of both entities, how was it he was showing up as both at the same time? Knowing that it was neither the time nor place to get to the bottom of the strange appearances, she made the mental note to ask him about it when he showed up as himself again.

She also had no valid argument for either of them because they were both right. Withholding and disguising her love was counterproductive but the truth was that Jarek's wish to leave the pack did not include her and if granted, he would abandon her at the end of their trip. Allowing him inside any further would be foolish.

They all fell silent as Raina led them to a bench that sat beneath a group of oak trees at the end of the long walk. The sun had set a couple of hours before but the lights from the plaza were bright and they illuminated the entire area but for the spot they were headed. She wondered again why Sam had chosen to take the form of two such opposite personalities during her greatest times of need but ultimately, the answer was all too clear. Joan was as cold and calculating as Lucy was warm and humorous and Raina needed both of their influences to make well thought out decisions.

Bowing her head and lowering her eyes to the ground, Raina stopped walking to collect her thoughts and steady herself. She watched as a group of ants worked as a team to carry a crumb back to their tiny village, when one of the insects turned away from the group and scurried in the opposite direction, leaving his family to find a way to struggle with the weight he left on them.

"That one must be a male," Joan said.

"Man hater," Lucy shot out.

"Goofy bitch," Joan insulted. *"Perhaps you can come back and help with less serious matters, like cooking or sleeping. Leave the bigger decisions to me."*

"Shut up!' Raina finally yelled. "Both of you!"

The ill-timed and vicious comment flew out of her mouth just as they were passing two women embroiled in their own conversation. A malicious giggle from Raina's left told her that Joan was amused by the unfortunate situation while an indrawn breath from her right told her that Lucy was not.

"What did you say?" asked the heavier set of the women. Hair shaped like a 1950s housewife and a tone that insinuated the need for constant conflict, she stopped abruptly beside Raina and put an angry hand to her hip.

"I'm sorry," Raina apologized. "I wasn't talking to you."

The woman looked back at her even less attractive friend and smiled dramatically.

"You see anyone else in hearing distance, Claire?"

Claire shot glances in every direction and then shook her head with a grin.

"Not a soul, Nance," she answered.

Both women looked back to Raina with a shrug of their shoulders.

"There doesn't seem to be anyone else around which must mean that you must have been telling us to shut up for some strange reason."

"Look," Raina began, trying to sound less annoyed with the pointless humans than she was letting on. "Why don't you ladies continue with your walk and I'll continue with mine, all right?"

"Punch her in the face," Joan demanded.

Her tone had become more aggressive and Raina worried about just how far her angrier ghost would go in such a situation.

"They're just bored, silly women, Raina," Lucy jumped in, obviously worried. *"Don't be angry with them. Pity them for their ignorance and their limitations."*

"Punch her in the face!"

Raina ignored both voices as best she could while maintaining unwavering eye contact with Nance, then Claire, then Nance again.

"I'm going to walk in that direction," Raina pointed ahead of them. "My friends are waiting for me and I'm not interested in arguing with you any further."

"Is that right?" Claire asked. "Guess you shouldn't have opened your mouth then, huh?"

The women looked Raina up and down before making eye contact with one another, as though they had discovered something amiss at the same time.

"What are you supposed to be anyway?" Nance asked, distaste woven into each word and in a tone that was both syrupy and patronizing. "I think you chose the wrong place for your little pit stop. We are a civilized community and we certainly don't carry on conversations with ourselves or dress like monsters here. Is someone lacking a little attention?"

"Knock her lights out, girl! If you don't, I will!"

"You can't touch them," Lucy yelled at Joan. *"You have no power in the physical world, you fool!"*

"I have all the power she gives me," Joan replied with a mischievous smile. *"Isn't that right, Raina?"*

Though it was becoming increasingly difficult, Raina continued to block out their words and concentrate on the problem in front of her.

"I'm going to keep walking, ladies," she said to the humans. "Enjoy your evening."

Upon her second step away from the abusive strangers, Raina felt hands on her back as she was shoved with mild force into a small puddle before her. As dirty water drenched the bottom of her gown, she felt her fury as it jumped many notches higher. Hearing laughter behind her, she pulled her dress up higher and stepped out of the puddle. With an entirely different look in her eyes, Raina met her assailant's stare with an intensity that radiated from her with a palpable heat. When her ghosts spoke again, Raina did not tune them out but listened with the alertness that comes attached to rage.

"This is why you despised the humans, Raina, remember? This is why you wanted a new world and this is the moment where you are allowed to let go."

"Don't do it, Raina. Don't bring trouble or attention this way. Think of your pack. Think of Leo and the rage that took hold of him."

Though reminders of Leo's torturous and anger-filled heart usually worked to dispel her need for revenge, she found that it did not work when her fist rounded her side and shot out so quickly that she didn't realize it was happening until it made contact with Nance's cheek. Claire's scream accompanied the sound of Nance's cracking bones and Raina allowed the sweetness of retribution to fill her while she inhaled the delicious scent of justice. The moment was cut short, however, by another, louder screech from Claire and the sound worked to snap Raina out of her trance. She noticed that the woman had knelt down protectively to soothe her moaning and blood-drenched friend.

"Don't worry," Raina comforted. "She's not dead. Nothing a little plastic surgery won't fix."

"You bitch!" Claire screamed without restraint.

Raina's leg sprang to life and before she knew it, formed a weapon of her knee. With brutal force, she brought it up to the bottom of Claire's chin and then listened to the woman's teeth as they fell to the ground and to the blood as it dripped from her wounds. Though she tried to scream, only groans of agony escaped her broken face. Her tears became lost amidst the blood.

"Awww, sorry," Raina mocked. "Guess you shouldn't have opened your mouth, huh?"

Spinning on her heel and lifting her dress carefully, she hovered slightly above the puddle before floating across it. Once cement was beneath her again, she touched ground and picked up her pace, trying to ignore the voices that gathered behind her as the other humans rushed to the women's aid. Raina knew that it was only a matter of time before one of them decided to pursue her so she ran back to the diner and crashed into Dominic and Jarek as they walked out.

"What the hell?" they asked, confused.

"Come on," Raina rushed. "We've got to get out of here!"

"Why?" they asked in unison. "What have you done?"

"It's not me," she answered quickly. "It's Joan. She won again."

When they returned to the car, Leo was asleep in the backseat, a *Maxim* magazine in his lap, a 20-ounce Mountain Dew nestled against his arm, and a single Combo hanging from his lips, which twitched with every snore. Christoph was just returning to the car as well and he appeared tired and in need of some rest. Dominic asked for the keys and gestured for him to sleep in the back.

"I'll drive," announced Dominic, as the others filed into the vehicle.

While his strategic planning ability was currently limited, taking the keys was a calculated move he had configured long before. By taking control of the wheel, Dom was taking control of their destinations. And there was an unannounced stop that needed to be made.

Chapter IX

After promising to never again leave them unaccompanied, Raina talked Dominic into making their first overnight stop. They were all exhausted, grouchy, and their legs had started showing imprints from the leather seats; they wanted nothing more than warm beds and a little privacy.

After checking in, Dominic exited the lobby and headed toward the car in a cool, slow stride. As he approached it, he extended his arm, his index finger rotating the metal ring of the room key in a circular motion. He hopped in the car and motioned for Jarek to drive forward.

"Straight ahead, all the way down."

Dominic got a thrill from the memories of past visits to resorts. He had enjoyed playing rock star and fantasizing that he had an endless bank account. The mere memory of room service and mini-bars made his pulse race. He had frequently enjoyed playing tour guide to his friends with each visit to various hotels.

As the car crept forward, Dominic playfully imitated the Count, while welcoming his crew to their location.

"Ladies and gentlemen... welcome to Hotel Royale. On your left, you will find our two luxurious swimming pools. Two! Ah ah ah... hot tub... sauna..."

With a slight glance to his right, he observed two young college girls dressed in their nightclub attire, fumbling with a slight stagger to navigate their room key into the door of their room.

"And on your right... continental breakfast... being served from 6 a.m. until..."

He paused slightly as his crew switched their attention to the two guests.

"Now!"

The doors of the car flew open and each one of them moved with a purpose, almost in time with the pulsating guitar melody coming from their stereo.

Having finally enjoyed a hot meal, Raina lounged on her motel bed thinking of the long journey ahead. Hoping there would be no reappearance from either of her ghosts, she closed her eyes and tried to stop thinking. Conflicted by thoughts of what could happen if and when they made it to Lucius, she finally fell into a deep and restful sleep just in time for the sun to awaken. It had been such a deep sleep, in fact, that she didn't hear a sound when her surprise visitor dropped by, quietly and unexpectedly as usual. Undisturbed by the click of the lock and deafened by her slumber, she didn't hear the slow creaking of her motel door and didn't stir a muscle when her sleeping body was pulled gently into a muscular hug. What did wake her was the feel of a strong chest against her cheek and the firm hand that held her head to it.

Most women would have been frightened and likely responded with a scream or a struggle or both, but not Raina. It hadn't taken her long to adjust to Jarek's intrusions and his need to overpower her in every way possible. Somehow, without becoming aware of it, she had grown accustomed to the continuous violations of a guest who possessed neither an invitation nor a key yet insisted on showing up during her most vulnerable hours.

She knew that her subconscious mind had registered his arrival and identity before her conscious mind had. If he had truly been an enemy, Raina would not have sensed such comfort and safety and would have gone automatically into fight mode. Instead, she buried her head deeper into his torso and felt her arms instinctively enclose his thick waist. She had always loved the feel of Jarek's body – all six feet and three inches of it. Two hundred and forty pounds of hard-earned muscle made for a serious embrace and she gave into it without a fight because his massive strength made her feel protected rather than scared.

In the beginning, she had been afraid of his sudden appearances, but as their intimacy deepened, Raina had come to realize that he loved her and would never harm her, physically any way. On the contrary, she would assign Jarek the role of captain of her personal army should anyone ever wage a war on her life. She had no doubt that his courage and strength would help her to conquer a bloody battle but even more invaluable, his intense love for her could one day become the sole weapon needed to win a war on her life.

Raina smiled against his chest and wondered why he always chose to sneak in when he could just as easily have knocked or planned the visit. He knew, though she was leery of his mysterious pop-ups, she wouldn't turn him away because she loved to be in his company as much as possible. Having decided that he was afflicted with an overdose of male privilege and entitlement, Raina found herself accepting that his sneaky arrivals were meant to remind her he could gain access whenever he wanted.

Raina tried to assess all she could from her limited position. Jarek's presence in her room told her the sky must have darkened and the rhythmic drops pelting on the rooftop suggested it was raining hard. With her lips still pressed to his shirt and his arms enclosing her affectionately, and possessively, she asked a muffled question.

"Is it raining?"

"Yes, darling."

"Are you sure?"

A short half laugh led his reply.

"Do you hear the drops pounding the roof?" he asked sarcastically.

"Yes."

"Is that not enough for you?"

"But the weather report said it would be a clear night."

"Which do you believe more – the weather report or the weather?"

She pulled her head back just enough to cut her eyes up at him from such a deep angle.

"I'm not sure," she joked.

Jarek clasped her chin between his thumb and forefinger, keeping her face tilted upward and her gaze in place. Had anyone else tried to utilize such dominating behavior with her, Raina would have laughed at them or punched them in the face but when Jarek did it, it was acceptable to her, normal somehow. Their relationship had always been marked by his domination and her submission; the resultant chaos caused Raina to wonder if the universe were just amusing itself with their coupling.

"How'd you get in this time?" she asked, knowing he wouldn't tell her. No matter how sturdy or how numerous the locks, he always managed to find a way in and it made her paranoid that he possessed powers he hadn't shared with any of them.

"Don't worry about it," he smirked.

Raina offered a weak smile.

"No, seriously," she tried again.

"Seriously," repeated Jarek, running a finger down her jaw line. "Don't concern yourself with such tedious things."

"You could have really scared me, you know."

His smile widened.

"I thought about putting a hand over your mouth but changed my mind at the last minute."

"Smart thinking," she said firmly and tried not recoil at the thought of it. "You don't have any smelling salts in your pocket, do you?" she half joked.

"No, darling. I'm a patient man."

She laughed despite herself. Jarek's wit and ability to make her laugh had seen her through some very tough times and she wasn't willing to give it up. Not yet anyway.

"You don't have your knife on you, do you?" she joked.

"Always," he answered. "Not that you'd ever have to worry about it."

"No?"

"Of course not," he said, offended. "I'm buying one for you though. You need protection, especially on this trip."

"I don't want one. I couldn't cut someone if I tried."

"I don't know about that," he grinned. "You never know what you're capable of until your survival's in jeopardy. Besides, it's actually quite enjoyable."

"What's wrong with you?" she asked.

Jarek laughed his long, heartfelt laugh that she had always loved. He so enjoyed when she asked him that.

Raina lost herself in the memory of the first time she had seen Jarek lying on their doormat. He had managed to drag himself through their yard, up their steep staircase, and to their front door before collapsing. Looking sadly upon his disheveled clothes and glazed eyes that day, she had known immediately that it would take him several days to understand and accept what had happened to him, what he had become.

Grabbing the fingers that caressed her face, she threw them away from her and disengaged herself from their embrace. Jarek loved to harass her. Most often, he was just looking for one of her trademark pouts but there were times he didn't stop until he saw tears. On the rare occasion when a drop would fall from her tear-soaked lashes, Jarek would switch roles with himself and comfort her. She had dubbed him the 'tear drinker' the first time he made her cry and he had accepted his nickname with delight.

"Why do you torture me?" she asked him softly.

He raised his eyebrows, as though he was really putting thought into it.

"You're like barbed wire and roses," he smiled, nodding to punctuate his statement.

Jarek cocked his head to the side and mimicked the sad expression reflected in her features before scooting to the side to allow her more space. Or at least to allow her the illusion that he was giving her space. She never knew what strategy was playing out inside of his head.

"What does that even mean?" she asked calmly.

Jarek's nod turned to a slow shake of the head but the smile never wavered for a moment.

"Oh, Raina," he continued in his soothing voice. "Do you know what my favorite part of you is?"

Her hands shot up to her ears in an effort to block out the rest of his statement but Jarek gently leaned forward to pull them back down and place them in her lap.

"What?" she surrendered more quickly than usual. She was exhausted and his games only drained her more. Raina feared she might have to feed twice as much to make up for the energy he had stolen from her, again.

"You're just a little girl inside," he answered affectionately.

"I'm not a little girl!" she argued.

"Yes," he smiled. "You are. There's an innocence about you, a sweetness and a vulnerability that's obvious to everyone who knows you."

Raina was shaking her head emphatically by the time he finished.

"No," she insisted.

She didn't want to be a little girl. She wanted to be a strong and independent woman and that he saw her as a child infuriated her. Raina put both hands to his chest and pushed on him for leverage. She scooted backwards over the lumps on her mattress and away from the bed-side embrace, stopping only when the back of her head bumped the headboard. She glared at him without a word while working hard to resist the urge to smack the snide grin off his face.

"What are you doing here?" she asked. "Don't you think Dom will notice you're missing?"

Jarek's grin contorted to a straight line and his frown marked a sudden change of attitude.

"I don't make my decisions based on Dominic," he answered, anger taking over the playful tone. She knew that reminding him of Dom's position in their lives would piss him off but, never one to back down in the face of confrontation, she proceeded with her lecture despite the consequences.

"Well, maybe you should start," she challenged, nervously.

Jarek stood up and it caused a nervous chill to run from the bottom of her spine all the way to the tip. Towering over her motel bed and obviously affected by her words, Jarek's protective stance became more intimidating and Raina realized she was getting nervous. She longed for her coffin and desperately missed having the ability to simply shut the lid to any unwelcome feeling or guest.

His expression softened as he sat beside her on the bed and he pulled her hand into his. With a firm but gentle tone, he went into the explanation that she always hated hearing.

"I love Dominic; you know that," he began in a controlled voice. Pulling her other hand into his, Jarek leaned forward and dropped a kiss onto her lips before he continued.

"I respect him but I can't answer to him or to anybody else, Raina. I'm just not built that way."

"But you found us!" she argued. "You came to us! You knew the rules and you accepted them, Jarek. Your place in the pack protects you from the leagues of vampires who would force you into captivity, a much worse fate if I might add."

She distanced herself from him both physically and emotionally by pulling both of her hands away from his and hugging her knees. It was the conversation she had dreaded. She had always known that Jarek wasn't capable of following anyone and that his time with their pack was limited because of it. She had been ecstatic when he befriended Dom and had allowed herself to grow more comfortable as their bonds strengthened throughout the years but always knew the day would come when he found himself unable to bear the constant inclusion and obedience required of him. Raina closed her eyes to his words but stopped herself from covering her ears lest he call her a little girl again. She wished desperately that she had a girlfriend to talk to, someone who could understand her anguish and offer her the support that only estrogen could provide.

At the sound of shuffling in the corner, she shifted her gaze to its source and saw that Lucy had popped in.

"It's all right to let yourself love him, Raina, even if it hurts later."

Refusing to acknowledge her presence, Raina looked back at Jarek and continued sharing her thoughts, whether he wanted to hear them or not.

"You've lasted this long. Why does it always have to come back to this?" she asked, though she already knew the answer.

"Because, it's who I am, who I've always been," he answered simply. "And it's because of you."

"Me? Why me?"

"Don't play dumb," he said in a patronizing tone. "You know exactly what I'm talking about."

Jarek stood and began to pace the small room as she pulled one of the hair ties from her wrist. A nervous habit since childhood, she threw her hair into a ponytail knowing that she would pull it back out within a minute or two. Those who knew her well knew that she would tie up her locks up and then pull them back out again several times throughout the conversation.

He approached her again and pulled her hands back into his, despite her obvious wish not to be touched during the painful conversation. When she tried to pull them back, he held them tightly.

"Come on, give me a break," he chided. "You had to know it would never work like this."

"Why?"

"Because you belonged to Dominic and now you belong to me and that makes for a very tense situation. You didn't seriously think we'd be able to just move past this without a problem?"

"I don't belong to anybody," she countered.

"You know what I mean," he threw back, ignoring her point. "It's caused a rift that can't be repaired, no matter how much we want it to. Besides, you always knew I would have to leave one day. I answer to no one but myself."

"It can be repaired. I know we can figure this out," she encouraged, knowing in her heart that she was lying to herself. Raina remained silent as she soaked in the words she didn't want to hear.

A chair leg scratched the floor from the door area and she sensed her guest's identity without even looking toward it. Since Jarek hadn't acknowledged the sound and the temperature felt as though it had dropped a few degrees, it could only mean one thing; Joan had decided to make an appearance as well. Refusing to look her away, she continued to stare at Jarek.

"Say it," he commanded with a grin.

"Don't do it," Joan demanded from the chair she sat in.

"No," Raina answered him, ignoring the voice from the darkness.

She pushed her face into the closest pillow, like an ostrich trying to hide itself by sticking its head in the sand.

"Say it," he insisted.

Talking into the pillow, Raina repeated her answer. "No!"

He pulled her face out of the pillow and placed a hand on each side of her face, cradling her jaw.

"Why is it so hard for you?" he asked gently.

"Because he's gonna leave you!" Joan interrupted again. *"Don't ever forget that."*

"I don't know," Raina lied, ignoring Joan but heeding her advice anyway. She hoped that her lack of participation in the conversation would force Jarek to abandon it altogether.

She looked past him and into the dark corner where Joan sat, relaxed. Her eyes shifted to the door where Lucy stood shooting angry glances toward her nemesis before addressing Raina one more time.

"It's better to have loved and lost...," Lucy said in a sing-song voice.

Raina bit her lip to prevent herself from answering either one of them and then looked back at Jarek quietly. She couldn't bear the sympathetic looks he gave her when she announced their arrivals and decided to wait until he was gone to yell at them. Still holding her face, Jarek penetrated her eyes with a stare so intense she almost winced.

"Say it," he told her again.

Raina stared back and wondered if he could see the love in her eyes. If he could, he would never feel the need to hear the words come from her mouth but she decided to give in anyway.

"I love you," she said quickly.

"No Raina, like you mean it," he directed. She smiled and closed her eyes and re-opened them before answering.

"I do love you, Jarek," she said.

"You see?" he asked. "Was that so hard?"

"Yes, kind of," she admitted. Switching gears as fast as possible, she decided a subject change was in order.

"You better go. If Dom wakes up and you're not there, it won't be good."

"Stop worrying about Dom," he said. "Besides, he left the room about an hour ago."

Raina's heartbeat quickened and it almost made her lose her breath.

"What do you mean he left? We made a deal: no venturing out alone. This is unknown territory!"

"This is unknown territory to you and me; not to him. Remember, this is his hometown, Raina."

She lowered her face so that he couldn't see the concern in her eyes. She didn't want for him to know how much she worried about Dominic. She just wanted to sit down and have a long chat with her pesky ghosts.

"I need to be alone," she half told, half asked, him. "Just for a little while?"

"Take whatever time you need, darling," he said.

Jarek pulled her up from the bed and held her without words for a long time. Finally, he kissed her sweetly and released her hands slowly as he backed away. Though he used the door to exit, Raina still had a nagging feeling that he had entered from a different place entirely.

She locked the door behind him and leaned her back against it to rest. She hadn't wanted to declare her love but her energy had diminished to a dangerous level and every cell she possessed screamed for her to go feed. If Dominic weren't back within the hour, she would head out into the city of Lansing on her own. She didn't like feeding in front of the rest of them because she wanted the memories of her sins to live inside of her mind only.

Chapter X

Dominic awoke in a haze. He acknowledged the enhanced tinted window screens and knew they must have been meticulously replaced by Raina as he slept. Dreams still clung to his conscious mind and he realized he had been onstage entertaining the masses again. He missed the feel of the cold microphone against his lips. Somehow, the mic had always felt as though it were an extension of him – like some instrument of veracity that tempted the truth out of him. Behind it, he was transformed to his most primal self and his creativity was given open rein over his entire being.

He admitted to himself, reluctantly, that the world he had chosen to immerse himself in appealed greatly to the intellectual and power hungry parts of him, the ones that wanted to supervise the minions and control public order. There was something about such control that was undeniably irresistible, but it did not have the power to fulfill the other parts of him and lately, the other parts had become hungry, loud, and very much in need of attention.

Though there were similarities between his position as a leader and his time spent onstage, it had become clear to him that it would not be enough to sustain him like he had hoped. Just like in the old days when he had controlled an audience, his new followers looked up to him with respect and a little bit of fear for his position. But it was the differences between his two worlds that were starting to get to him. Rules and boundaries were forcing him into distraction and because of it, he was becoming more careless. Something nagged at him from within and he knew that if he didn't make a decision by the time he made it to Lucius, one would be made for him and it might not be the one he wanted.

Dominic followed the same path that he used to take when he and his band mates were headed to a gig. He had left his pack behind, sleeping comfortably in their motel beds and completely unaware that he had broken his own rule to stay together. Thoughts of Raina and Jarek finding each other in his absence forced his hand to his pocket and he stopped to pull a cigarette from its box. His pack was not a part of this. This quest belonged to him and him alone. He lit the cigarette and inhaled the delicious toxins until visions of his new life dissipated entirely; only then did he continue walking.

The simple act of following his same old steps seemed to awaken the sleeping memories that still lived deep inside of him into an almost violent state of awareness. The familiar thoughts that arose shook to life the old feelings that used to be attached to them and before Dominic knew it, he was experiencing the path to the bar just as he used to. In his new awareness, his band mates were trudging behind, weighted down by their instruments but energized by their excitement. He became excited by the old sensations and couldn't fight the impulse to turn around and check on his friends, but saw instead that he was alone. The mission was still a solo one and he did not have the power to think them back into existence, something he had wished for since the day he'd left them.

Though his senses were all on high alert, the one that led him with such conviction of direction was the auditory army that seemed to march heavily throughout his awareness, leaving notes and lyrics in its wake. He allowed his ears to direct his legs as he took in the Gothic, greaser-punk, rock-a-billy sounds emanating from the same club they had passed on the way to the motel, the same club that was going to visually show itself to Dominic at any step.

He hadn't told his pack why they had come to this place, to this state. He hadn't really needed to search for a believable lie; they trusted him implicitly. They believed him when he insisted they come to this place – that they must travel to Lansing to save someone. He hadn't really been lying. He just hadn't shared that the 'someone' to whom he referred was him, the leader of their confused but passionate little pack.

Dominic could not feel temperature but he knew it was cold by the way the rest of the street occupants were dressed. Gloves and hats covered every head and every hand; their knitting worked hard to ward off the chill that tried to penetrate them. Not wanting to appear different and therefore attract any unwanted attention, Dominic pulled his arms in toward his torso and tried to appear pained by the frost that bit at his skin. He bent forward just a little, trying to appear a regretful man punished for his inability to remember a jacket before leaving the house. Just as he started to get into the spirit of playing with the humans, instinct told him to look up.

It was the club where Dominic believed he had initially made his mark on the music scene. It was where he had experienced the most freedom, a world that had allowed him to lead an obedient and grateful army where boundaries did not exist to suffocate him and threaten to destroy their glory. It was where all boundaries were checked at the door or one would not be allowed entry. They may as well have had a sign out front, announcing their truest intention as their one and only rule.

No Boundaries Allowed

He walked closer toward the front doors but then turned sharply toward the left and headed for the back. He hadn't really thought it all through yet. He just took for granted that he could rely on the warrior within that always seemed to wake up during times of trouble or peril. The problem was that, for the first time, his inner warrior appeared to be sleeping and Dominic felt no guidance from within. He had no plan on how he would explain his perpetual youth to band mates who would surely have become middle-aged men, hopping onto the stage for the intermittent show in their otherwise grown up and scheduled lives. He had no more idea of what he would say to their shocked responses than he did when he had stared at the article of their reunion show that he had ripped out of Lansing's local daily newspaper.

He had ordered the rag to be delivered to his New York home from the moment of his turning. It was how he remained connected to his human ties; how he had followed the accomplishments of friends and the deaths of family members throughout his years away from them. He had returned for the occasional funeral but had hidden behind the trees from mourners who would surely have fallen to the ground, clutching their hearts at the sight of his presence. They believed he had fled to Hollywood alone and had ended up on the floor of a motel room taking his last breath – a needle in his vein pulling out his last vestige of life and a stomach full of narcotics promising to do any job the needle couldn't handle. It was a story he had fabricated himself as a gift of closure to those who would not accept his loss without a body.

When he had happened upon the article of his old band and their plan to play a reunion show at their old stomping grounds, he had stared at it for hours. He knew that nothing would stop him and had planned it from the moment the roadtrip was mentioned. And now, hiding behind the place that had offered him true purpose, Dominic had no earthly idea what he would say to them when he finally gathered the courage to venture inside.

He climbed up on a crate to peek through a back window. Squinting his eyes, he tried to concentrate his vision through the only piece of glass that wasn't blocked by dirt, dust, and grime. There was room for only one eye at the small clearing that he wiped into existence with his sleeve, so he closed the other to give strength to the one he planned to use. His line of vision led directly to the middle of the bar. The owner had moved things around since his last visit so many years ago. Dominic felt a tightening in his gums and the urge to fly headfirst through the window. He fantasized landing directly upon his old spot on the stage with his guitar magically strapped to his body and his cold microphone back to his lips. His thoughts were cut short, however, at the thought of their shocked expressions and he decided instead on a more discrete means of entry.

Walking back around the side of the building, he knew that once he turned the corner and was seen again by the heavy bouncer who sat bored to death at the front door, there wouldn't be enough chance to maintain the cover of a confused passerby. He would have to answer for himself and explain his presence one way or another. Dominic's heart beat faster than it ever had and paranoia set in, making him wonder if the doorman could hear.

Gathering the biggest burst of courage he could muster, he propelled himself forward and turned the corner. Just as he figured, the bouncer's head arose from his preoccupied stare and he made direct eye contact with him. Because of the bouncer's sudden role as opposition, he had to push away the urge to tear him apart and drain him of every last drop of blood from his body.

"Hey man," Dominic laughed. "Took off in my thoughts and walked right past the door."

"Happens to the best of us," consoled the guard.

Rising to his full height, the man's large stature made Dominic admit to himself that he might have become intimidated in his human form. In his new one, however, it only taunted him with the reminder that he could not feed off anyone in this place. He should have thought to eat before coming to the show. Arriving at a nightclub that was filled with excited and sweaty bodies while he was struggling with starvation hadn't been a smart move.

Dominic advanced toward the towering man who stood holding out a hand to collect his money. There was indeed a cover charge and Dominic was grateful that he had foreseen the need for cash. He reached into his pocket to pull out the twenty dollar bill he had borrowed from the pack's dwindling roadtrip money. Handing it to the guard, his gaze roved over toward the front door where he had a perfect view of the stage that had once served as his second home. It still had the same haunting draw and still beckoned his presence as it always had.

"Forget your jacket tonight?"

The bouncer's voice pulled Dominic back to attention. He was obviously in need of more conversation than Dominic had offered so despite the raw nerves that jumped around inside of him, Dominic smiled and gave in to the necessary small talk.

"Yeah, like I said," he answered slowly, his head turning back toward the stage as he spoke, "I'm in another world tonight."

"Hey, no worries," the bouncer said, returning his smile "That's what we're here for. Come on in and let it all go for a little while."

Without the distraction of further conversation, he walked past the bouncer and through the front door, becoming instantly overwhelmed by the sensation of temperature. He had lost the ability to discern one degree from another upon his turning but here, in this room, he felt it again. It was warm, almost hot, and it radiated throughout his body and into the tips of his fingers. They itched to feel strings beneath them as he stared longingly at the bass onstage. It was shiny and sturdy in its stand and it welcomed him, almost dared him to jump onstage to grab it and just start playing. He worked hard to reel the wish back in and dispose of it in his mental room of discarded fantasies.

The music he had heard playing from outside was coming from the jukebox and he felt a sense of relief that he wasn't late for the show. Dominic walked toward the bar, trying hard not to let anyone see the nervous glances he shot in every direction. He wanted to find his friends, his band mates, before they found him.

It was just as crowded as it had been in the old days and Dominic felt a stab of envy at thoughts of the band's new vocalist. The fans had always come to listen to Eight Ball Grifter with Dominic at the mic and not some outsider they had been forced to find to close out the circle. It should be his voice meshing with the sounds of the instruments and creating an aura of excitement like no other band in their area ever could.

Dominic stood in the shadows at the back of the bar, staring at the stage and envisioning his band when they were at the height of their music career. The combination of talents had brought fans from afar to shows that were well known as the underground sensation of the punk-a-billy world. Trying to fight another shot of contention for the man who would stand in his place, singing his music with his boys behind him, he felt his right incisor puncture his gum. Dominic knew that he if he didn't act soon, his old crowd and his beloved band mates might all become witness to the monster he had become.

Walking out of the shadows and toward the middle of the bar, he realized the trail wasn't an easy one. Too many bodies were invading his personal space and the conflict began to make him dizzy. Part of him wanted to penetrate the closest vein available but the other part felt a rush of pride that his boys could still pack a house. Forced to squeeze himself through the middle of a couple, he ignored the annoyed expressions directed his way and envisioned the drink that had always been in hand in the old days. He could almost taste the Jack and Coke sliding down his tongue, burning his tonsils along the way to inebriation. The memories soothed him and the knowledge that his drink would soon be in hand overpowered his increasing desire for blood.

Instinctively, he looked toward the table where they used to sit and the sight of its occupants forced him into a backwards stumble that he barely controlled. There they were – sitting at the table just as they used to, gearing themselves up through toasted shots as they prepared themselves to rock the crowd out of their minds, and possibly clothes. He ordered his drink and sat at the furthest table from his band mates, never taking his eyes off them. Glancing around, he observed the employees were unfamiliar and the layout had changed, but the environment remained the same as so many years ago. Still dark, dirty, and boasting the same broken guitars, cymbals, and drum heads on the walls that he had gazed upon in years past. Dominic looked down and stared at the liquor that awaited his consumption. He wished desperately that he were sitting at the table with them, where he belonged. Lifting the tiny glass to his lips, he tilted his head to accept its initiation back into the world he was forced to abandon so long ago.

He slammed the glass onto the table and stopped pushing away the strong draw toward the table, toward his boys. The energy of the crowd and the sight of his friends reconnected him with the life he had walked away from and the happiness that had been attached to it. Staring across the room, his eyes fell on Spades and he shook his head with regret. It was the emotion he despised the most and it always came attached to memories of his old friend, who had moved from another city to join their band. He knew that Spades' disappointment had no doubt turned to anger at Dominic's premature leaving and he wanted to run through the bar, apologize for his absence, and gain the forgiveness he knew he didn't deserve.

Instead, his mind wandered back to the days with his old guitarist, recalling the various mini-tour travels and late night driving conversations. He remembered the demons his friend had wrestled with, wondering if he had ever found a way to overcome them or if he could ever find it in his heart to truly forgive Dominic for the decisions he had made for himself. Allowing himself to just stay in the moment, Dominic fed from his old friend's endless energy and hoped their reunion would be a positive one.

Dominic shifted his gaze toward Knuckles. A pretty brunette with a big white smile sat beside him laughing at something he said. Dominic felt a surge of happiness and pride for his friend and hoped he had not only found love but that he had finally learned to hold onto it. Their shared memories hitched a ride on Dominic's thought waves and his smile widened at the old visions that emerged from his mental time capsule.

When the band was young, Knuckles had struggled with self-esteem issues and had subsequently down-played his own abilities on the guitar. He hadn't truly accepted the power of his talent and together, they had shared their insecurities and questions about life over copious amounts of alcohol in abandoned bars long after everyone had left. Over time, Knuckles had become an icon – a werewolf of the music scene, with a following that hung onto every story of every tattoo he had allowed to be punctured into his skin.

Again, Dominic had to shake away the regret that tried to pierce his momentary happiness with its sharp needle full of killjoy. Dominic had been plagued with the guilt of taking that life away from his band mates and he started to wonder if he should show himself at all. Their reception might not be as welcoming as he hoped and their rejection would be devastating.

Where's Diablo?

The question echoed up to him from his subconscious and he stood up to head to the bar for another shot. He needed courage and didn't care in what form or fashion it came. Ordering was easier for him than the rest of the customers as he had the ability to command the bartender's attention with no problem. He drank his second Jack and Coke at the bar and then slammed the glass back onto the bar before heading toward the front window. He watched the people as they milled around outside and knew they were just waiting for the first strum of a guitar or the first beat of a drum to invite them inside.

Both inside and outside, the crowd was filled with familiar faces and Dominic felt a connection, an inexplicable solidarity with each and every one of them. He sensed they somehow knew he would be here and that the band, in their nature of brotherhood and forgiveness, would help him to materialize on stage.

Like the old days, the drinks flowed quickly through the crowd. Beside him, beer bottles were raised high and were accompanied by drunken sing-alongs. The comic harmonies would stop abruptly as the friends and fans shared communion through shots of Jagermeister. Close friends and loved ones sat nearby to offer support and more alcohol. Dominic felt a pang of jealousy to see the waitresses bring his buddies round after round, despite the several bottles and shots in front of them, already lined up in waiting.

He leaned against the wall and tried to block out thoughts of feeding, admonishing himself to allow only happy memories inside lest he make a quick entree of the blonde at the end of the bar. The song playing from the jukebox came to an end and the last remnants of Sid Vicious vanished faster than the punker had in real life. As the next song pounded itself through the speakers, memories came rushing back to Dominic.

Johnny Diablo jumped into his head again and it brought Dominic back to an earlier time in their band's career. It had been at this same exact club, when while loading out guitar cases after the show, a man he did not recognize had stepped in front of Dominic from out of nowhere and pushed him on the shoulder, yelling at him even though his rage was completely unsolicited.

"Hey asshole!" the guy had screamed.

Not recognizing the man, Dominic's mind had scrambled to think of a quick response to the sudden tension and the implied threat.

"Did I sleep with his girlfriend?" he remembered wondering.

Before he could even process the question, Diablo had pushed him aside and placed himself in front of the angry stranger. Just the sight of Diablo made the guy forget his rage as well as his need for the restroom. An angered and protective Diablo, standing six feet, three inches and weighing two hundred and sixty pounds, had forced the guy to drop his head shamefully to examine his crotch area moments too late. He had pissed himself noticeably and, without another word, had fled the embarrassing scene, providing Dominic and Diablo with a hearty laugh and a great memory.

Dominic remained thankful for the years of Diablo's friendship and wished he had not taken it for granted. He heard the internal snap and knew that his subconscious mind had made a decision that his conscious mind hadn't been part of. He was shocked and terrified to feel himself walking forward, straight into the line of light that would make him clearly visible to anyone looking his way. Sturdy legs and an apprehensive heart led him toward the band's table and he recoiled from the power of his sudden conviction. He knew that his plan was to take his rightful seat beside his band mates, a seat that had always been meant for him.

As he neared their table, the smiley brunette looked up, her smile faltered, and her mouth ceased moving in mid-sentence. At the sight of her incredulous expression, everyone at the table turned backward to follow her line of vision. It was too late to turn back as Dominic found himself standing over them in silence.

Spades' face turned increasingly pale as the color drained slowly out of it. Knuckles had already bypassed the whitening stage and had come full circle to an expression of horror. His gaping mouth and shaking hand made it difficult for him to drink the shot that had just been laid before him but he forged on and drew it unsteadily to his lips anyway. Without taking his eyes off Dominic for even a moment, he downed the liquid and slammed his glass on the table.

"Where ya been?" he slurred, and then started to laugh. It was a typical reaction as most humans broke when the moment became too surreal to wrap their brains around.

Spades reached a shaky hand toward Dominic's arm, undoubtedly believing him to be a ghost from beyond. He knew their vocabulary didn't have the words to encompass their shock. Finally making contact with Dominic's arm, he pulled his hand back so quickly he almost fell out of his chair but was steadied by Diablo, who appeared at just the right moment as he always had in their history together. His old drummer pulled the only free chair out from the table and offered it to Dominic quietly.

Accepting the seat and looking around at the faces that stared back at him, he still had no idea what he would tell them and had decided to rely on instinct to guide him through the rest of the night. Dominic bowed his head guiltily when he noticed Spades look to Johnny for support and comfort.

"Please tell me you're seeing this too," he pleaded of Diablo.

"I see it," Diablo answered, leaning across the table to place his hand on top of Dominic's. "I mean, him. I see him."

"How can this be possible?" he asked his long deceased friend after a twenty-year absence. "We thought you died. What's going on here?"

Dominic found his voice and when he spoke was impressed to find that his vocal chords didn't fail him.

"I did die," he answered cryptically.

"Then how is it," hiccupped Knuckles, "that you're sitting here at our table?"

"I had unfinished business," Dominic smiled.

His band mates looked to one another before focusing their attention back on the ghost that shared their table. They shook their heads in disbelief and raised their eyebrows at each other in desperation. They needed an answer that they seemed to understand Dominic couldn't offer them for some reason. They had to decide whether or not to allow his mysterious presence to remain in their circle.

"I'm sorry. I didn't mean to leave you like I did," offered Dominic, making eye contact with each of them before hoisting the nearest drink.

He knew that if they didn't welcome his presence, he would be crushed and crushing a vampire's borrowed spirit could prove to be a fatal mistake. Dominic would fight hard to keep the change from happening here. He could never live with himself if he ever harmed one of them so he kept his leg muscles at alert for any sudden command to take off.

"Bartender!" Diablo shouted to the bar. "We need another Jager over here!"

"No need for sorrow" added Spades. "Shit man, I ain't mad atcha."

As Knuckles provided a hearty slap on the back, Dominic allowed himself to breathe in their acceptance and it filled him with an euphoria he had never known. He asked questions of his old friends, wanting to know how they had spent the last twenty years. He needed to find out if they were regretful or angry or fulfilled. They answered him with honesty and showed him the same air of respect that they had shown him in their youth. When they asked questions of him, Dominic would just remain silent. His lack of explanation did nothing to dampen the moment and his friends, buzzed from their shots and drunk from their shock, invited Dominic to join the stage with them.

"What about your singer?" Dominic asked, hoping that whoever it was would spontaneously combust. His band mates looked to a tall, thin guy at the corner of the table. With a wiry arm, the guy raised his own shot glass to the group and nodded his blessing.

"Go," he said simply.

Without need for further encouragement, the four original members of Eight Ball Grifter jumped up onto the stage and grabbed the instruments that had made them almost famous. The feel of the bass in his hands was like a shot of adrenaline to his heart and Dominic strapped it to his body the same way he always had. Jagermeister still in hand, he turned backward to face his band mates and smiled the knowing grin that only they would understand. He moved in to tighten their circle so that they could commence the moment properly.

"Have a shitty show" each of the four announced as shot glasses raised and they heard the clink of their connection.

Highly superstitious, musicians treaded carefully over the words they threw at each other prior to starting their show, and the familiar words they uttered now wouldn't fail to produce success; it never had. Dominic already felt the same comfortable flow, as if the past twenty years had never separated them. Keeping with old customs, each band member tossed his glass to the side of the stage as the demon Jager made its way through their already clouded systems. Its creeping effects helped to transform them into their more aggressive and controversial stage personas.

"A one, two, three, four!" yelled Dom, as the drums thundered and piercing guitars rumbled onward. The voices from the audience matched the decibel of the drums and the screams from excited fans almost drowned out the taunting and sporadic strums of the guitar.

Excited fans thrust drinks into the air as an offering of their devotion. In their heyday, Dominic had played it cool when shot after shot had been gifted to him by a grateful crowd but he hadn't always been able to consume all of the alcohol they presented him. While his intent was never to offend them, he knew that on any given night of any show, if he drank all the liquor offered to him, he would lose all ability to play and sing. He had relied on the trick of turning his back to whichever generous fan had asked him to share a drink and then tipping the shot back with a tilt of the head. With the glass pressed against his lips, he would allow only a tiny bit of liquor to pass while letting the remainder soak his bowling shirt and his wife beater and, at times, the floor beneath him. But on this night, Dominic drank in each and every drop of years' past experiences.

As the introductory song came to a close, the crowd exploded with cheers and yelled random comments to the stage. "Muchos Grassy-Ass!" Dom slurred, in response to the crowd's approval, happier than he'd been in twenty years. "This next song is called… Spit on My Grave!"

As the night played on, Dominic was renewed by energy through the sheer excitement of the reunion show, of enjoying the brotherhood and the chemistry that had gone on mercilessly unmatched throughout his life. For a brief moment between songs, Dominic zoned out and silence engulfed the room. His attention was focused in a trancelike state on the faces in the crowd. They were looking at him, expecting him to entertain… to do something….

'Thwap!'

Without fail, Diablo's drumstick was thrown meticulously to the back of the head and it worked to bring him out of his daze. Diablo always had a way of knowing when to intervene and Dominic threw a wink his way before looking to both Knuckles and Spades, each one standing beside him as they played to the crowd's every cheer. Dominic always enjoyed seeing the mischievous grin that always spread out upon Knuckles' face and the determined and energetic grin of Spades.

He drifted in and out of memories, remembering how the band members had once prided themselves on being rockers, not musicians. How they had tried to explain they weren't musicians with their technical distractions but instead, rockers who could care less. As they had always declared, *"Give the band three chords and a melody, tell them to rock it out, and they will – every time."*

Their energy brought him back to life and filled him with memories of his lost soul, one that was not stolen or borrowed but entirely his own. It was the reason he had agreed to join his pack on the roadtrip and it was the exact trigger he had needed to make his most important decision of all. The night was not encumbered by debauchery or murder. It included no robbing of blood banks or subsequent worry about the consequences of his meal. The music was real and it was pure and it was what had remained his lifeline to the world he had almost forgotten. The music had always saved him, had always re-energized his spirit and made him whole again. It was in the music that their salvation lived and he knew that it was the driving force that led him to Lucius.

Dominic smiled his first real smile in over two decades. He pulled the mic toward his lips and allowed it to draw out the mysterious lyrics that joined the frenzy of music all around. He knew that because of this night and this reunion, he could return to his pack stronger, more motivated, and ready to head to their destination with true purpose.

Chapter XI

Dominic returned to his motel room with more vigor and energy than when he left. His pack wasn't happy about his absence but he just continued to smile throughout their demands for an answer. Though his respect for them was enormous, he didn't feel they were entitled to know everything about him. Maintaining a sense of mystery and keeping parts of his life quiet had always been his way and he didn't plan to change it so close to the end. He knew they would benefit from his experience in a positive way and simply remained mum about where he had been and what he had done. Raina gave him the hardest time of all but he refused to break, even in the face of her threatened punishment of coldness and silence.

"Come on!" he simply called out to them as they abandoned their rooms and pulled their luggage behind them. "Let's hit the road!"

Raina crawled into the car and threw dirty looks his way whenever he made eye contact. Christoph gave him a knowing smile, seeming to somehow understand that his leader's absence had provided him with the necessary fuel to continue. Jarek eyed him suspiciously but didn't ask for details that he knew he wouldn't get and Leo rushed to catch up with all of them, extra bags in hand and a shirt that protruded with the loot he had stolen from the mini bar in his room.

"What ya got there, Leo?" Dominic asked, even though he knew the answer.

"Nothin," he answered guiltily. "Why do you ask?"

"Oh, no reason," he answered. 'It's just that you seem to be leaving with more than you came with."

"Neh," Leo replied, sarcasm edging his tone. "You're just tired from your long night out."

Jarek advanced on Leo and pulled his shirt up high causing tiny bottles of Bacardi, cheap wine, and candy bars to tumble onto the cement. After leaning over to pick up the stolen items, Jarek stood back up and glared at him with an expression of warning.

"I'll just hold these for you," he said in a voice that implied his statement required no answer.

"Asshole," Leo muttered under his breath, heeding the warning not to debate their shared thievery.

Dominic turned away, in no mood for an argument that would strip him of the high he was still feeling. He threw the keys to Christoph and told him to just head west until further notice. The rest of the pack took their seats and drove in silence away from the motel that had saved them from the daylight. Although no one but their leader knew where they were headed next, they refrained from questioning him any further. Once he had made a decision, they relied on their belief in his integrity and their innate faith in him to quiet all concerns. Though forced to follow him on his whims, the pit stops didn't impact them individually aside from causing a twenty-four hour delay in reaching their destination.

The inside of the car was quiet as they stared out the windows at the passing trees and unfamiliar territory. Exhausted from travel and physical strain from last night's show, Dominic fluttered in and out of a dream state that teased his subconscious mercilessly. As the memories of human-like pain set into his back and his knees, Dominic could not distinguish between what was real and what was just a detailed mortal memory of the backlash that had always followed energetic performances.

With Christoph at the wheel, Dominic was grateful for the time he had to reflect on the previous night's experience and of similar shows of years past. He looked back on his days with the Eight Ball Grifter boys with fondness and allowed himself to become immersed in the memories of the band that had defined so much of who he was. The chemistry that had existed between him and his band mates was truly one of a brotherhood that even death could not destroy. Internally, he commended his old comrades for their forgiveness of his sudden departure and their willingness to let him share the stage with them one more time.

The droning of the tires against the pavement lulled Dominic into a daydream where he could experience the vivid emotions of earlier past. For years, his stage persona had allowed him to play a different role on stage and within the social interactions of the venue. Their live performances had always brought him to an emotional high that he never experienced again in quite the same way. He listened to the rumbling of the engine and felt comforted by the vibrations of the car as he reflected on the previous night. He could still see the faces from the crowd as they sang his own words back to him, hands gripping bottles and glass that they thrust toward him as an offering and tribute. It fueled the fire in all of them just as it had in the past and he could still hear the words of the crowd ringing in his ears.

"Som'Bitch!" they had shouted.

Dominic shifted his position in search of more comfort and he felt a small smile escape his face. Although gifted with the perfect combination of elements that allowed one to feel like a God, in the morning it was always the same. The highs dissipated, his persona always transformed into a mere shadow of reality and he was left feeling empty and average. No fame or fortune, no limelight, no special attention from the ladies or endless mingling from the fans. Instead, the euphoria was replaced by a cracking back and knees that snapped, reminding him of each aggressive pose and movement in the most painful way possible. Tendons aflame in his forearm and arthritis that curled his hands in agony took over the glory, the lights and the reverence that had only just rumbled through the crowd beneath him. Whiskey-soaked vocals created a hoarse and weakened voice, which in turn created mild panic that the melodic blessing with which he'd been gifted would never have the opportunity to be utilized again.

As a human, his only choice had been to lie on the couch, seemingly half dead, while his natural recovery system worked to replenish him both mentally and physically. Dominic winced against the aches that called out to him from different parts of his body as the torn upholstery of the car's seat presented no such comfort.

"Hang a left here onto the highway," he instructed Christoph from his horizontal position on the backseat. "We wanna be headed south from here on out."

"No more surprises, right Dom?" inquired Leo, not bothering to shield his sarcasm from their tour guide.

"Actually... there is, my good man," he replied. "I've arranged for a little roadside tourism."

"I hope it involves partaking in some extracurricular dinner activities," added Leo, his increasing hunger evident in each word.

"McDonald's?" Christoph piped in.

"Sorry boys, neither one," Dom answered with a compassionate smile. "Think of it more as a little midnight gravesite visit."

"Where?" Raina asked, her excitement taking over the anger she felt. "Where, Dom?"

"Just trust me," he answered, chuckling to himself as he settled back into his seat again. "Look for the large billboard of a dead celebrity and wake me when we're there."

Closing his eyes and preparing to transport himself back to the stage, he knew that his pack wouldn't mind the detour. They found his games amusing and needed the diversion anyway. For the next half hour, they bantered back and forth at the sight of every billboard that loomed ahead.

"The Tidy Bowl Man!" Jarek laughed. "He's dead, right?"

"I think so," Raina answered.

"There's one!" Leo announced, somewhat disgusted. "Who is that?"

"It's Joan Rivers!" Christoph said excitedly.

Smirking, Raina interjected. "Uh, she's not dead…."

"Coulda fooled me," spouted Leo. "Jesus…."

Raina poked Dominic in the arm playfully but he lay still.

"How about a little hint, Mr. Mysterious?" she asked. "Come on, where are you taking us?"

He opened one eye slowly, barely cognizant of the conversation going on around him. Pointing off at nothing in the distance, he closed it again and let his head fall back onto the seat.

"Thanks," she joked. "Lotta help you are."

When the game died down, the car grew silent as the pack decided their destination wasn't within close enough proximity to keep playing. They turned their attentions inward again and hours passed, all of them sleeping but Christoph.

Just past a cornfield, a large billboard began to come into view and gradually, they saw that it displayed the face of Fairmount, Indiana's most legendary celebrity. With a knowing laugh, Christoph woke his companions.

"James Dean you guys… Dom… I think we're here."

"We're *where* exactly?" asked Raina groggily as she peered out the back window. "This place looks deserted."

Christoph followed the signs that guided tourists down the exit ramp, along a thinning road and directly into a cemetery.

Finally sitting up and transporting himself back to the present, Dominic let them in on his plan.

"Let's go pay him a visit!" he said, pulling himself into a sitting position. He had known the location of the deceased celebrity as he had visited it with his band mates during his human years. Upon their arrival, he realized that his interest in taking his pack to see it was not driven by his willingness to share the iconic experience but, indeed, another connection to his past.

The pack got out of the car and made their way through the hills and down the paths of the cemetery, admiring the grave markers and statues with the same interest of an architect observing the Sistine Chapel.

"You think that's something... wait 'til we get to New Orleans," remarked Christoph.

The statues seemed to come to life in all of their splendid glory as though grateful to be housed in a place where the souls roamed freely. Dominic reached into his pocket and produced an oblong pressed penny in his palm. After staring at it for a long moment, he returned it to his pocket and instead positioned a silver dollar at the base of the grave.

"That's it?" Leo laughed. "That's your big roadside ball of twine?"

"Almost..." he replied. "I've arranged for an old friend to open up the James Dean Gallery for a late night tour."

Intrigued by history and American pop culture, the pack appeared at least somewhat amused as they headed back to the car. Arriving at the museum a short time later, they saw the owner's shadow behind the front door of the two-story Victorian home turned museum, obviously awaiting their visit. As they made their way down the sidewalk, a duck jumped out from behind the bushes and bit Leo on the ankle before waddling off.

"Son of a…!" Leo yelled as he jumped backward.

The pack tried to subdue their laughter but to no avail. Dominic and Jarek especially appreciated it when the universe ganged up on their friend in the most unexpected of ways. Noting the angry look on his face, they tried to pull back their amusement.

Dominic led the group to the front door, where they were met by David, an old friend from his days with the band and a loner who hadn't left his house for several years. He never questioned Dominic about the fact that he hadn't aged in twenty years and his lack of interest, or awareness, was greatly appreciated. He appeared tired but excited to see his old friend. After a quick handshake between the two, he greeted him with the same line he had always used.

"So, you're passing through town on your way to a show?"

"Yeah, thanks so much for openin' up for us. Sorry it's so late," apologized Dominic, using the guise of his band to protect the identity of his pack.

"Not a problem. I know you musicians have crazy schedules. Have fun…," David told them. "Let me know if you have any questions."

Over the next hour, the group perused the artifacts that depicted the life of James Dean, peering through glass windowed cabinets at the items reflecting the once king of cool. As an archivist, David had begun collecting in 1974. His movie posters were impressive and the assorted novelty items were amusing, sparking the imagination of what life was like so many years before, but the most fascinating items were the collection of photographs that were scattered throughout the various displays. Some had been taken by Dean while others showed the man himself in various settings with a variety of individuals. Dominic strolled slowly down the aisles, taking in the expressions and the body language of the great actor and the most famous Indiana native in history. His eyes caught Christoph staring at a black and white photograph, a hint of confusion and evaluation upon his face. Breaking the stare, Dominic waved his hand between Christoph's eyes and the photo.

"You all right?" he asked him.

"Sure, just a little tired," he answered with a weak smile.

Sensing no imminent concern, Dominic started to turn away, intent on enjoying some more visual treasure hunting. He knew that his friend deserved his own private thoughts, just as he had deserved his night on the stage.

"Someone just really looks familiar in this picture," Christoph said, distracted.

Dominic turned to acknowledge him and Christoph continued talking, though he seemed to be addressing his comments more to himself.

"Naw, that couldn't be," he added with a shake of the head. Pulling his eyes from whatever intrigued him, he followed his leader for the rest of the tour. Though Dominic's concern for his friend was mounting, he didn't feel that prying would do any good just yet.

"Hey!" he announced instead, circling the floor so the whole pack could hear him. "There's one last place I wanna show you guys."

Breaking their glances from their respective items, each of them looked his way.

"It's just down the road about five miles," he continued. "After that, we should be ready to secure a place for daylight and then make some miles after some sleep."

One by one, they thanked David for his kindness and hospitality and scurried back to the car, speeding off down the dirt covered back roads. Large oak trees lined the sides of the road, serving as a gigantic natural picket fence that led them to their next destination.

"Just ahead here on the right," directed Dominic.

Ahead was a small one-story building with a red neon sign in the window that blinked 'Closed.' The larger sign next to the road indicated a restaurant named Piper's Grille, boasting a pub style menu, brew, and spirits. Just behind the restaurant, peeking out from behind a fortress of oaks was an old run down lumber mill, its walls and foundation built from thick heavy wood and stained from years of water damage.

"Another breakfast feast?" asked Raina, figuring that he was once again in the mood for food similar to the truck stop.

"No... we're going back there," Dominic answered pointing a finger toward the mill. "You gotta see this place."

The pack piled out of the car lazily and walked toward the trees, pushing various bushes out of their way to reveal an old path that lead to the entrance of the mill.

Buried in the dirt and moss along the way were random pieces of rusty old farm equipment and as they approached, a large lumberjack saw spanned the width of the building, which hung over double wooden doors that were latched by a two by four. Leaving the sealed doors undisturbed, Dominic led his team of roadtrip explorers to a side window with glass that had long since been busted out. Lending a hand to each, Dominic lowered each of them through the window and down the small drop to the wooden floorboards below.

Inside the rundown mill, they realized that it was just as impressive as it was dilapidated. The size of a modest airplane hanger, visions of multiple mill workers exerting themselves amidst their trade product entered each imagination. They inspected the area and the log beams that ran the length of the building at various heights, supporting the roof and creating a maze like infrastructure above. Below, workstations surrounded by piles of sawdust sat untouched, as though at one moment in time all work ceased simultaneously and no one ever again entered to resume the project. The boards creaked beneath their feet as they made their way forward to examine further. Mice scurried past them in curiosity, looking up as they passed, examining their intruders.

As the group continued, the path of wooden planks began to slope downward toward the main floor. In the distance, a slight rustle could be heard and Dominic paused to raise an index finger to his lips, motioning for the others to stop and listen. To their left they heard a sudden loud clank, as if something had hit a large tin can lying in wait. As he slowly looked up to the rafters, a small rock zipped past Dominic's face and landed on the board in front of his feet. It was obvious they were not alone; all they knew was that it was not the mice sending warning signals their way.

Squinting through a high window to get a clearer view of the distance, Christoph caught a glimpse of something in the moonlight. Narrowing his eyes more, he could see what appeared to be three human figures bound together by ropes; their backs to one another and their hands and feet bound to lightning rods. They were tied at their waists to a piece of metal equipment and the sight brought him to an abrupt halt.

"Uh, Dom?" Christoph whispered.

Before he could share what he had discovered, a large dark figure descended from the shadows of the rafters and landed directly in front of them.

"Intruder!" it called out loudly.

The pack was stunned to find another vampire in the middle of nowhere, especially during their innocent excursion through the mill. Indiana was the last place they had expected to find trouble, yet they realized they had somehow stumbled upon a strange nest of turned mill workers. Watching quietly but intently, two others joined their predecessor.

"Greetings," announced Dominic. "We mean no disturbance to you or your home."

From the shadows, a thin, muscular man dressed in jeans and a flannel shirt appeared before them. His fashion statement depicted the deepest of the south, having torn off the arms of his shirt to display his biceps and tattoos. A ragged brown baseball cap with a large golden fish hook wedged within the side covered his brow. He tipped the brim to reveal his eyes.

"Yer damn right," responded the figure in a slow southern drawl. "What the hell do you want?"

"My name is Dominic and this here is Raina."

He chuckled inside at his inadvertent adaption to the southern twang that took over his real accent. Pointing behind him, he continued.

"And that's Christoph, Jarek… and Leo."

Interrupting him, the figure became more aggressive. "What are you doin' here? Why the hell would city folk from… New York, I assume… be interested in our mill?"

"Look, we didn't know you were even here," Raina interjected. "Our leader knew of this place from his human years and he just wanted to share its vision with us."

Stepping closer to her side, Jarek spoke next.

"Yeah, man, relax. We're not here for you."

From their approach, more than their appearance, Dominic surmised that all three of them were lower level members to the vampire world. It was a safe assumption they hadn't yet developed most of their powers and it was evident that they didn't care about any form of social grace.

"Let's get rid of 'em!" yelled the one positioned to his leader's right, holding a sickle in his hands and bearing a grimace that was less than friendly.

"Easy Larry… don't get yer panties all in a bunch," replied their leader with an eye roll. Leaning forward to speak into Dominic's ear, he whispered, "Don't mind him much… he feasts on the cows. One time, got himself a case of the hoof 'n mouth… not sure he's ever recovered."

The mood lightened as the figure grinned. Though Dominic tried to smile back, his attempt was cut short at the realization that his new acquaintance only sported one incisor and three teeth.

"The name's Clive," he introduced himself. "You've just met Larry… and that there is Vincent. And this here is our mill."

The one identified as Vincent was quite intimidating. He was large in stature and had the muscular build of a young farm hand who had seen many days of endless manual labor, lifting, hauling, shoveling, and potentially moving large buildings fully intact.

"T'aint another one like us for miles 'round these parts," added Clive proudly.

"What a shame…," Raina whispered under her breath, obviously disgusted at the sight of dirty redneck bloodsuckers.

"Come on and join us! Yer just in time fer the eats," Clive invited, launching himself from the wooden plank to the main floor and followed obediently by Larry and Vincent. The pack exchanged confused glances but accompanied their hosts outside.

The three victims that Christoph had seen moments before wriggled against the ropes that held them to the pole behind them, their backs to the pole and positioned in a triangle formation. Bandanas, made into homemade gags, covered their mouths.

"Looky here…," announced Larry, still clutching his sickle.

Its blade gleamed from the light that was produced by a small campfire in the corner. Looking closer, the group realized the three captives were teenagers; two males and a female. Larry began dancing around all three in jubilation and the smile on his face hinted at the enjoyment of his impending meal. Though the teenagers made attempts to scream, they only succeeded in releasing whimpers and squeals that managed to sneak past their gags.

"This here was supposed to be fer just the three of us, but since yer here...," began Clive.

Dominic interrupted, trying hard to keep his cool at the sight of the terrified kids, "Actually, while we appreciate your hospitality..."

Larry, who stood closest to Leo, turned the sickle and held it against Leo's face. "What are you saying?" he asked. "Not interested? No stomach for it, son?"

Shoving the sickle aside, Leo's anger mounted.

"Screw you redneck! I'm not as politically correct as my leader and I have no problem tearing you apart right here, you disrespectful low life piece of shit!"

The two began to scuffle as Clive moved slowly to the left side of his first victim.

"What's yer problem, city slicker?" he questioned them, his attention mainly on Dominic.

"We're not fond of taking the lives of the young or the innocent," he replied.

"No?" Clive answered angrily, leaning in closer to the neck of the teen girl. "Then I guess they're all mine!"

Before the pack realized what was happening, he thrust his fangs into her neck and smiled widely as her body twitched and then fell limp against her ropes. Blood trickled down his chin and he stared back at the pack with glazed eyes.

Raina watched as Leo and Larry continued their fight, oblivious to the events going on around them and she noticed that Vincent had not moved to respond to either situation. His eyes remained focused on the three teens and he seemed more sad than excited. Moving in closer toward him, she whispered.

"You had nothing to do with this, did you?"

"No, ma'am," he said morosely as he stared at the floor. "I knew those kids once upon a time. They're locals. I wished them no harm."

Raina knew that her pack would not stand for the behavior of their hosts whether it was their home or their cultural norm or not and she whispered quietly to Vincent.

"Go," she warned him. "Get out of here quickly. Your friends won't make it to see the next darkness, I guarantee it."

His eyes expressed gratitude and a sincere aura of caring that was non-existent in most of their species.

"You don't really want this kind of existence, do you?"

"No ma'am, never did," Vincent replied.

Without another word, he turned and headed toward the exit as Raina turned back to see what was unfolding between Dominic and the toothless leader. She realized that, although they had made a move to intervene upon Clive's self-indulgent feast, they had acted too late. Though a lower class and lacking in any type of intelligence, the hillbilly had moved with a quickness that ensured the victims' demise before the pack could interfere.

Dominic's rage was building, the actions of the rednecks fueling his anger to its boiling point. There was enough evil in the world that they needn't feed off the undeserving but their meal of the teens was not what had him so enraged. While not a personal preference for Dominic and his pack, he still acknowledged the need for their kind to feed and to survive. It was the disrespect toward his pack and the rude interruption of their peaceful tour that had caused him to lose his high and grab hold of the monster inside.

What had been planned as an enjoyable sightseeing visit had turned into not only a disappointment, but an immense frustration at the ignorance before him.

"Jarek, now!' he instructed, knowing that his wing man was just waiting for the word.

Spearing his opponent with his thick shoulder, he sent Clive flying backwards against the thick wooden walls. Jarek ran toward him and after a brief fracas of flying fists and gouging nails, he reached down to his belt and pulled out his new knife. Holding it to the throat of his enemy, he stood in position quietly until Dominic gave his next instruction.

As Jarek maintained his threatening stance, Christoph and Leo wrestled Larry The Cowslinger to the ground and Raina watched as his arms flailed amidst the sawdust.

"Pick him up," directed Dominic. He walked toward them slowly and peered into the eyes of both of the lost and wretched creatures.

"To the roof!" he yelled and his pack obeyed, lifting their hostages into a short flight and making their way through a large open door hidden among the maze of beams above.

It didn't take long for the pack to know what Dominic had in mind as he had always proven himself to be the king of irony and the prince of karma. Staring briefly at the two large lightening rods that stood adjacent to the east end of the mill, he motioned with his arm for the others to follow him. As Raina walked by his side, the males forced their weary adversaries in a direction they didn't want to go.

"Where's the other one?" Dominic asked.

"Um…. Dom?" she tried to explain. "He wasn't really one of them."

Dominic already knew of her decision and her actions as they transpired and had only asked to test her honesty. The truth was, he trusted her judgment.

"Good for you," he commended simply. While she was thankful for the accolade, her facial expression remained serious. She was devastated by the actions of the residents of the rundown mill and would never be able to rid herself of the teenagers who still wriggled behind the ropes in her memory.

"Still carry those cuffs with you, Jarek?" Dominic asked.

"You know it," Jarek answered.

"I'll replace them for you."

"No need," Jarek smiled. "I have more than one of everything."

He pulled two sets of silver handcuffs from his back pocket and threw one of them to Raina. Snatching them from the air, she walked with purpose toward Christoph and Leo, who had already positioned Larry to one of the lightning rods. Immensely grateful at her job of cuffing his dirty hands to the rod, she pulled the bracelet tight enough around them to ensure no possible escape. Jarek followed suit with Clive nearby and forced a few extra clicks for added enjoyment, digging the steel into Clive's skin.

"There," Dominic said with a smile. "As you can see, you'll have a perfect view of this morning's sunrise."

Turning his back to them, he made his way down the sagging tiles of the roof as most of his weary pack followed. Leo, however, remained standing behind the two ill-fated vampires and his pack began counting as they waited for him to complete the ritual he so enjoyed.

"I will sweep away everything in all your land," he chanted loudly. "I will sweep away both people and animals alike. Even the birds of the air and the fish in the sea will die. I will reduce the wicked to heaps of rubble, along with the rest of humanity!"

Finished, he spun around and ran to catch up to his pack.

"Sweep away?" Dominic asked with a grin.

"Yeah, Dom… Zephaniah 1:2-6: I will sweep away both people and…"

"Better get yourself a damn big broom," Dominic cut him off jokingly.

Looking up toward the lightening sky, the pack jumped into their hearse and made a quick exit in search of a secure place to rest.

Chapter XII

The closest place that offered respite from the sun came in the form of a bomb shelter only five miles from the mill. Christoph's empathic abilities and Dominic's power to read the minds of passersby on the road led them there without incident. They spent the entire day underground, safely hidden from the daylight. It didn't take them long to fall into a deep and restful sleep as the exhaustion from their unplanned adventures had drained them of every ounce of energy they had. The entire pack slept for so long, in fact, that when they awoke, they discovered that the sun had already packed up for the night and that darkness had already masked the sky for several hours.

"Shit!" Dominic yelled after pushing against the heavy door that protected them. "We've lost time... a lot of it! Get up, let's go!"

Renewed from sleep but starving from having gone so long without feeding, the pack quickly abandoned their shelter and piled into the hearse with Jarek at the wheel. The overriding thought in all of their minds was nourishment in any form possible.

"We have to eat, Dom," Jarek said, stating the obvious.

"I know," he answered, his voice filled with concern. "I know."

"We could have at least had a nibble on the teens," Leo complained from the back. "The rednecks already killed them; it wouldn't have been a terrible thing to do."

"Don't talk like that, Leo," Dominic warned.

"I hate to agree with the idiot, Dom, but he's right," Jarek said.

"That's how it starts," Dominic admonished. "It would have been the same and you know it. I'm hungry too. We'll find something."

Dominic felt a stab of shame because deep down, he agreed with them. Looking behind him at Christoph, he knew that his friend could sense his desperation.

"What now?" he asked his leader. "We can't keep going without eating."

"We'll head to a place with food, real food, and we'll try to sustain ourselves until we find the right blood."

The pack remained silent as Jarek sped as fast as the hearse would allow and Dominic navigated from the passenger's seat. None of them spoke because if mention of their hunger came up again, it would only strengthen the void they were all suffering. An exit sign came into view and it offered both restrooms and a Dairy Queen. Dominic turned around to address his hungry pack with forced enthusiasm.

"Look!" he said, ordering Jarek to follow the ramp that led to their salvation. "Food!"

"All right!" Leo exclaimed. "I love rest areas! They always have such a variety of selections because of the tourists. I could go for anything right now... Chinese, Spanish, American!"

"No, Leo," Dominic answered firmly. "We're going to Dairy Queen."

"What?! Why?"

"Because we're starving right now and being around humans will be too tempting."

"It's a rest stop, Dom," Jarek added quietly. "There's always evil lurking around rest stops."

"Yeah, there are also children and families stopping for potty breaks. What if we go there and there's nothing wicked in sight? You know what'll happen then!"

"Fine," Jarek answered, trying to disguise his contempt. "I want a Dilly bar anyway."

"Are you kidding me?" screamed Leo from the back. "What's a Dilly bar gonna do for us right now? Besides, it's like four a.m.! What Dairy Queen is open at this time?"

"Well, if it's closed we can always break in," Raina offered. "I'll cook for us."

"Oh, Jesus Christ!" Leo said angrily as he lit up a joint.

"That's only gonna make you hungrier, stupid," Raina chastised.

"Go to hell."

Jarek tried to focus on his love of Dilly bars. It wasn't just the taste of blood that satisfied them but also the smaller pleasures that made their extended lives worth the living. Cheeseburgers, Dilly bars, and music had not lost their power just because their souls had taken up residence elsewhere.

The restaurant came into view and he opened his mouth to announce their arrival when red and blue bubbles appeared in the rear view mirror.

"Shit," he said instead.

Too hungry to deal with some silly cop with his idiotic laws and his stupid notepad, Jarek tried to fantasize about his teeth crunching through the chocolate shell that protected the sweet, cold vanilla. He was failing miserably, however, as his thoughts kept returning to what the cop's blood might taste like. Staring through the side window, he watched as the police offer approached their hearse and he worked hard to push away images of popping his veins and draining him of everything he had.

Rolling down the window and calling upon his more charming and endearing side, he reminded himself to remain on his best behavior lest they call more attention to themselves. He had promised Dominic that he wouldn't kill an innocent and he planned to make every effort to stick to that vow. As it was, the cop made it a difficult feat.

"Hi, officer, can I help you?" he asked, forcing out a laugh that lacked sincerity. His tone was too friendly and too syrupy; its phoniness called more attention to them than his fangs would have.

"What is this, Halloween?" the cop asked with the arrogance that Jarek despised in the humans. Burly, buff, and dressed in all blue, his attempted authority made Jarek's taste buds start to tingle against his will.

"No, sir," he answered. "Just a Gothic band headed south for a gig."

"Really," the officer answered sarcastically, drawing out the word for as long as he could. "Does your trip include smoking so much marijuana that I can barely see you through the haze?"

Jarek felt the familiar sensation of growing incisors but he fought hard to control his instincts. He felt Raina's hard kick to his seat from behind and when he glanced next to him at Dominic, he noticed that he was just staring quietly through the windshield. Looking back into the eyes of the cocky cop, he couldn't help but to envision him on a plate with eggs and English muffins and civility slipped away from him at a pace he couldn't seem to stay ahead of.

"Bacon," he blurted out before he could stop himself.

"What did you say?" the cop shot back, angry and offended.

"Sorry, officer, I was just wondering if you wanted to join us for a meal."

"Are you trying to be cute?"

The cop's hand dropped to his side and Jarek wasn't sure if he was going for his radio or his gun. The weapon didn't scare him but the possibility of calling attention to his pack did. He carefully eyed each move the officer made and when he saw his right hand make a beeline for the radio, Jarek clutched his wrist before it made it to his waistband.

He pulled the horrified cop through the window by his neck and angled him below his jaws so that he could bite down into the soft flesh. Envisioning the unfulfilled Dilly bar, he became angry that he had been forced to break his vow to Dominic and was unable to finish drinking. Instead, he threw the half dead body to the back to let the rest of his pack enjoy their unexpected meal. After a minute, the drained and mangled body was thrown back up to the front and Jarek jumped out of the car with a loud sigh and the rest of the police officer in his hands. Knocking the corpse's head against each handle on the way to the trunk, he used the long nail of his pointer finger to unlatch the trunk lock and then threw the remainder of the officer's body inside for the munchies he knew would hit later. It was only after he slammed the trunk door shut that he noticed Dominic standing beside him – very close, very quiet, and very still.

"Are you mad?" Jarek asked him.

"I'm pissed."

"What else could I do, Dom? He was getting ready to make a scene."

"I'm not talking about that. Of course you had to kill him."

"What then?"

"Why don't you make things easier for both of us and just stay out of Raina's bedroom?"

Jarek didn't answer. A memory of his and Raina's shower scene popped into his mind and he wondered if Dominic meant the bathroom as well.

"Do you think that's funny?"

"I can't control my thoughts, man," Jarek answered, defensively. "Play fair and stay out of my head during this conversation."

"You play fair and stay out of Raina."

Jarek felt his eyes flash with a rage that he tried to keep subdued. The more he felt Dominic crawl around inside his mind, the more difficult it was to hide the memories. Their hunger, their exhaustion, and the bad blood they had ingested had started to affect them all in a very bad way.

"Didn't we already have this conversation?" he asked calmly.

"We did but I think we're due for another. We'll talk later."

Jarek didn't have his leader's telepathic powers but he didn't need to. It was obvious what Dominic wanted to do to him in that moment and it only strengthened Jarek's resolve to finish the trip with as little trouble as possible. He just wanted to grab a Dilly bar, hop back in the car, and drive even faster toward their destination. The conversation was a reminder to never forget his place in the uncomfortable triangle. Even though he and Dominic had been close friends for a very long time, there was still an imbalance of power that could turn a two-man battle into an all out war of the Underworld.

"We have about three hours 'til daylight so we'll deal with this after we find a safe place and get some rest," Dominic suggested. "Go get your Dilly bar."

Jarek led the pack into the quiet parlor and glanced at the clock on the wall. It was four-thirty a.m. and no one was in sight but for the young cashier who was still in the process of opening the store. Knowing their hours of darkness were limited, he didn't allow himself to ruminate over the guilt of taking someone so young. His anger toward Dominic was infecting him and their rule to spare the innocent was overpowered by one thing and one thing only. Survival. As much as he wanted the Dilly bar, his need for more blood was just a little bit stronger. Passing the deep buckets of mint chocolate chip and vanilla ice cream, Jarek knocked over the cone rack with his left arm and went for the pimple-faced cashier with his right. The pack walked out of Dairy Queen minutes later with boxes of Dilly bars in hand and one unfortunate cashier, in the wrong place at the wrong time, rolling on the floor, clutching his throat.

The next half hour was spent in relative silence as music streamed through the speakers; working its magic to soothe their inner beasts. Then, with a click from the dash, the CD ejected from the car stereo.

"New tunes," Jarek demanded calmly.

Glancing over his shoulder to the backseat, Dominic extended his hand.

"Johnny Cash...," he said, as though he expected for the CD to be in his hand before even concluding his request. Leo fumbled through their disc cases and other random roadtrip car debris with no success.

"Find it," Dominic enforced impatiently.

"It's not here..."

Staring out the window, Christoph added lazily, "Ahhh... Cash... the necessary soundtrack to any good roadtrip..."

"Not helping," Leo whispered. "You're a cheese-ass... you sound like a damn commercial. Can you even name more than two songs of his?"

Looking back up at Dominic, he noticed that his hand was still held out, open and expectant in an odd backwards position.

"Sorry Dom… no Cash."

"What else could go wrong, seriously?" Dominic asked, pulling his empty hand back into the front seat with a sigh. Raina stopped applying her lipstick abruptly at the question.

"Don't ever ask that," she scolded.

Tapping the dash, Jarek announced, "Runnin' low on fuel, guys."

"So pull over and fill 'er up." Raina suggested.

"No cash," replied Jarek.

"Thought we'd established that," said Dominic.

From the back, Leo chimed in. "Still no luck, Dom."

Raising his right hand and pressing his index finger against his forehead, Dominic shook his head in frustration.

"Worthless," he mumbled quietly.

The motor sputtered and clicked before completely turning off and the pack coasted slowly to the side of the road. Each looked to the other for an answer but none of them had one. Raina was the first to speak.

"What now?" she asked.

"I don't know," Christoph answered. "Something happened."

"You think?" Leo mumbled from the back.

"Lay off," Jarek spit back at him.

"You're always protecting the weak, Jarek. It's getting boring."

"You don't see me sticking up for you, do you?

Without hesitation, Leo leaned in toward Jarek and scratched at his face like a wildcat to his prey, causing a long thin gash that glistened with blood before it disappeared. Each injury still caused instinctual pains and scars that turned vampires carried over from their human lives. For most of them, complete acceptance of their immortality was impossible and Jarek had always had difficulty letting go of his soul. His eyes darkened and he jumped backwards into his seat before falling into a deep crouch and a position of attack.

"Enough!" Dominic yelled.

They rarely heard him raise his voice so his command grabbed their attention almost violently. Raina pulled her resting head from Christoph's lap and sat up straight. Christoph kept his focus on the trees outside and Leo backed into the seat as much as the vinyl would allow. Jarek focused on the steering wheel and sent a prayer to hell that he would at least make it to the end of the roadtrip without killing one of his pack mates. It was an important journey for all of them and they knew they had to find a way to keep it together.

"I'm sick of this constant bickering," Dominic continued in a calmer tone.

"Find a way to entertain yourselves, go to sleep; I don't care... but I don't want to hear anymore fighting tonight. In case you hadn't noticed, we're stranded on a long strip of nowhere with an hour left before the sun wakes up and fries us. Maybe you guys could even help come up with an idea or two."

Dominic looked to each of them and they could feel his deep stare assaulting their minds. Though he had the power to do it, he could never bring himself to violate Raina by intruding on her thoughts. She was the first woman in a long time that he felt such fierce protection over and he wouldn't hurt her any more than he would allow someone else to hurt her.

"Let's go," he said, getting out of the car and flipping his wrist for them to follow.

They walked down the side of the highway, each caught up in their own dark thoughts. Jarek trudged along slowly with the cop's corpse dangling over his shoulders and boxes of Dilly bars clutched in his angry grip. Leo mumbled complaints as a joint clung to his bottom lip. Christoph walked quietly, lost in deep thoughts while Raina floated alongside of them quietly. Nobody spoke until Dominic stopped suddenly.

"What's up?" Leo asked.

He didn't answer but just pointed toward an empty Corvette that had been stranded on the side of the road, just as they had been.

"Come on," he said as he led them toward the flat tired vehicle. Looking through the windows, they saw that sandwich wrappers, empty cans, and napkins were strewn all over the front seats.

"Pigs," Christoph said in disgust. He believed in keeping everything immaculate and didn't understand the sloppiness that seemed so inbred in the humans.

Dominic opened the door and sat in the driver's seat and Leo climbed in beside him. In the backseat, Jarek and Christoph sat on each side of Raina with the corpse resting across their legs as they looked to Dominic for further instruction. Their abilities to leap wouldn't get them out of danger any faster because their powers had weakened as their pack's unity had diminished.

"Damn," Dominic said. "Nobody even slowed down. I think our appearance might be freaking them out."

"Prejudiced jerks," Leo shot out angrily, shaking his head back and forth to exacerbate his disapproval.

"Jarek and Raina," Dominic began. "Go to the side of the road and try to flag down someone; anyone. Pretend to be a married couple out of gas. We don't have much time."

Raina applied a new coat of lipstick and then flipped her hair back as she held onto his stare. Grabbing the joint from Leo's mouth, she stuck it between her lips and took Jarek's hand into her own.

"Come on, let's go," she finally said.

After watching them walk away, Dominic turned to Leo and Christoph.

"I hope this works," he told them, trying not to show his concern. "I'm getting hungry again. It's coming faster."

"Me too," Christoph agreed.

The cop and the cashier hadn't been enough to satisfy them. Only when his hunger turned to physical pain did Christoph ever give in to his urges. He could deal with the shakes that overtook his body and he could handle the sensation of ice that rushed through his sore veins. He could even deal with the stomach cramps that brought him to his knees with their increasing tightness and their relentless lack of mercy but it was what came after the pain that Christoph had a hard time dealing with. It was the emotional aspect that worked as a gravitational pull toward the closest blood source and it was the hollowness that usually caused him to lose the internal battle.

He grabbed one of the juice boxes from the cluttered floor and jabbed the tiny straw into the aluminum that covered its drink hole. After emptying it of what liquid it had left, he carefully angled the small hole beneath the cop's last squirting vein and filled it to the top with the blood of the fallen lawman.

"What are you doing?" Dominic asked with raised brows.

"Preparing snacks," he answered as though Dominic should have known.

Dominic shook his head but didn't respond.

Grabbing the remainder of the carcass, Leo pulled both arms out of their sockets and threw one up to Dominic before tossing the rest of the corpse over his head. He smiled when he heard the thud that marked its landing beneath the back window.

"Why do you always feel the need to top me?" Christoph asked, annoyed.

"It's not like it's difficult," Leo answered between mouthsful of flesh. Taking another bite of the cop's severed arm, he smiled at the sound of bones crunching inside his mouth.

"Feel better?" Christoph asked.

"Much."

What Christoph really wanted to tell him was that he was just an angry little runt and that he always would be but decided to keep quiet. He had once learned the hard way that, although small, Leo's lack of height and muscle did nothing to diminish his ferocity when his pride had been hurt. The night Christoph had compared Leo's size six shoes to the button inside of his boxer shorts had not been a productive one and he winced at the memory as Leo continued to glare at him, chomping through bites of meat and gristle.

"Want some?" Leo asked in between bites

"No, thanks, I'm good."

"Look," Dominic said, a hint of excitement outlining his tone.

Following the direction of his glazed stare, they saw that a van had pulled over to the side of the road several yards behind them. Christoph sighed audibly as they exited the car to join them. Though he felt a sense of relief for their rescue, he also felt sympathy for the driver and passengers, who wouldn't make it away intact.

"I'll do the talking," Dominic said firmly.

As they neared the van, the writing on the passenger door became visible.

First United Church.

"Christians are delicious," Leo said excitedly. His pace picked up speed at the thought of the fresh, young blood.

"Calm down," Christoph said. "Look closer. They're children."

Leo responded with the hearty laugh that always thoroughly annoyed him.

"And?" he asked dramatically.

"And we don't kill children," Christoph answered defensively.

"No, YOU don't kill children. I kill whomever I want," he snapped back.

It never took long for his temper to reach its maximum and Christoph wondered for the hundredth time what the little creature's life had been like before he'd been turned. He imagined that Leo's inability to accept his small stature had always made him the asshole of every group.

"Shut up, both of you," Dominic jumped in. "We're catching a ride, not killing kids. We have exactly one hour before daylight and don't have time for your arguments right now."

Both of them held their tongues at the flash of anger that shone through his blue-eyed glare.

"Wait, slow down," Dominic whispered at the halfway mark. "Raina's got this."

He watched the way she maneuvered herself toward the van. There was seduction in everything she did and Dominic wondered if the driver noticed she wasn't walking toward him as much as she was floating. The tips of her shoes quietly scraped the cement as she inched closer to his window.

"Let's go," Dominic said, picking up the pace again.

"Wait! My snacks!" Christoph nearly screamed, thoughts of wasted cop and spoiled blood unacceptable to him.

Leo stopped walking and stood very still before turning around to burn a hole through Christoph's corneas with a rage filled glare.

"You're not serious," he said.

Christoph didn't answer. Instead, he ran back to the car that housed their homemade party favors and grappled with the pile of juice boxes on the floor. Glancing at a mangled leg of cop, he wished they had brought mint jelly. Struggling to carry all of the juice boxes without spilling them, he decided to forego bringing along the few pieces of policeman that remained.

As he shifted his weight to accommodate his coveted snacks, he heard singing and when he looked up, saw that Dominic and Leo had already made it to the van. Standing on the passenger's side beside Raina and Jarek, he noticed how all four of them stood immobile as they stared at the young choir group inside. The sliding van door was opened all the way and the children were staring back quietly. All might have gone well had the children not started singing.

"Kumbaya, my Lord, Kumbaya. Kumbaya, my Lord, Kumbaya."

"Oh, no," he said to himself.

Dropping the juice boxes, he half ran and half leapt toward the van, traveling as fast as he could. He was fueled by the dread one sensed upon the discovery that they were too late to make a difference and upon the next verse of Kumbaya, watched as his pack's faces morphed into the dark and ugly images that accompanied their thirst.

Upon their turning, they had come to despise those who worshipped God because of the hypocrisy attached to their lost souls. The Lord had abandoned them all and had left them to fend for themselves for an eternity. He knew the song had set them off and wished he had been closer to the van, believing he could have prevented the third verse, which had subsequently become the young group's death sentence. Not even Dominic had the power to diffuse the pack once the change hit.

He watched as Dom's head dropped into a bow and noticed how he turned away from the van and his rapidly morphing pack. Though neither of them could stop the massacre, neither would become a part of it either. They had always been stronger and better able to fight their urges than the others.

Christoph grimaced from a distance at the sight of Leo's teeth growing into fangs, longer than a tiger's and sharper than a new blade. He tried to close his eyes to the scene but realized that the scent of their fear and their sweet blood wafting his way was a temptation that even he couldn't fight. Drawn in against his will, he stared at the carnage through spread fingers.

Watching in horror, he found that he couldn't turn away from the sight of Leo as he plucked a little girl from her seat and held her in the air above his head. Her scream never got the chance to escape her vocal chords because she had still been securely fastened by a belt when he'd pulled her out and her lower half still remained attached to the seat.

Christoph covered his ears to muffle the horrified screams of the children as each one of them accepted the reality that monsters did exist after all. He could almost taste the blood vicariously as he continued to peek through his fingers against his will.

He watched as Jarek bit into the throbbing jugular vein of a teenage boy and stood frozen in his spot as he watched him drink almost every last drop from the innocent youth. Through his empathy, he could feel his friend's conflict and desperate desire to stop himself and the transfer of shame and guilt only strengthened his despair. He cursed the inability to dull his senses.

He felt his own hunger increase and intensify and tried to ignore the threats of pending hollowness for his lack of participation. He told himself repeatedly that he would not take a child, matter how strong the need became and then heard his own shoe tips loudly scraping the concrete as he headed toward the petrified driver.

The short, chubby man simply stared at him through the windshield with eyes opened so wide that Christoph envisioned his eyeballs falling out. His gaping mouth was as still as the rest of his body and it intrigued Christoph how some humans froze during fear while others reacted with aggression and still others tried to flee. Despite the driver's reaction, he knew the man would become his breakfast within the minute.

Punching effortlessly through the windshield, he found his incisors inside the man's fat neck before he even realized what he had done. The driver's frozen stance turned to aggression upon the bite but it did him no good. Teeth still inserted inside the man's vein, Christoph's line of vision stopped on Raina and he watched her with intrigue. Dominic had been right. She was a true seductress; her movements were almost fluid-like as she caressed a little boy's tear stained face.

"It's okay," he heard her coddle him sweetly. "Just let go."

He was about twelve years old and Christoph knew the suffering that she would experience when it was over. He knew that she would remember how the boy's tears forked off in different directions and how they fell from the sides of nose and he knew also that she would punish herself for it for eternity. Wiping away his tears, she started to hum a bar of Kumbaya as Christoph closed his eyes to finish off the driver. When he opened them again, Raina was staring directly at him with a look of pain that, he knew, she would never be able to release.

Chapter XIII

The massacre silenced all of them and they drove in silence until their hunger returned. They were awake, alert, and energized by the feeding but scared and ashamed because of how they went about it. After stealing the cash from the driver's wallet and swiping the plastic gas can from the back of the van, Jarek had left them roadside in pursuit of the closest gas station. Within minutes, they had refilled their tank enough to make it to a gas station and then put as many miles as possible between themselves and the carnage they left behind. None of them referenced the destruction of the children or the damage they had caused within; they did everything they could do to block out the memories entirely.

With Dominic back at the wheel of the hearse, Christoph sat in the back and thought about the dangers that still lie ahead. He forced himself to concentrate on only positive thoughts and refused to let himself get sucked into the darkness that called for him. He had one wish and nothing would stop him from his meeting with Lucius. His request was long overdue and the time had come to ensure that his greatest desire was finally granted.

Christoph thought about the little things in life that had always inspired him. He appreciated his ability to still appreciate the smaller things. The loss of their spirits had only strengthened their desires because feelings of longing lived within their hearts and not their souls. He still felt his nerves jump when they passed towering trees and open fields and fast food restaurants. He craved fast food almost as much as he longed for blood and knew it would be a struggle if ever he had to choose between a midnight massacre or a McDonald's cheeseburger.

Each time they passed an interstate sign that invited drivers to a salty and delicious exit he would become as excited as a five year old. At the wheel, Dominic tried everything he could to keep Christoph's attention on the left side of the road rather than the exit signs. Knowing they were low on money and pressured for time, he quickly thought of ways to divert his attention from the golden arches he saw coming up on the right.

"Hey guys, look!" he exclaimed, pointing a finger through his driver's window toward absolutely nothing.

Christoph sat up straight. Squinting his eyes, he peered out into the darkness through his back window but saw nothing but the occasional silhouette of an elm tree flashing by.

"What is it, Dom? I don't see anything but trees."

Dominic glanced toward Raina and motioned with his eyes to the upcoming burger joint as way of seeking some help. They had done well on time because of his ability to thwart any more unplanned stops and didn't want anything to waylay their schedule, not even a quick stop through a drive-thru. Catching the near desperate plea in his eyes, she jumped in to help.

"Wait a minute!" she exclaimed, leaning over Dominic's lap to share in the roving eye search. "I thought I something too!"

Jarek remained quiet in his seat behind Raina but found the situation amusing. Bored to tears, he had kept himself entertained by making games out of anything he could. Noticing the fast approaching McDonald's and their pathetic attempts to divert Christoph's attention, he decided to make a small wager with himself.

"Christoph wins or I take a shot," he thought to himself, eyeing the flask that was hugged between his knees. It shone back up at him and he smiled at the inscription Raina had personally engraved for him on its smooth metal surface.

To My Devil, My Angel, My Sequel

He had never asked her exactly what it meant but had loved it almost as much as Dominic had despised it. Beside him, Christoph suddenly whipped his head to the right.

"Damn. I wanted that shot," he thought.

The familiar tingles began to race one another down Christoph's spine when he saw it come into view and he had to place mild pressure on his knee to control the excited shakes. Shooting an angry glance toward his front seat cohorts, his lip curled into an angry sneer. If looks could kill, his would surely have generated their spontaneous combustion but he worried that his hostility might inadvertently have the opposite effect so he decided to change tactics before Dominic applied more pressure to the gas pedal instead of less. Praying hands replaced frustrated fists and he simply mouthed one word.

"Please?"

Exasperated and annoyed but guided by compassion, Dominic let his head fall back against the headrest and hung a sharp right into the long circular drive-thru line. He started crunching deadlines in his brain as Christoph unfolded his hands and flattened them on his knees. His tongue darted out of his mouth and licked at the corner of his lips, leaving a long sturdy line of saliva dangling in its wake.

"It's like traveling with a friggin' child," came Leo's muffled voice from somewhere in the back.

He had been resting comfortably in the coffin at the back of the hearse when the sudden change of direction knocked his face into the inner panel painfully. The annoyed twitch in his right eye told him there wouldn't be a chance in hell of closing them restfully unless Dominic gave into Christoph's needy and childish demands. Leo pushed too hard at the inside of the coffin lid and it slammed into the back window with enough force to make the rest of them jump in their seats.

"Was that really necessary?" Raina asked with a pronounced scowl.

"Necessary? No. Fun? Absolutely," he retorted angrily.

"Bite me, Leo," she said.

"Don't tempt me, Scarlett," he insulted. He could usually get under her skin with insinuations of her disloyalty but this time, she laughed.

"You'll forgive me my inability to ever fear you, little man."

Without further ado, Leo hurled his body through the car's interior and directly toward Raina's head. Just before the painful collision, Jarek brought Leo's flight to an abrupt end with a one-armed block, its force shooting Leo back into the coffin in a loud, clumsy fall.

"Oops," Jarek said with a chuckle. "Sorry 'bout that."

"Enough!" Dominic finally interjected loudly and they quieted.

Jarek wasn't hungry, not for a burger anyway. His cravings were geared more toward another shot of whiskey or the pulsating jugular of a tourist. The drive-thru was brightly lit and he recoiled from its shine, willing his system to adjust to the fact that it was illumination, not solar.

Having made the same trip on many other occasions, a collection of food orders was unnecessary. Dominic pulled up beside the speaker and waited for the invitation to order.

"Welcome to McDonald's, would you like to order one of our delicious value meals this evening?" crackled an obviously Hispanic female voice, boredom evident in her tone.

They could hear Leo laughing loudly from the inside of the coffin as he amused himself with gruesome fantasies. Each one included a different method of sucking the cashier dry but all of them ended with serving her decapitated head to some horrified customer expecting an ordinary happy meal toy. Dominic threw a look to Jarek who happily obeyed the silent command by slamming his fist on the coffin lid, hard. Leo stopped laughing immediately.

Focusing his attention back toward the squawking box, Dominic delivered their order with the same respect he would use to address an authority figure. He treated the humans based not on their race or status but instead on their level of kindness.

"Good evening," he said in a voice that could soothe nations. "Could we please get seven rare cheeseburgers and five small cokes with no ice?"

The cashier was quiet for several seconds before speaking again.

"Rare?" she finally asked.

"Yes, ma'am."

"I don't think we make them that way," she answered, mystified.

Dominic tried not to roll his eyes at her limited thought capacity. It was the same conversation every time. Minding his patience, he continued.

"Please tell the cook to just throw them on the fryer for ten seconds; just long enough to unfreeze."

"Is this a joke?" she asked, doubt saturating her tone.

"No, ma'am," he answered gently.

Dominic had the patience of a saint and the manners of an old-time gentleman. He wasn't quick to annoy and could effectively diffuse most situations with the tone of his voice alone. Both melodic and hypnotic, it usually had the power to get him what he wanted without too much effort.

"Okay but if you're playing me, they're gonna make me pay for this."

"I wouldn't let that happen," he said kindly.

"Okay, you got it," she answered skeptically. "That'll be thirteen dollars and twenty-seven cents."

"Thank you," he said to the cashier as he fumbled for his wallet.

Dominic had started to pull forward but stopped abruptly when he remembered something else. Reversing the huge hearse back to the speaker, he was rewarded with an angry response from the driver behind them. The man pressed down on his horn for a ridiculous amount of time before sticking his head out his window.

"Stupid ass!" he screamed, holding out a tightly pointed bird that he waved toward each of them.

Dominic ignored him and leaned into the speaker as he waited for confirmation that their cashier hadn't quit after their order.

"Hello?" he asked the quiet box.

"I'm here, sir," she answered timidly.

"Sorry about that. I forgot to ask you to leave the pickles off two of the burgers, please?"

"No, just one," Jarek advised from the backseat.

"Sorry, no pickles on one burger please," Dominic corrected. Neither he nor Jarek had ever liked pickles so his friend's decision to keep them on his burger had him ruminating in suspicious thoughts.

"Yes, sir," the cashier answered. "Please pull up to the first window."

"Thank you, ma'am."

Dominic pulled forward once more and when he came to a complete stop at the second window, he turned around to check on his pack. Noticing that Leo had his face pressed against the back window, he felt a sickness in his gut to see that he had crawled out of the coffin to stare down the chubby driver who had honked at them.

Apprehension invaded his nervous system as it usually did when Leo was quiet.

"What're you doing, Leo?" he asked, trying to keep his tone light.

"That asshole just called us a car load of greasers, punks, and drunks," Leo answered, referring to his supersonic audio abilities. "I was just trying to figure out how I'm gonna rip his throat out."

"You're not. You're gonna turn down the volume in your head and enjoy a cheeseburger with us," Dominic instructed. "Now, turn around."

Leo ignored him and pressed his face harder into the back window, his stare never wavering from the man's reluctant eye contact. The driver had a clear view of his squashed and indented appearance and the disconcerting sight was making him restless. He turned away, breaking the eye contact, and tried to appear unaffected by the stare down. His nervousness made Leo smile. Disarming the humans was his foreplay and had always been his favorite part of the kill.

The driver, trusting his words were protected by physics, continued to make nasty comments under his breath but Leo could hear his whispers as though they were screams. The change started to take form through the reddening of his eyes, the growing of his incisors, and the sharpening of his nails. He could smell the driver's fear as it wafted in from his car and he could sense it further in the man's abrupt cessation of whispered ramblings.

Leo had once enjoyed his power to manipulate sound waves but it was a gift he wished he could return. The ability had become more of a curse than a blessing after realizing he was forced to hear things he preferred not hearing. He despised the humans with their phony smiles and the unkind words they were usually muttering beneath them.

Though the pack had often advised him to not to concern himself with the ignorance of the mortals, Leo couldn't let go of his hatred for them. The seed of his disgust had been planted when he was one of them. He was often treated with cruelty and had harmed him in ways that he had never disclosed to anyone else until meeting and falling in love with Collette. Having known only disgust and vengeance, after discovering his love for her and accepting hers for him, Leo had realized the rage was only relative to his happiness. As his hatred had slowly dissipated, he had begun to discover the awesome potential of humanity until his spiritual awakening was cut short by the merciless and selfish act of a coward who refused to show his face before biting him. After awakening from his death, the rage had rushed back into him with intensity and Leo had never been able to rid himself of it again. At thoughts of the love he would never know again for all eternity, he became angrier and energized by the lost memories and he climbed out of the coffin entirely.

Perching himself on top of it, he continued to stare out the back window of the hearse, pushing aside the curtains that were drawn to show respect for the dead. Tilting his head in amusement at the driver's increasing discomfort, Leo offered a huge smile that took up most of his face. His eyes, however, remained dark and shone with thoughts of retribution.

"Why did you get pickles, Jarek? You hate them as much as I do," Dominic asked from the front seat. Not wanting to hear the answer since he'd already surmised the reason on his own, he asked it in the hopes of drawing Leo into their conversation and taking his focus off the man that followed them.

"Because he likes to give his pickle to Raina," Christoph answered, too delirious with thoughts of beef and ketchup to realize he should have just kept quiet.

"Hey, Christoph," Leo said distractedly, never taking his eyes off the car behind him. "Anyone ever tell you're a complete idiot?"

When Christoph turned around, he noticed Leo sitting on top of the coffin Indian style and peering through the curtains they were supposed to have kept drawn.

"What are you doing?" Christoph asked the back of his head. "You haven't moved for a little while and you're starting to freak me out."

"I'm fine. Mind your own business," came thr rapid reply.

The driver behind them readjusted his glasses and turned his baseball cap to the side as a way of ignoring the putrid creature glaring out from the hearse at him.

"Freaks," he whispered to himself.

Dominic paid the cashier and she handed him the bag of burgers before leaving her post again to retrieve their drinks. He held one out to Raina before tossing the bag over his head and into the backseat. Unfolding the paper that housed her burger, she lay it carefully on the napkin she'd spread out on her lap, pulled off the top bun, and cut her eyes over to Jarek. In turn, he peeled the two flimsy green slivers from his own cheeseburger and dropped them onto her meat.

"Thanks," she grinned.

"You're welcome," Jarek winked.

Dominic mumbled something inaudible to all of them.

"What was that, Dom?" Raina asked sarcastically.

"Nothing."

Dominic wondered, and not for the first time, why she was so intent on torturing him. He had never wanted to leave her and had only made his choices for the greater good of their pack but she would never come to accept it. Instead, she flaunted her relationship with Jarek in front of him and seemed to almost relish his discomfort and pain. Just as he started to fall into a memory of sweeter times, their cashier was back with two of the cokes.

"Sorry, sir. Your other three drinks will be right up."

"No doubt about it, Dom," Christoph said with mustard dripping from his chin, "she's taking her time cause she has a crush on you."

The girl's goofy smile didn't fool any of them. Dominic's blue eyes and penetrating stare affected all the ladies the same way.

"Yeah," he mumbled back absentmindedly.

Knowing that he should heed the warning that nagged at him to pay attention to the situation at hand, Dominic closed his eyes to tune them all out. Trying to block out the affectionate banter between his former lover and his best friend, he fell into a memory of his last intimate moments with Raina. He could still feel the warmth of her skin and could still hear the soft cries that had escaped her as she lay beneath him on their last night together. Whispering curses in his own mind for his past decisions, Dominic was pulled violently from his sad reverie when the hearse shook with sudden and brutal force. Though the movement had been jarring, it stopped too soon for any of them to properly assess the cause.

"What the hell was that?" Jarek asked first.

All four heads turned backwards at once, hoping to see Leo still sitting vigil atop the coffin. They were startled to find him squished in between Christoph and Jarek, sitting up straight and attentive. Though he smiled innocently they could sense the guilt that emanated from his entire being.

The cashier reappeared with the last of their Cokes and a dorky smile. She had missed the excitement in her short absence.

"Thank you, miss," Dominic said. "You've been very kind."

Concern and distraction had knocked the charm out of his tone as Dominic wondered how long it would take for Leo's crimes to get them arrested.

"Do you know what that was, Leo?" he asked with as much patience as he could muster.

"What what was?" Leo asked innocently.

Knowing he wouldn't divulge anything until it was too late, Dominic tried another tactic.

"Did you get your burger from the bag?" he asked.

"Oh, no thanks," smiled the diminutive vampire. "I already grabbed a snack."

All four of them turned around again, slowly and carefully. Nothing was different or noteworthy but for the pair of glasses and baseball cap that sat quietly on top of their closed coffin.

Dominic shook his head and then bowed it deeply. He had known the complete prevention of unnecessary carnage was impossible but had hoped it wouldn't occur in plain view of the humans. Vampires were killers and even he didn't have the power to squash their most primal instincts, he did prefer that their treacherous acts not be witnessed by innocents or recorded by security cameras.

A muffled cry sounded from inside the closed coffin and they all knew it was Leo's snack calling.

Dominic pulled out of the McDonald's drive-thru, leaving an orchestra of beeping horns and a car with a missing driving in their wake. He didn't say a word as he pulled away as discreetly as possible and headed for the closest exit out of the state.

Chapter XIV

"Tennessee is gorgeous," Raina marveled as she stared at the passing greenery from her back window.

"Yeah," Christoph mumbled from the driver's seat. "I sure wish we could see it in the daytime."

It hadn't escaped their attention that he had grown melancholy over the last few hours but the pack knew better than to ask why. They all knew from experience that their mysterious friend with the fondness for cheeseburgers and crossbows would share his feelings in his own time and in his own way. Raina simply scooted up closer behind him and encircled his shoulders with her arms in her quiet manner of comfort. Even Leo had backed off from harassing him, evidently deciding to give his favorite target a break for the time being.

"Well, don't get used to it," Dominic said, turning around from the passenger's side to return the bottle of whiskey back to Jarek. He had nursed it for longer than he'd planned but was enjoying the warmth it provided nonetheless. "We're heading into the city in a few minutes and it's not all pretty trees and quiet beauty; take my word for it."

"Which city?" Leo asked from his seat atop the coffin.

None of the others would be able to get away with perching themselves on such a high platform without pushing the tops of their heads right through the ceiling but their small friend looked as comfortable as he could be. His mood had become much more positive and upbeat since his last snack and he still donned the baseball cap as a souvenir after discarding the driver's body.

"Oz, stupid," Jarek piped in though they had all thought him to be asleep. His head was thrown back against the back of the seat and his breathing had become heavier, like one in a deep slumber. "We're almost in Oz and your new name will be Toto when we arrive."

Though he continued to berate Leo, the words were delivered with more humor than malice.

"What city do you think, moron?" he continued.

"I don't know, asshole," Leo threw back. "History wasn't my best subject."

"Geography, you idiot," Jarek muttered with an eye roll. "Geography wasn't your best subject."

"How do you know what I did good in?" Leo snapped back, throwing a candy bar wrapper toward him and wincing when it only fluttered in the air and landed on his own lap because of its weight.

"Forget it," Jarek answered, frustrated.

Head still back against the seat and body still slumped in preparation for a nap he turned his face toward Raina and stared at her profile. Watching how gentle she was with Christoph made him love her even more than he already did but it was not a feeling he would ever share in mixed company. Instead, he turned his face toward the window again and closed his eyes.

"See what I mean?" Dominic asked, pointing through the windshield and ignoring their petty arguments. "And they call us freaks."

A dark hooded figure stood at the corner a few yards ahead, counting out money and handing a small package over to a tall skinny man with stringy hair and pockmarks over more than half his face. They didn't even try to disguise their drug deal nor did they appear particularly concerned that a pack of vampires had their faces glued to the glass as they watched it play out. Once his goods were purchased, the pitiful customer strode away with a limp and an obvious case of the shakes, no doubt in search of a dirty needle and a quiet spot in which to fill it.

"Where are we exactly?" Raina asked.

Dominic eyed the intersecting street signs and opened the detailed map that had taken residence on his lap. Thumbing through it to find the statistics of their current city at the bottom of the page, he read aloud to the pack.

"Let's see... Warford and Mt. Olive... Warford and Mt. Olive," he slurred slightly. "Here it is! We are currently driving through the seventh most dangerous neighborhood in America. And we're only sixteen miles from Graceland."

Somewhat amused by the information, he chuckled to himself before continuing.

"Looks like there's an average of about four aggravated assaults, two rapes, eight burglaries, and one murder every month," he continued. "Right here in this very spot!"

"Lovely," Raina said.

"Hey, sounds like my kinda place!" Leo threw back. "I wonder how the real estate is here."

"Dis-gust-ing," Jarek said, annunciating each syllable with more repugnance than the last. His gaze was directed out the back right window and his expression had contorted into a look of sickened disapproval.

Four pairs of eyes followed his glare and they watched as hapless stragglers loitered at the front of a strip club that was less than enticing. It boasted worn and bedraggled signs that invited customers to enjoy both full frontal nudity and a full liquor bar. It was difficult to determine whether the building or the occupants were more decrepit and Christoph slowed down so they could absorb the seediness of their surroundings.

Feeling the same internal stirring that he always felt around such a venue, Dominic changed his mind quickly after getting a closer look at the scene. More than happy to pull his attention away from such ugliness, he stared at Christoph to assess his mood instead. He became just as disheartened by the sudden change in his friend's posture when he noticed that Christoph's hands had been overtaken by mild shakes and noted the manner in which he stared off into some unknown and distant thought. Aware that his friend's burdensome abilities always became stronger when in close proximity to sin and debauchery, Dominic decided his empathic powers must be working at full capacity.

Unable to turn away from the club anymore than they could turn away from a train wreck, they each stared open-mouthed at the barely clad women milling around the front of the bar. Chain-smoking their cigarettes and sneaking hits from a crack pipe, the pack watched as the drug and sex infested dancers worked half-heartedly to lure in the leering patrons with promises of discounted lap dances, and more – much, much more. A far cry from the higher class establishments he had become accustomed to in his past life, Dominic noted the sad group of strippers before him would never be accused of being beautiful or graceful. These dancers boasted scabs, hickeys, and bruises, which were unfortunately their best assets. Regardless if their marks were an occupational hazard or merely tangible proof of their unhealthy lifestyles, he felt a sick chill run down his spine. The place felt more like the final stop on the way to a lonely death than a Mecca of entertainment and excitement.

"Jesus Lord Almighty!" Jarek exclaimed with disgust.

"Yeah," Raina agreed. "Christoph, you wanna step on the gas a little harder and get us the hell out of here, please?"

"Oh, come on!" laughed Leo. "They're not so bad! I say we pull over for a quick snack!"

"Sure!" Jarek answered sarcastically. "And when we're done, we can stop off at a Methadone clinic for a little nightcap. You just don't care what you put in your body, do you?"

"I'm with Jarek and Raina on this one," Dominic agreed with a hint of sad compassion in his voice. "Please speed up."

"Yeah," Jarek added, distaste etched into his expression. 'I think I caught an STD just by looking at them."

"Who cares?" Leo shot back, amused. "It's not like we're gonna die!"

"You guys suck, you know that?" Christoph finally interjected, his harsh tone surprising them all. "They're lost and they're hurting and you all just sit there in judgment? Why don't you take a good long look at yourselves?"

"Huh," Raina said softly. "Wish I could."

"They're wretched," Leo said.

"It is their choice, Christoph," Raina said. "They don't have to be there, doing what they're doing."

"How do you know? None of you know what they have to do or don't have to do just like nobody knows our real story!"

Raina grew silent. She wasn't used to Christoph becoming so heated and she definitely wasn't accustomed to him yelling at her. His accusatory tone hurt her feelings.

"All right, relax," Dominic commanded.

Christoph pressed his foot on the gas but just as they began to move forward, a ratty guy with an enthusiastic attitude popped up at Christoph's window unexpectedly.

"Can I help you?' he asked the odd looking stranger.

"Hey folks!" the guy greeted eyeing each one of them individually. He handed Christoph a flyer and continued to smile but his delighted attitude seemed less than sincere.

"Just inviting passing tourists, and locals of course, to a little rave we'll be holding at the abandoned warehouse down the road. That is, if you're in the mood for a little fun and adventure! Lots of drink!" he yelled before cupping a hand over his mouth to whisper, "and lots of drugs."

Raising his voice again, he continued the ranting invitation. "Lots of pleasure on every level you could imagine, if you know what I mean."

He threw them a wink that lacked playfulness or seduction and just left them feeling dirty. The speed of his words and the shaking of his hands hinted he had just snorted a fat line before approaching them.

"Love your car, by the way!" he added.

"Yeah, thanks," Christoph said in the friendliest voice he could muster. "Appreciate the offer."

He stepped on the gas again and did so with a newly inspired urgency. Raina snatched the flyer from his hand and read the invitation out loud.

"It seems that a local abandoned warehouse will be serving as a hot party spot for those in search of *all seven sins,*" she read. "Can we go? Please, please?"

"What?" Dominic asked. "Why would you want to go there?"

"Think about it, Dom. Lots of sin, lots of wickedness; bunches of evil people gathered in one place... lots of blood! It would be like a buffet! Just like old times....," she smiled.

Dominic stared back at her with a knowing look in his eyes and grinned.

"Damn," Leo agreed. "She's right. It's perfect!"

Dominic looked to Leo and Jarek and both of them answered his silent question with a nod of the head.

"We have time for the rave or we have time for Graceland," Dominic said. "Let's take a vote."

"Rave!" they yelled in unison.

"Okay," Dominic confirmed. "Rave it is! Doesn't start for an hour though so we've got some time to kill, which is fortunate for me because I have to take a piss that'll last about that long. Pull over to the side, Christoph."

The alcohol intake had caught up with his bladder with a vengeance and he had no time for social graces.

"What, here?" he asked. "There is no side. You can't wait until we find a bathroom?"

"Seriously, pull over; can't wait," he whimpered, holding his side and sitting uncomfortably upright in his seat.

"But Dom, I…"

"Right there… there's some bushes. Just pull over or I'm gonna piss in the car!" Dominic pleaded with urgency.

"There's nowhere to stop," Christoph exclaimed, his eyes jetting back and forth from the road to Dominic and his untimely bladder. "Look, there's a Tupperware container in the glove compartment. Can't you use that?"

Without argument, Dominic opened the glove compartment and, amidst several CD cases and gum wrappers, saw the clear Tupperware container large enough to hold a sandwich staring back at him. Half drunk, he pulled it out and held it up in disbelief and contemplation, ignoring the snickers from his companions in the backseat.

"All right! I'm doing it," he decided aloud. "Holy crap!"

Realizing the complexity of such a task, Dominic refused to back out. He had already accepted the challenge and refused to quit before he started. He was determined to figure out a way to urinate into such a shallow container while in a moving vehicle and while wearing leather pants. It was a simple decision of whether to attempt the seemingly impossible or to allow his bladder to explode. The former decision won hands down.

Leaning forward over the front of the seat, he unzipped his leather pants and angled the container in front of him as best he could while snickering to himself over the ironies. He could lift a car one-handed, leap higher than an oak tree, and read the mind of a human being but for the life of him, he couldn't figure out how to successfully relieve himself in a sandwich container. Without the luxury of further contemplation, he went for it.

As he began to urinate, the pride of his temporary success turned quickly to concern as he realized the container was already half full and that his bladder was less than half empty.

As he made the painful attempt to stop mid-stream, Christoph slammed on the brakes and the hearse jolted almost violently.

"Son of a bitch!" Christoph shouted as he shared his attention with the road and with his passenger. Dominic had unfortunately lost control of his own situation and urine dripped and drizzled from the dash of the car, spilling generously into a new make shift urinal on the front seat floor.

"Dude! My car!"

"What the hell was that?" Dominic yelled, fumbling to balance the container as well as his dignity.

"I don't know," Christoph answered, his eye on Dominic more than the road. "Something jumped out in front of me; doesn't matter... are you finished?"

His tone had turned to near panic at the thought of the stains that might accompany them for the rest of their trip.

"Okay, okay, I'm good," Dominic answered. "You got a wet nap or something?"

"A wet nap?" Christoph asked incredulously. "Seriously? Grab a tissue from the glove compartment or something!"

Finding the lid amidst the mess, Dominic secured it to the top of the urine-filled container. As he rustled through the various compartments of the sedan looking for something to clean up the mess, he ignored the rest of the pack laughing in disbelief from the backseat.

"Aaah," Leo chortled gratefully from the back. "Thanks, Dom. I needed that."

Dominic looked apologetically to his driver.

"I'll clean it up when we get to the warehouse, man," he promised with a hiccup. "And you might wanna wash out that container before using it again."

"You can go ahead and throw it out the window, thanks," Christoph retorted.

Chapter XV

The pack walked into the warehouse and felt the threat immediately. The eerie silence in the massive hall was louder than the music they had expected to hear and there wasn't a body, a bar, or a sin in sight. There were no drunk, dancing humans, intent on losing themselves in liquor, drugs and sexual exploitations that they would regret in the morning. Instead, a pallor of death clung to the atmosphere and the odor of decay drifted passed the pack's nostrils in a manner that was disturbing to even an immortal.

Dominic's first internal reaction was surprise that he hadn't sensed the peril from outside and his second was a rush of panic that he refused to show his pack. He knew if their hidden enemies had the power to camouflage their essence, they were up against a more powerful coven than any they had ever faced together, as only old, aged vampires had the ability to disguise their presence.

The door they had entered slammed behind them and all five turned backwards as one, amidst the darkness. Seeing no one, they instinctively aligned themselves into a position of battle with Dominic taking the lead, Leo bringing up the rear, and the others meticulously placed in the middle. None of them spoke because their rules established they dare not speak aloud in unknown territory or under the possibility of threat. Fortunately, their leader had the power of mind-speak and it didn't take them long to adjust their frequencies so that each one of them could be party to the silent conversation.

"Don't move, don't speak; just prepare yourselves."

They obeyed his commands and remained immobile, quiet, and alert. Though Leo didn't make a peep, the pack could feel his rage and for once, they were grateful for it. His ire was transmitted through Dominic's telepathic powers and it infected each of them with its energy. The power of his fury prepared them to fight, like a steroid injected into a murderous mental patient, and they accepted it gratefully. A noise sounded from a loft above them and when they drew their attention to it, they realized the opposing pack had decided to reveal themselves slowly and dramatically rather than as an ambush.

"Trust nothing."

Leering at them from different locations, the quiet enemies came out slowly from their hiding places but did not advance on them. Dominic and his pack scanned the room with all of their senses and absorbed every detail they could with their combined abilities. Eyeing their surroundings with quick, darting glances, they counted their enemies and planned internally but with as little communication as possible. They had no way of knowing who else might be picking up on Dominic's mind-speak and the last thing they wanted to do was alert any of them to their intentions.

"Fifteen," Dominic said to their waiting minds.

Outnumbered three to one, they made the silent and collective decision to begin discerning which items in the warehouse they might be able to use as weapons. The opposing pack leered at them from their different positions around the warehouse but still, none of them spoke. A male and female pair smiled down at them from their perch on the top stair of the loft. Placing a long, sturdy finger to one side of his neck, the male grinned as he slid it gradually across his throat until it reached the other side. The gesture seemed to appeal to the female's amusement and she threw her head back with delight before mimicking his movements by drawing a feigned incision across her own slender throat.

The enemies' attentions seemed to be focused mostly on Christoph but he calmly returned their leers and threw in a playful wink of the eye. All the while his mind scrambled to wrap itself around the most creative and crafty idea he could conjure up on such short notice. Jarek began choosing his targets based on the strongest and largest members of the opposing pack and he cursed himself for leaving his new knife in the glove compartment. Knowing their situation had taken a dire turn, he worked hard to hide the chest heaves that threatened to give away his angst. Though he wanted nothing more than to reach his hand out to pull Raina closer, he remained still and forced himself not to look at her at the risk of the enemy realizing his weakness and finding a way to use it against him.

"Well, hello there," greeted a somewhat amused male voice to their right. "Come to join the party?"

"We have; thank you for the invite," Dominic answered, holding up the flyer. "Got it from what I can only assume was one of your pack members."

A gangly vampire with bad acne and crooked incisors stepped forward to join his leader. Though his true appearance differed somewhat from the ratty one he had exposed to them at the strip club, it was obvious he was the same vile customer who had leaned into their car to offer them the flyer and compliment their ride.

The opposing leader laughed and it sounded warm and welcoming, much like his appearance. His dark wavy hair had a sheen that could only be attained through time and attention, a possible reflection of his vanity and sense of image. The cornered pack of five scrambled to assess every detail available to them when devising a plan. Discerning an enemy's weakness had always been their greatest ability as a team and it was most likely what had kept them alive for so long.

"That's right. You two have met, I'd almost forgotten," their leader answered in a voice that dripped with sarcasm. "This is Jacob. Jacob, meet our timely guests. They've traveled quite a ways from their own home in… where is it you're from? New York, right?"

"That's right," Dominic replied, never dropping his smile. "I see our reputation has preceded us. To what do we owe the pleasure of such an intriguing invitation?"

"Oh, let's not just jump right into business," the leader said, gliding forward to stand before Dominic. "At least allow me to introduce myself before we begin exchanging unpleasantries. My name is Aurelio."

He loosely gestured behind him to his scattered flunkies before he continued.

"And this is my pack. We are not only the oldest tribe in Memphis but also the most powerful."

"You forgot the ugliest," Leo piped in from the back of their battle formation.

"Shut up!" Dominic demanded internally.

Aurelio's grin fell away at the insult but he replaced it immediately with another, much less sincere one. After a glare toward Leo, his eyes fell on Christoph and he fixated on him for a moment before directing his attention back to Dominic.

"The big mouth must be the infamous Leo," he continued.

"I feel at suh a disadvantage," Dominic answered. "Here, you have all this information about us yet we've heard nothing at all of you."

"There's not much I plan to tell you, really," Aurelio replied as he took a step forward. "Allow me to elucidate. We plan to kill you and have looked very forward to doing so since the moment we heard of your trip. You will not leave this place. Your journey ends here, my friend."

"Why, may I ask… friend," Dominic began, "have you chosen a small, unknown pack from so far away to focus your attentions on? You certainly have gone to a lot of work to get us here, Aurelio. Your name means Golden, correct? Implying you're the golden boy of this crew before us?"

"Silence!" Aurelio demanded and then calmed himself swiftly before continuing. "You can't tell me you don't know."

"Once word of your intentions to find Lucius hit the streets we have all hoped for the chance to meet you. You sure threw us all with your visit to Lansing, but it kept us on our toes. I know that our pack, personally, has awaited your arrival with baited breath."

"What did you bait yours with?" yelled Leo from the back. "Tuna fish?"

"Have you no control over your pack, Dominic?" Aurelio asked with disapproval. "Such disrespect to speak out as he does! If he were one of mine, I would have killed him already, before the words even tumbled out of his heinous little mouth. But of course, I suppose we can't expect much more from a pack of misfits who believe they can travel to the headmaster and make a bunch of wishes as though he were a genie rather than the most powerful vampire in the country."

"Leo, if you speak again, I will kill you myself."

"Aurelio!" a female voice yelled proudly from the top of the loft. "They're talking to each other!"

"Is that right?" Aurelio asked intrigued but without turning to acknowledge her. "And what might our special guests be saying to one another?"

"I don't know, I can't tell... I'm sorry. I just know they're talking. It's interrupting my frequencies!"

"That's okay, Gwennie," Aurelio answered. "That's a good girl."

Directing his next statements to Dominic, he maintained a tone of civility and kindness which might have been believable to a human. To the pack, however, the hardness of his eyes and the rigidity of his stance said otherwise.

"Females," he complained to Dominic as he shook his head back and forth to show his exasperation. "I only keep two, myself. They're not always the greatest help but they sure do come in handy at times, wouldn't you agree?"

Eyeing Raina with a look that made her shiver, he peeled back his lips to show her his fangs and then snarled in an effort to scare her but she showed no reaction. Despite Dominic's commands, she spoke within before one of them made an error in judgment in their efforts to protect her. She knew that traveling with them made her their biggest liability and it filled her with regret that she had difficulty containing

"Don't react on my behalf, any of you," she pleaded to her pack.

"They're doing it again, Aurie!" screamed a proud Gwennie. "This time it was her! The girl!"

"Is that right?" Aurelio asked Dominic as he floated gradually to stand before Raina. He continued to speak to Dominic but as he did so, he gently placed her chin between his thumb and forefinger. "We heard about this, allowing a female such a lengthy leash. Appalling, if you ask me."

Raina slapped his hand away from her rather than cowering as she knew he was hoping for. To her right, she could see Jarek's hand begin to flinch as he did when he was angry and from the front, she realized that Dominic had turned to face her. Both were potentially fatal moves and she knew that if something didn't happen quickly, they would be taken down by their new enemy within a minute's time. Aurelio's face contorted to a look of anger and disgust.

The pack, quickly realizing the imminent danger they found themselves in, knew they had little hope for escape. Remaining silent, they turned their thoughts inward and made note of the limited options around them.

"Not good..." Dominic projected amidst his team.

"What now?" Raina responded, knowing that despite their enemies' awareness of conversation, some form of game plan needed to be devised if they were to stand any chance.

"Leo?" Dominic inquired with his comrade for ideas, noticing the rage in his eyes and admitting to himself that traditional methods of retreat or creative strategy were no longer an option.

'Take 'em out!' Leo yelled aloud for all to hear.

As the remainder of the pack braced their bodies for action, Leo began running wildly, his head bent forward to guide him in his race toward a forklift. Though his boots periodically touched the floor during the maddened rush, his body seemed propelled by a different force as though he had no intention of wasting valuable time adhering to the laws of gravity. Trying to determine his plan was difficult for all of them because he didn't seem to have one. His reaction was born of pure rage and instinct; by the time any of them realized what he was doing, he had already climbed behind the wheel of the monstrous machine and flipped the switch.

Just as quickly, an acrobatic and incredibly limber male from a beam above flew swiftly toward him but his effort was thwarted by Dominic, who had grabbed hold of the hanging hook he'd strategically placed himself beneath. Utilizing every muscle in his calves and his legs, he pushed off Jarek's waiting hands and propelled himself toward Leo before the enemy could reach him. Only a second before the blond-haired, red-eyed vampire reached the driver's side of the forklift, Dominic slammed into him mid-flight and jammed the arced blade of the hook through the flesh beneath his chin. He then took him along as an unwilling passenger for the rest of his swinging ride.

Once Dominic had pushed off him, Jarek used all of the strength in one arm to push Aurelio away from Raina and with the other he pulled a loose and pointed board from the floor. The silence of the warehouse was filled by the cranking of the forklift and the groan of Dominic's punctured enemy and it seemed to work as a soundtrack for the rest of the quickly unfolding massacre.

As Aurelio worked to regain himself, Jarek stabbed the board into his heart and looked back just in time. A female in flight was speeding toward Raina and she wore a disturbing grimace reminiscent of the Joker or an evil clown. As Raina ducked to avoid the collision, Jarek wrapped a muscled arm around her waist and half ran, half flew with her toward the corner.

Realizing the forklift was too slow to keep up with Leo's plan, Christoph called out to Jarek and both raced toward the machine together. As Jarek utilized all of his strength to manually force the claws of the forklift into position, Christoph used the large sheet of broken glass he had pulled from a window in an effort to shield himself. Using himself as bait, he backed himself against the wall and taunted four of the enemies to stand before him and block his exit. Blades readied, Leo hit another switch and called out to him before making his next move.

"Christoph, now!" he yelled.

Dominic swung toward Christoph just in time for Leo to pin the four enemies against the wall. He scooped all four into the sharp and unforgiving clutches of the blades and laughed heartily at the crunching noises they made.

The throat slicers from the loft flew in a synchronized fashion toward Raina, still in the corner, but the male was caught painfully unaware by an oncoming Jarek who rushed from his place at the forklift. Pulling the hidden knife he remembered having stuck into his boot, he sliced the steel blade across the enemy's neck.

"You like the real thing?" he asked before spitting on him and tossing the knife to Raina.

The female stood before her, smiling sweetly, before baring her fangs and making a move to strike. Rather than running or fighting as expected, Raina pulled her into an embrace and changed their positions so that the female's back was to the wall instead of hers. Then, pulling back and using the anger inherited from Leo as well as some of her own, she used Jarek's knife to slice her foe's throat from end to another. Breathing hard, she faced Jarek and spoke.

"You're right!" she called out nervously. "That does feel good!"

None of the wounds the pack had inflicted on the enemy was mortal but they worked to hold them off in their attempt to flee the warehouse. Jarek pulled Raina toward the door they had entered as Dominic and Christoph arrived by swinging hook together. With the forklift, Leo held off the enemies who remained standing between him and his pack. Remaining still in the driver's seat, he looked to his pack to ensure their safe positions.

"Leo, come on!" Dominic yelled.

A group of four had formed a line between the pack at the door and Leo in the forklift so it was no simple feat for him to simply join them and run out of the warehouse. Dominic still held his swinging transport in one hand, Jarek still brandished his knife, Christoph still held his broken pane of glass, and Raina had picked up the pointed floorboard in their run for safety.

As one, they flew at the four whose backs were to them as they faced Leo, and allowed the sharpest parts of their weapons to puncture each of them in the back of the head. Had they not been energized or strengthened by Leo's fury, their efforts would likely have caused less damage. However, they had rage on their side and by the time they stuck their respective blades into their enemies, the blows were powerful enough to bring them down long enough for Leo to meet them at the door. They fled the warehouse and slammed the door behind them before racing to the car.

"Be careful!" Dominic yelled. "There's still one left. Keep an eye out!"

The pack jumped into the car, with Dominic at the wheel, and burned rubber on their way out of the parking lot. Their vehicle, though screeching and smoking and almost tipping to the side because of their speed, accelerated forward until the highway was beneath them and the warehouse was a distant memory. Only then did any of them speak.

"Whew!" Leo yelled. "That was a blast!"

Chapter XVI

The streets were filled with an array of cultures that blended together in a mesh pool of intrigue and sin. The excitement from the humans and the vampires alike could be felt on every block as each species plotted out their nights very differently. The masks hid their faces, concealed their truths, and blurred their boundaries as liquor flowed freely and the shared drugs gave free rein to their darkest of fantasies. With each drink, the idea that God's eyes could not penetrate their party was only reenforced further.

After the warehouse debacle, Dominic had decided to take them on one last pit stop before finishing their trip to Lucius the following day and Mardi Gras seemed most fitting for the time and place they found themselves. He intended to make sure each one of them had fun as he was uncertain whether or not they would all make it out of Lucius' mansion together or even alive. He felt he owed it to each of them to spend one more night of joy in each other's company.

Part of him wanted to call off the trip before it was too late but he knew the decision would be a selfish one.

He simply didn't want to lose any members of his pack, his family, and the task of trying to keep them all safe had started to wear on him. Dominic feared the outcome of the trip more than he had ever feared anything.

He glanced backwards at his pack as they followed him through the crowded streets of the French Quarter. A quick scan told him they were all deep in thought and he tried to guess where each of them sat inside of themselves. They'd dressed comfortably in the garb they normally tried to conceal; black capes blew backwards with each gust of wind and all five jaws expanded to house the hungry fangs they usually kept hidden.

Creole spices wafted toward them, a silent and mouthwatering invitation to dine on crawfish stew, jambalaya and shrimp Creole. Dominic stopped to assess the crowd and allow his pack to begin their dinner preparations. As the humans lined the concession stands in a long wait for authentic Cajun dishes, the pack stood quietly as they sized up the humans.

Dominic eyed Leo, who stood in silence with his gaze concentrated upon the herds of pointless, nameless people stumbling by him and spilling drinks on his new boots. They remained unaware of his attention to them or of his thirst for their pulsating veins. Dominic watched the slow smirk that took over his lips as he salivated for their liquor-filled bloodstreams. He plugged into Leo's mind without letting him know and as always, his heart became heavy over what he saw inside.

Who did this to me? Dominic could hear him ask himself, over and over again.

Leo would surely discover who turned him and Dominic had no way to foresee how it would play out or how it might impact his own wish. He bristled from the thoughts that tumbled from Leo's head and caught in his throat as he listened to the curses that his small friend cast upon the One who had turned him just when he'd come to understand the world and had finally known the love of a woman. Collette danced around his mind, her long dark hair blowing behind her, and he longed for her touch as he had every day since he'd been forced to leave her behind.

Dominic pulled his stare from Leo and allowed it to land on Christoph, whom he had never been able to clearly read. Thoughts so deep that he couldn't quite reach them, Dominic had often wondered what secrets his dear friend had kept hidden from him for so long. He wished that Christoph would just share his pain and allow for him to bear some of the load but he never did. Dominic suspected deep down that he had lied to them about his real age because his heart was too noble and his constitution too strong to have been born into any of the recent generations. Dominic allowed him his secrets though. He would not disrupt his friend's journey and would do everything in his power to make sure that Christoph's wish came true.

Dominic resumed their walk through the streets with Raina and Jarek following directly behind him. Alert and prepared for anything, Christoph followed while Leo maintained his post at the back. When he glanced behind him, Dominic noticed that Raina's hand was clasped by Jarek's and he felt a stab of remorse for his own decisions. It was part of the reason he needed to make things right somehow. He loved them both deeply and he feared their outcomes more than those of the others as their wishes would have the greatest impact on his own.

At the next intersection, Dominic stopped to tighten their unit as the humans made way for a new parade. He wanted to see the faces of his pack together, smiling and laughing and having fun as they let go of their heavy hearts and their painful thoughts for just one night. He laughed to himself when he saw Raina cringe at the white porcelain face templates that whizzed past her, knowing that their drawn, phony facial features were the reason for her dismay. She cringed the same way at the clowns and he remembered the words she had once used to explain her apprehension toward them.

"Humans who feel the need to paint on smiles are the most dangerous of the bunch."

A tap on his shoulder pulled him from his reverie and he turned his attention toward the source of disruption. Though Jarek's mouth was at his ear, he still had to scream in order to be heard by Dominic over the horns and the music and laughter that filled the streets.

"Can you watch her for a minute?" he asked. "I want to check something out."

"Where are you going?"

Jarek gestured with his head to a stumpy, white haired man across the street. The hippy had set up shop selling imported knives and it was all the answer Dominic needed.

"Don't be long; we shouldn't split up here."

"Come on, Dom, loosen up," Raina said, pushing her way into their conversation. "This could be our last night alive!"

"That's not amusing, Raina."

"I wasn't kidding, Dominic."

"Listen," Jarek interjected. "I'm just running across the street. Why don't you two grab a bite and I'll find you before the next major intersection."

"Fine," Dominic relented. "Don't get lost!"

Jarek dropped a kiss on Raina's lips.

"Be good," he mouthed silently before turning away and squeezing through the crowd that stood between him and the weapons.

"I want to go too!"

Christoph, suddenly at their side, seemed more antsy and distracted than usual.

"You don't even like knives!" Leo accused, rising up from the middle of their circle.

"Where did you come from?" Dominic laughed as he backed up to allow him more space.

"Yo mama," Leo joked.

Happy to see Leo in the rare chipper mood, Dominic caved. "Beat it, both of you. Meet up at the next intersection, okay?"

They agreed and took off quickly before he had the chance to change his mind. Dominic and Raina regarded each other quietly before resuming their walk. Transforming back into tour guide, he started pointing out landmarks, vampire haunts, and secret markings on some of the buildings they passed. At Lake Street and Prien, she tried to turn left but he pulled her back quickly.

"No," he advised firmly. "Not that way."

"Why not?"

"I can hear them down there," he answered, pointing to his head. "They're trying to stay quiet but I can sense their organization and their tactics."

"Whose organization and tactics?" she asked impatiently.

"The vampire police," he explained. Dominic told to her that immortal officials roamed the streets of Mardi Gras in search of their own for breaking vampiric law. Irresponsible kills or unauthorized turnings could wreak havoc on their species. They had organized groups to enforce the peace so that they could continue to dine on their chosen blood without police or media intervention. As his explanation wound down, Dominic stared at her as an idea formulated itself inside of his mind.

"What?" she asked.

"Feel like playing an old game?"

She tried to restrain her excitement but he could see it in the sudden shine from her eyes.

"Really?" she asked. "Don't tease me."

"Really," he confirmed with a smile.

"Well… Jarek did tell us to grab a bite," she reconciled aloud, more to herself than to him.

"Let's go!" he said.

Ten minutes later, they descended toward the lower level of a dilapidated building and found the secret door that led to the private party. Vampire raves weren't difficult to find, nor were they difficult to infiltrate. They were, however, very hard to escape from which was why the two had made a game of it so many years before. Sharing their penchant for risk and adventure, they had made a habit of crashing the bloody galas, uninvited, after local packs had spent a year planning the human feast for themselves.

The humans enjoyed risk and secrecy. They searched out underground parties in search of the seediest and most wicked of all Mardi Gras sins and it was their own violation of soul that gave Dominic and Raina permission to feed off them. Glancing at one another, she raised her eyebrows and waited for his direction. He answered with a shush finger to the lips and knocked twice on the steel door.

When a thick face with huge jowls and a round nose appeared at the glass partition, they both smiled and Dominic held up two fingers to announce the number in their party. The guard used a hand to slide open the small window but he did not smile. Raina watched Dominic's eyes narrow as he wandered through the guard's thoughts and peeked into his subconscious. He was massive, powerful and muscular but, as most doormen at vampire raves, would never be regarded for his intellect. His ignorance would give them the edge they needed and they comforted themselves with the knowledge that muscle rarely won out in a battle of wits.

"Password?" the guard asked, stifling his yawn with a loose fist.

"Illuminati," Dominic answered calmly, reading his mind.

The glass window slammed shut and they heard a click from the door as it opened to allow them entry.

"Welcome," greeted the massive guard, with less enthusiasm than a patient in a dental lobby. "Have fun."

He backed up to allow them in before slamming the door behind them.

"What's his problem?" Raina whispered in Dominic's ear.

"He's distracted," Dominic answered.

"By what, his own odor?" she asked, fanning the air beneath her nose with her right hand.

"Something about a teenage suicide pact later tonight," Dominic answered as he glanced toward the door that had been tightly secured. Pulling her into him protectively, he continued the explanation through a whisper to her ear.

"It seems there's a lost and misguided group of teens that revere the Underworld and they're roaming Bourbon Street tonight," he said. "They plan to hang themselves by daybreak as some misguided offering to vampirism and he's itching to find them. He doesn't seem to have much by way of a brain but he could still be a strong adversary, so be careful."

Raina understood the guard's lure. Willing souls were powerful and therefore, easy to absorb. To happen upon a group of them was a rare treat for any vampire.

"They're calling themselves the Sunday morning suicides and he craves them," Dominic finished. "Badly."

Raina hesitated for a long, thoughtful moment before she spoke.

"Ready to come in?" she finally asked.

Dominic nodded with an apologetic smile as he accepted the invitation to merge with her frequencies and enter her mind. She only allowed him to use his powers on her during times of peril because she was uncomfortable with him walking through her thoughts, never sure which torrid one he might trip upon. To play the favorite game, however, he would have to be allowed entry.

The smile on his face was smaller than the one he felt inside. Dominic always enjoyed the opportunity to peruse the thoughts she refused to share with him and he secretly hoped for the chance to sneak around undetected if the situation allowed.

"Hang on," she warned quickly. "I have to clean up."

Raina panicked as she ran around the confines of her mind trying to sweep away anything she might be mortified to have him stumble upon. Closing her eyes, she willed away all thoughts of both he and Jarek and visualized putting them away in a trunk with several padded locks.

"Okay," she said. "Ready."

Without a word, Dominic's eyes narrowed and he made eye contact that she met with intensity. A familiar shiver ran up her spine as she felt him come inside and make himself at home.

"Tsk tsk," he teased through the voice in her head. "You are a naughty girl."

"That's not funny," she yelled back within.

"Then why am I laughing?"

"Cause you're a little bit twisted?"

"Look who's talking," he laughed into her thoughts.

Then he spoke out loud but only loud enough for Raina to hear amid the loud, banging music that blared out from speakers in the ceiling.

"Remember," he warned, "real messages stay inside but don't stop moving your lips entirely. They'll notice."

"Duh," she said out loud.

They walked deeper into the club and looked around at the sights around them. Taking it all in at once was impossible so they fell into their old pattern with Dominic scanning the left side and Raina assessing the right. Both of their gazes moved slowly upward as they eyed the two cages suspended from each side. Inside of each one danced a barely clad stripper who gyrated to the techno sounds with an expression of ecstasy etched into her face.

The two strippers wore matching outfits with high black boots and shiny, tight red shorts that failed to cover anything more than their most private areas. Their matching leather bras sported low cleavage and connected to the bottom half with a thin strip of material in the back. Raina turned back to Dominic and raised one eyebrow at him.

"Having fun yet?" she yelled, feeling the hunger and temptation that emanated from him.

"Mmm," he mumbled, never taking his eyes off the caged girl who had wrapped her leg through one of the bars.

"They look delicious," Raina agreed.

"They sure do."

"You take one, I'll take the other?"

"Let's take a look around first. If we don't see anything better, we'll come back."

"Deal," she agreed without further prodding. Raina was hungry but also interested in what was on the rest of the menu. "Can we split up?"

"I don't think that's a good idea."

"Come on!" she begged. "You're hooked in, you can't lose me!"

"Look," he nodded toward the huge clock that took up the top third of the wall. It read eleven forty-five, only fifteen minutes before the feast would begin. "Almost time."

Raina looked toward the clock and became instantly excited. Trying to keep any type of inappropriate or erotic thought from entering the doorway of her mind, she diverted her own attention by reaching out for Dominic's hand. She had only planned to give it a quick kiss goodbye before racing off to find dinner but when she made contact, he held it tightly.

"Be careful," he spoke to her thoughts slowly.

"Aren't I always?" she whispered back. She tried to pull her hand from his but he pulled back.

"I couldn't take it if anything happened to you."

Suddenly, a vision of herself trapped amidst an angry circle of vampires, took over her thoughts so completely that it almost felt as though she'd been transported to another place entirely. Just as quickly, she forced it out and blinked her eyes at Dominic, trying to think of a lie as fast as possible.

"What the hell was that?" he yelled over the music.

She could hear the fear in his tone but held to her previous decision to not share the repeated vision with him. She was never certain which visions were real and which were just a trick of the imagination and had made embarrassing mistakes in the past.

"Nothing," she answered quickly before turning away. She tried to walk off just as fast but felt herself being tugged back by her long red ponytail.

"What?" she asked guiltily, without turning to face him.

"What was that?" he repeated, calmer than the first time. "Have you seen that before?"

"Yes," she answered truthfully before turning around. "But it definitely wasn't here, in this club or on this night so... see ya!"

She turned again and tried to run but he hooked an arm around her waist and pulled her in toward him.

"Sorry," he said. "We stay together."

Raina pouted but didn't resist any further. She had been shaken by the vision just as she was when she had dreamt it in the backseat of the car. Besides, she liked how it felt to have Dominic hold her again and didn't want to pull away from the forced embrace. She let herself stand there with his arm around her for as long as possible before the feeling turned to a conscious thought that he would be able to read. As soon as she felt the emotion start to slip from her heart and float toward her brain, she pulled herself from his grip and turned to face him again.

"Let's go," she said before breaking eye contact, grabbing his hand roughly and pulling his arm so that he could follow her through the dance floor.

They passed a couple making out on the floor, caring nothing about the audience they had for their intimacies and then continued past an all female human group that sucked on lollipops with closed eyes while they swayed their hips to the music.

When they reached the end of the floor and touched carpet again, both of them were drawn to the bar where an angry boyfriend admonished his embarrassed date for having danced with another man. The berating became so obnoxious that mascara began to seep from the poor woman's eyes as she fought tears that threatened to shred the rest of her dignity to pieces. Without need for conversation, they walked slowly toward the bar and Raina placed herself in the angry boyfriend's line of vision.

Hooking into his stare without a struggle, she cooed at him seductively and spoke with her eyes.

"C'mere."

Holding her arms high above her head, she moved her hips to the music as the next song began to play. The techno sounds ended and the song they had been waiting for began to roll from the speakers as the dark lights dimmed even lower. Anger falling away from his eyes, the man rose from his bar stool and moved toward Raina without turning from her stare for a second. When he met her on the dance floor, she pulled her raised arms down gently to his shoulders and smiled. Raina could feel herself begin to salivate as she envisioned his jugular vein: throbbing, fat, and ready to burst with the blood that filled it. She couldn't wait to wrap her teeth around his neck and she sent Dominic the message that he stood in wait for.

"He's the one," she whispered to his thoughts before letting her head fall backwards to the sporadic drumbeat she knew was coming. The dark tune had been a favorite at vampire raves for years as its slow melody and suspenseful, climbing beats helped one to experience the climatic moment in its entirety. When she leveled her eyes with the stranger, she began to murmur comforting words to remind him of the pleasures she would provide. Able to pull her eyes from his for only a moment before her power weakened, she used the break in their stare to glance over at Dominic, who still stood at the bar with the dejected and humiliated girlfriend. Raina's attention rose higher toward the clock and she saw that it was only a minute from striking midnight.

"Get her out of here!" she screamed to Dominic's mind and she watched as he hurried the girl to a curtained door before reappearing again. He threw Raina a quick wink and a half wave before heading back across the dance floor to the cages. Standing beneath his chosen entrée, he allowed his gaze to travel slowly up the pole that led to the stripper and felt the atmosphere in the room become charged with a simmering excitement. From his position at the side and from Raina's on the floor, they carefully counted out the vampires from the residential coven and made a quiet pact to keep a watchful eye on them at all times.

Dominic wrapped his hands around the pole and began to climb, one hand over the other, using his powers to jump and slide to fuel the way. At the same time, Raina moved in closer to her own target and giggled softly. The formerly enraged man lacked all lucidity and remained hypnotized by her trance. The music climbed higher and a symbol crashed at the same moment the clock struck midnight.

Dominic smiled at the pretty stripper who was shocked to find that she suddenly shared a cage with someone else. Shock turned to horror when his smiled widened to accommodate his growing incisors and he caught her at the waist when she tried to jump from the cage to the floor.

"Sssssshh, it's okay," he comforted quietly as he readied her neck into the necessary position.

He moved her backwards against the bars and gently pushed her head to the side to expose her neck as his eyes scanned the dance floor in search of Raina. She wasn't far off down below and her own teeth were held in a high snarl as she prepared to bite. When her stare caught his, she allowed him to hold her gaze so that they could share the moment together. At the exact same time, they each sank their teeth into their victims, one screaming in horror and the other unaware of anything but his own warm blood as it spilled onto his blue silk shirt and saturated it. They never broke eye contact and because of their attention on one another, failed to become aware of their own audience. Blood dripping from their faces as their victims fell from their hands to the floor, they continued stared at one another from across the room, unaware of everything else around them.

Screams pierced the air as the humans watched on in horror. Friends and dates were mauled by a pack not as compassionate as Raina and Dom and one by one, the human pleas were cut short as the resident vampires tore out their throats and drank their blood with gluttony and unrestrained thirst. Seeing nothing but each other's eyes and hearing nothing but their own unspoken words, Raina and Dom smiled at one another until the music stopped. Cut short like a needle dragged across an album, they tore their eyes from each other and looked out at the crowd to find every vampire in the room staring at them with disapproval and disdain. Their meals had been interrupted by intruders and unfortunately, Dominic and Raina were the intruders. Their eyes met once more and they mouthed one word to each other across the room.

Shit.

Handcuffed to chairs with backs touching, they found themselves alone in a deserted room at the back of the club. Dominic and Raina spoke to each other's minds as they tried to think of a way out of their predicament.

"Okay," Raina started, "that went well."

"Let's not argue," he advised. "I have an idea."

They had been fortunate enough to escape an immediate takedown on the dance floor but their luck did not hold out for long. After being corralled by more pack members than either of them could fight off, they were dragged into the storage room and left until further investigation by the opposing leader could determine a fitting sentence for their violation. Aside from finding a way to make it out of the club, they also knew it was imperative to escape before the pack caught wind of who they were and where they were headed. So far, they hadn't answered any questions but once the leader walked in, their choices would become much more limited.

"What's your idea?" she asked, just before the door opened and the meaty guard from the front walked in. He appeared much more enthusiastic about their possible torment than he had their entry into the club.

"Well, well, what do we have here?" he said happily. 'I thought there was something strange about you two."

Neither of them answered aloud but Dominic spoke to her within.

"Just follow along."

"Okay," she answered, blindly trusting him as always.

He shook his head and addressed the guard.

"Sorry about this whole thing," Dominic apologized. "We didn't realize it was a private party."

"Were you invited?" asked the guard sarcastically.

"No, not really."

"Well then, it's a private party," the guard finished. "Funny how that works, isn't it?"

Dominic sighed audibly and then addressed Raina quietly, as though he were trying to tell her a secret.

"Now, we'll never make it to the Suicides," he said with the most disappointed tone he could muster.

"Thanks to you!" she replied, feigning a attitude of blame.

"Me? It was your idea to come here!"

They argued back and forth but both noticed that the guard's expression had become inquisitive and thoughtful and though he outlasted both of their predictions, he finally broke down.

"What are you talking about?"

"Oh," Dominic said, pretending to have been caught unaware. "Nothing."

The guard glanced at the door he had left open and walked over to close and lock it. He turned back to his captives and spoke again.

"I might be able to help," he said. "Depending on what you say to me right now."

"It's just a group of teenagers we stumbled on; probably just a hoax anyway."

"What did you hear?" the guard rushed.

Raina piped up to make the story more believable. Unaware that his charges were carrying on a conversation right before him and lacking enough intelligence to figure it out, he would buy their story more because they both shared the information.

"We ran into some teenagers and heard them talking when they didn't know we were listening," she lied. "They said something about a suicide pact so we thought we'd try to find them. The children are always sweeter and their souls will be ripe."

"Did you hear where they were going?" the guard asked, as sweat dripped from his forehead. He reminded Raina of a lecherous old pedophile in search of a kindergarten class with an absent teacher.

"Of course," Dominic jumped back in. "It's where we were headed when we ended up here. It's actually very close by."

"Can you take me to them?" the guard asked, almost desperate. "Please?'

"We're a little tied up now, sorry," Raina complained.

"Don't be rude," Dominic advised her aloud. Inside, his words were different.

Good one.

"We can take you with us," Dominic said to the guard as he nodded downwards toward their cuffs.

The guard walked around them slowly but remained silent. Afraid the guard might deviate from her plan, Raina called him to stand before her.

"Think," her eyes said to his. "Think of the river of blood you can swim in if you like."

His eyes glazed over with yearning but Raina knew it had nothing to do with her. Though she was the one empowering his hypnosis, it was the young group of suicides that would make him risk immortality to get them out. The guard stuck his key into the lock that held them to their seats and upon the click of its release they heard the pack's leader from the end of the long corridor outside. The sound of heavy shoes, and many pairs of them, echoed throughout the outside hallway and it told Raina and Dominic that their sentence had been decided upon and was on its way.

"Hurry!" she whispered loudly to the guard. "Open a door!"

Dominic had already sprinted to the wall to run his hand down the length of it trying to feel for a secret passageway that led outside but found none.

"There is no way out!" the guard whispered back. "It's all brick. The only way out is the way you came in!"

While their strength was abundant, Raina and Dominic knew it wouldn't be enough to knock the wall down in time. No amount of telepathy or mind-speak or mesmerizing would take down a brick wall as fast as one whose gifted power was physical strength. They regretted not having asked Jarek along after all. Dominic and the guard saw the same conclusion in the other's eyes and the guard rushed to the wall, fists drawn. Maniacally, and with the force that could only come from one in true desperation, he pounded at the wall until the bricks began to move. Three hard pounds to the weakened area brought the whole section of wall crashing to the floor, bricks smashing to pieces upon their impact with the cement outside. Fearful for his disloyalties to his own pack, the guard squeezed himself through the newly erected hole and disappeared into the alley outside. Dominic dismissed his annoyance, filing it away for later. A man who saved himself before a woman or child did not deserve to live but Dominic had no time to ruminate over the thoughts. Voices in the hallway told them their visitors had arrived and Dominic lifted Raina from the chair and carefully aided her through the hole.

From the outside, she jumped from one foot to another and paid no attention as newly loosened bricks fell on her feet.

"Come on, come on!" she yelled to Dominic, no longer worried about keeping her words quiet. Keys could be heard turning in the lock at the door and Dominic was still inside. A sinking feeling replaced the joy she had felt only moments before and Raina pulled at Dominic's arm as he tried to make his way out through the hole before the wall collapsed on top of him. No sooner did his boots hit the pavement than the inner door to the storage room swung open to reveal a very angry leader and four more guards. Unsure of the sentence decided upon for them, neither cared. Dominic grabbed her hand tightly and pulled her into a run that led to a main road only a few yards ahead.

The guard who had led himself away from danger first waited at the corner of the road and he smiled when he saw them coming. Though their breathing was labored from the escape and the run, the fear they had worked so hard to contain slowly turned to uncontrollable laughter. The guard joined in and the three of them cackled even harder when the entire exterior wall of the building they had just escaped collapsed in on itself. It was minutes later that their merriment finally subsided and the guard spoke.

"So?" the guard asked. "Where are the teens? Let's go!'

"Of course, of course," Dominic answered happily. "It's actually not far from here at all."

Walking in perfect step with Raina, they led the guard through the thick crowd and passed the shops they had memorized on their way to the club. At the intersection of Prien and Lake streets, they rattled off phony coordinates to the guard and bid him a fond farewell before watching his dark shadow disappear into the dark surprises that awaited him.

"Why are we killing the guard after he helped us out of there?' she asked, scrunching her nose.

"Bad manners," Dominic answered simply.

"Gotcha," Raina responded. "Now, get out of my head."

'Already?" he teased. 'I was just starting to have fun."

'"Now… please!"

"Fine," he relented but he wasn't really angry.

He only wanted what she gave him anyway, nothing more and nothing less. He did not need to steal her thoughts to know what she felt, but it hadn't harmed him any when he caught one that she hadn't yet locked away. He smiled at her and she stared back at him without saying a word.

"Come on," he finally said, grabbing her hand and tugging her back into the busy streets. "Let's go find our pack!"

Chapter XVII

"Which way, Christoph?" Dominic asked.

"Just keep following," he answered.

"I'm tired," Raina complained.

She had tried not to take on the role of the typical girl, doing her best not to whine in the face of their challenges but the truth was, she was exhausted. Mardi Gras had been fun but it had also zapped her of the necessary energy she had needed for such a journey. Even though their New Orleans motel had provided them with beds and hot meals and much deserved relaxation, it hadn't been enough. The need for blood had become stronger during their trip and she had found herself having to turn away from even the youngest of humans they passed so as not to take a quick snack along the way.

"It's been hours, Christoph," Leo griped. "Are you sure you know where you're going?"

"Yes."

"I'm starting to wonder," he muttered under his breath. "Stupid empathic abilities gonna lead us nowhere…."

"Back off, little man," Jarek warned him.

"Come on, you have to admit this is ridiculous! We've been walking for hours; we should have driven if he knew it was this far!"

Christoph ignored the comments and just continued walking, leading his pack to an undisclosed location while throwing them the rare cryptic bone every once in a long while with bizarre ramblings about forests and pixies and hidden mansions. Dominic caught up to him and kept an even pace. He stared at his friend's profile as they walked and he wondered which abilities and instincts Christoph was really relying on to get them there.

"I trust you," he said to him simply.

He wanted to say more. In fact, he wanted to ask a thousand questions that might shed some light on why his friend's mood had changed so drastically since they had left the motel for the last leg of their trip toward Lucius, but he didn't. He knew, somehow, that Christoph would not steer them in the wrong direction and his growing anxieties and apprehension came more for his concern for his pack's increasing hunger than over a lack of faith that they would eventually make it there. He knew they were all starving and he knew that their hunger had turned purely to the need for blood over anything else. It hadn't escaped his attention how they ogled the last group of humans they passed a couple of hours earlier. The truth was, it had been difficult for even Dominic to walk past the small family without fighting the urge to tear them to shreds – the husband, the wife, and the baby alike.

"Did you guys ever see that movie 'Alive?'" Leo asked by way of disturbing conversation. "They crashed their plane in the Andes or some shit and had to eat each other to survive."

"What are you saying, wee one?" Jarek asked. "You thinking of eating one of us to stay alive? Ha! Good luck!"

"It's amazing what one can do when survival is threatened," Leo defended. "That's all I'm saying."

"What good would it do you, stupid? We don't spill blood!"

"We do upon our deaths," he answered quickly.

"So you would kill one of us to survive?" Raina asked, disgusted. "That's what you've been thinking about as we walk together?"

"I didn't say that."

"Yeah," Jarek added. "You pretty much just did say that and you can wipe those thoughts out of your head because you'd have to get past me to get to anyone here and I don't see that happening in even your wildest fantasies."

"You never know," Leo mumbled to himself, though they all heard him clearly.

Dominic turned around to face them but he continued to walk backwards. Shutting down their conversation with a warning look, he turned back toward Christoph and decided the time had come to start asking questions, but just as he opened his mouth, Christoph stopped quickly.

"What?" Dominic asked instead.

"We're here," he answered.

"Huh?"

All five stood outside what appeared to be a dilapidated, dirty, gray building that wouldn't pass an inspection code if a million dollars had been invested in it. They looked to one another with open mouths and skeptical stares but no one spoke except Dominic.

"Are you sure, Christoph?"

"I'm sure," he answered quietly. "Open the door."

"That door?" he asked, pointing to a weak wooden plank that had been placed carelessly in front of the entrance to the building. "But it doesn't have any hinges."

"Then push it aside."

"If you say so," Dominic relented.

Walking to the end of the dirty walkway, he gently pushed aside the thin piece of wood that barely worked to block the entranceway. Upon being touched, the makeshift doorknob popped off entirely and fell onto the cement, rolling into the high brown grass underfoot and disappearing entirely.

"If Lucius lives here, I'm turning around and going back to find that baby," Leo declared.

"Sshh!" Raina insisted. "Just shut up!"

"Don't tell me what to…."

"Both of you!" Dominic whispered as loud as he could before making a silent motion to cover his mouth, a quiet order for them both to stop talking. He then took the lead and guided each of them through the doorway toward fates unknown.

The tired pack walked through the doors only to discover they were back outside again; but it was a different kind of outdoors altogether. They felt as though they had walked into another world entirely as the scenery was a complete contrast from the dismal path that had led them there. Though sunlight appeared to shoot its rays upon the beautiful pasture and magnificent trees, its power was weak and it created a more muted effect than solar light would create. It was nothing more than magic and its falseness alone instilled a different type of fear in each of them. They realized that within this new and bizarre world, the occupants were trying to pretend they hadn't traded immortality for darkness. They were pretending that God still gifted them with light and because of their inability to see the truth of their realities, Dominic decided they might be even more dangerous than he had prepared them for.

The lush greenery was the first of many details to catch their attention. Thick grass and the dark blue sky seemed to stretch out much farther than the eye could see. Hundreds and hundreds of unknown species of trees stretched their branches out liberally over the forest. Though the appearance was intended to tempt intruders and instill an illusion of sanctuary, the pack refused to submit to its glory. They were leery to travel any deeper inside because they sensed the danger that hovered nearby.

Thick, sturdy branches reached out like long fingers beckoning them to feel welcome. The breeze that whistled through them was befitting of a horror soundtrack and seemed an entity all its own. The tree perched closest to the group seemed to take on the role of butler, its trunk serving as a torso as it leaned forward in a deep bow.

Raina tried to keep her fears at bay, knowing that if the residents, wherever they may be, picked up on her hesitation, it could be the end of all of them. She sidestepped her spot as discreetly as possible until she stood directly behind Dominic. When he looked back at her, she saw the message in his eyes and heard the inflection in his thoughts.

Stay close, stay aware, stay brave

Raina wanted to wink her understanding at him but her lid muscles seemed to have stopped working. Instead, she adopted the most courageous stance she could and faced the scene again with a newfound resolve to stay strong. It didn't escape her attention that Jarek closed in on her left side and that Christoph closed in the right as Leo protected her from behind. No matter what the race or species, the male instinct always seemed to dictate that the stronger gender protect the frailer one and Raina decided that within the context of her current situation, she was just fine with that.

The complete absence of any other life form was what made Dominic the most uncomfortable of all, above all the strange situations presenting themselves. The presence of another pack was strong and their refusal to show themselves right away felt intentional and taunting.

Suddenly, movement caught all five sets of eyes as it demanded their attention with its repetition. When their eyes stopped on it, they realized it was a leg and that it swung back and forth as its owner remained perched upon one of the higher branches of the bowing tree. In any other situation, in any other setting, the swinging leg would have appeared innocuous, even benign but not this leg and not this situation. This one swung with purpose and intent.

As their eyes rose from the leg to the face, the pack realized it belonged to a male. Even if they hadn't made eye contact and even if they hadn't been able to clearly observe his carefully chiseled features, they would still have known he was of the male species. Though testosterone and estrogen no longer marked their differences, gender was the one aspect of the vampire that could never be hidden as the ability to disguise gender was nearly impossible.

"Welcome," he said kindly to his new guests. Though his tone couldn't have been friendlier, the amusement weaving through it hinted at restrained malevolence.

"Good evening," Dominic smiled back. With his right hand, he gave a dramatic sweeping gesture and directed the conversations toward the false light. "Or morning perhaps?"

Their host laughed heartily and Dominic heard the tone for what it was – a tactic designed to instill comfort in the humans. To the pack, however, it had the effect of nails on a chalkboard and each of them fought the urge to cover their ears.

"Come in, come in. Don't be nervous," he said.

"Don't worry," Dominic smiled. "We're not."

He fixated his eyes not only toward their host but also toward the seemingly empty branches that surrounded the forest. It became clear to the pack that the other branches in the strange forest were also inhabited but that they had camouflaged themselves carefully into their surroundings.

"I'm Lucius," said the vampire as he fell from the tree in one fluid movement. He landed perfectly upon two very strong, very sturdy legs. "We were expecting you."

Dominic offered a smile that felt sincere to his own heart but knew would be construed as patronizing and condescending to its recipient.

"No, you're not," Dominic challenged, his smile never wavering. "Let's not start off on the wrong foot here."

Their host laughed again and the pack could still hear the echo of his laughter even after he stopped. He disappeared and reappeared again only two inches from Dominic's face, almost instantaneously and then began clapping the slow and increasing applause that was customary after a significant cinematic conclusion. The rest of his pack followed suit and the collective applause had the effect of a sudden flash of rain without any of the droplets. When all stopped suddenly upon the same clap, the subsequent silence instilled a surreal sense of horror in each of the visitors.

"Very good," he said to Dominic. The compliment was sincere and the penetration of truth into a world filled with lies was an odd contrast for him to struggle with.

"Thank you," Dominic answered.

"How did you know?" asked the imposter.

"I would have sensed greatness," Dominic replied without apology.

Their host narrowed his eyes into slits but it did nothing to keep his humor at bay.

"Be careful," he told Dominic as he backed up a few paces, using legs instead of magic this time. "I'm still the leader of this very large pack you see before you and will not tolerate even an ounce of disrespect while you are here in our home."

His gaze fell upon each of them but it lingered on Christoph the longest.

"From any of you," added the host.

"No, no," Dominic answered. "We are prepared to show you the upmost respect while we are visitors to your Den. Isn't that right?"

He looked back at his relatively small pack and commanded them silently to do nothing more than nod and smile. His stare lingered upon Leo the longest, as he could feel the rage and hear the pending growl emanate from the least controlled member of their pack. Four heads nodded silently but their eyes took in everything they could about the strange world they had stumbled into.

Dominic tried to communicate to his pack within the confines of their minds but found that his powers, while not completely absent, had weakened greatly. Individually, they tried to count the enemy but found there were too many of them to tally.

"We seek no trouble," Dominic added, "and we ask only the same in return."

Their host walked to stand before Jarek and he looked him up and down, seemingly trying to absorb all he could about him.

"Yeah," Jarek confirmed, uncomfortable. "We come in peace."

"And that you shall receive," said the host, focusing his attention back on Dominic. "What brings you such a long distance from your home?"

"We need to see Lucius," Leo blurted out from the back of their formation.

Though Dominic was furious that Leo had disobeyed his commands not to speak, he refused to alert their host to his anger. The enemy could not know that a pack member had ignored the commands of his leader as it would be just cause for severe and immediate punishment of both of them. Instead, Dominic used all of his strength to send a painful migraine to his wayward minion with an instruction attached to remain silent lest he put them all at risk. Leo apologized and they cut the communications quickly before anyone from the opposing pack caught on. Their host began to circle the pack, eyeing them suspiciously. He had a cane clutched in his right hand that he seemed to depend on not for movement but for some other reason they did not understand.

"And why, pray tell, would a miniscule pack from New York City believe themselves to be worthy of seeing the head of all masters?"

When he laughed mockingly, his laughter was echoed by his enormous pack.

"I didn't realize that Lucius left his screening process to his pets," Dominic said, smiling sweetly.

At once, their host was an inch before his face but this time, his protective pack inserted themselves into the possibility of a fight by leaping from their respective branches. They advanced toward the small group slowly, still restrained however, behind their leader.

What are you doing, Dominic? Raina thought as loudly as she could. *Why are you making them angry?*

Though their frequencies seemed difficult to align, she knew that he could still hear her.

Hush!

It was Jarek's voice that reached her mind rather than Dominic's.

He has to show them he's not afraid. Stay strong, Raina. Stay quiet.

And so she did. She cut the sound of all voices from within, including her own, knowing that she would never forgive herself if she placed any member of her beloved pack in danger.

"Is this type of insulting banter considered respectful in New York City, Dominic?"

Upon realization that their host knew not only from where they had traveled but knew their names, each one struggled against revealing any concerns. If Lucius' men knew so much about them, the possibility existed that they also were aware of the pack's individual purposes for having come there. Since vampires were forbidden to make requests for the individual as opposed to the pack as a whole, their visit would be less than appreciated.

"It's always nice to know that my reputation has preceded itself," Dominic smiled.

"Ah, but you might want to first know what your reputation says before making such a brave statement," answered their host. "Although, I might say that you and your pack were quite impressive back at the warehouse."

Warning bells went off in Dominic's mind and each of his pack members could hear it.

"So, you were the one who got away," he said without a hint of fear to give away what he really felt.

Their host had still not introduced himself and they were beginning to wonder if he planned to at all before ripping them to shreds. Without even turning to see the slow moving advance of his own pack, their host held up one hand and seemed to command them with his fingers alone. Like the conductor of an obedient orchestra, he was rewarded with their compliance as his massive pack stopped abruptly in their tracks.

"I'm Stephan," he said to Dominic only. As customary in most packs, the leaders did not refer to the members as individuals and therefore, would never allow for the others to address him by name.

Stephan began to circle them again, but this time, focused his attention entirely on Raina. He moved toward her with a sickening leer and she could see the frigidity and sense the changing posture of her pack. Knowing that their protection for her could quickly, and painfully, become their downfall, she forced herself to play up to the beliefs of this old-fashioned pack with its old school principles. As with every other species she had ever encountered, male privilege needed to be nurtured and coddled so that it could remain ultimately controlled by the female.

Don't react, she repeated inside of her head, talking to herself as much as her pack.

Cutting the communications quickly, she adopted a blank expression and tilted her head at Stephan. If he were to discover Dominic's willingness to share his power of internal communications with his pack, she knew it would be the death of them all. Rather than rely on messages from within, she continued to portray the role of the non-thinking and non-reactive female the other pack believed she should be.

"Do you all keep her?" asked Stephan, his eye contact boring a hole through her corneas. He stared at her as though she were his next meal and when he opened his mouth to bare his incisors, Raina could see the long strands of drool that hung from each one.

"No," Dominic answered quickly. "She's just mine. Special permission from the League."

Stephan knew he was lying. Special permission to solely maintain the pack female could only be given by Lucius and it was more than obvious they had never made the trip before. The humor that had previously accented each of his words multiplied with his next words.

"Is that right?" Stephan asked.

"That's right," Dominic answered.

"Well then, why is it when I asked the question, I got the clear impression there is another involvement here?"

"Perhaps your little antennae is broken," Dominic shrugged.

The inference that Stephan was perceived as an insect was not respectful as promised and Dominic knew he had hit a nerve when Stephan used his strange conductor signals to inform his pack that advancement had become acceptable.

Dominic and his pack remained in their spots but they tightened their small circle, knowing their small army had absolutely no chance should combat actually ensue. Something told him, however, the real Lucius wouldn't let them be mauled before he had his chance at some fun for himself. Just as he heard his pack start to wish one another fond farewells within the confines of their minds, a car began to wind slowly down the long path that stretched out before them. Its sudden appearance caused a marked fear within Stephan and his pack and they retreated slowly backwards. Without another word, they climbed back into the trees from which they had emerged and disappeared behind the branches.

As the car got closer, Dominic began to recognize the make and model. It was a Porsche 550 Spyder. He had remembered from the many news reports he had watched that it had only been produced by its maker for four years. Tumbling toward them over small dirt mounds that wouldn't disturb a larger vehicle, grating noises emanated from its weak chassis. Grayish silver in color, it was extremely low to the ground and its presence filled Dominic with a strange sensation of foreboding. He knew the car well.

Known as the 'Giant Killer' in its heyday, this particular Spyder had been dubbed the 'Little Bastard' and was not only reminiscent of the one James Dean had been killed in thirty-five years before, it was the same one exactly. Resurrected somehow for this grand and dramatic entrance, it pulled up beside the pack and stopped quickly.

"Woohoo!" yelled the driver excitedly. "Stops on a dime!"

Each pack mate looked to the next but none of them spoke for fear that the other didn't see the same. As if their meeting with Stephan hadn't been surreal enough, their newest pending introduction was enough to make them start questioning their sanity. All they knew for certain was that the excited driver of the doomed Porsche that pulled alongside their group could not be Lucius, the headmaster of all vampires. Yet, somehow, they all knew that it was.

He looked up at them with a huge smile and hair that stuck out in all different directions, as though he hadn't combed it throughout his entire lifetime. His skin was fair but not nearly as pale as the rest of their species and it brought forth disturbing images of the great leader lying in a tanning bed or on a beach in Aruba. Deep wrinkles lined his face, yet it didn't give him the appearance of old age. On the contrary, Lucius was incredibly handsome and he emitted the strong aura of both wisdom and a very lengthy stay on their planet.

"Aaaahhh..., love the way the air feels after a good ride," he exclaimed excitedly. His focus fell upon Christoph for a long moment but his expression remained intact. "Wait, hang on!"

Still sitting in the driver's seat, he leaned down toward the passenger floor in search of something, as though the presence of a strange pack in his Den was commonplace and completely acceptable. When he raised himself back into position, they saw that he was holding several eggs in both of his hands.

What the . . .?

Shut up!

Raina was no longer certain who was saying what but she didn't care. Having expected to face fears that she had never known existed, she hadn't made preparations for entrance into the Twilight Zone.

The pack remained quiet but open-mouthed as Lucius jumped over the driver's side door and stood before them. They had expected to feel lost in the power of his presence and were shocked to find him not only approachable and quirky but quite possibly, insane. Still half expecting to hear greatness and wisdom fly out of his mouth upon his next words, they recoiled visibly at his introduction to their conversation.

"Why do we measure things the way we do?" he asked, a quizzical expression taking over his features.

"I'm sorry?" Dominic responded, beyond stunned.

"Inches, feet, meters, liters, it's all ridiculous!" Lucius pushed on. "Why don't we just measure everything in eggs?"

Words were neither necessary nor available and with raised brows, Dominic turned to face his surprised pack. Doing his best to subdue his amusement, he tried to utilize his mind-speak, if for nothing else, confirmation that he hadn't been the only one to hear the question. Realizing his powers were impossible so close to the headmaster, he turned back to Lucius and spoke the only two words he could muster.

"Eggs, sir?"

"Yes, eggs," Lucius answered, tossing a raw one to their fumbling leader. He grappled with it so as not to drop the fragile shell to its death and succeeded, just barely, in not losing it from his tight grip.

"For example," Lucius continued as he sized up his vehicle, "I would say this car is about two hundred and fifty two eggs in length, width, diameter, and weight, wouldn't you?"

He smiled proudly at his own crazy calculations and looked to the pack for agreement.

Though Dominic's abilities were on the fritz, his pack knew exactly what he was thinking. Although they wouldn't dare utter the words out loud, collectively, the pack had one overriding thought.

He's lost his mind.

Chapter XVIII

Dominic turned his head away from Lucius but not for long. Despite the oddities he'd witnessed so far, he couldn't forget that the man standing before him had risen to great power through very violent means. If the rumors were true, and there was no doubt most of them were, the seemingly harmless vampire standing less than a foot away had committed unspeakable monstrosities, instilling justifiable fear in a great many vampires. Endearing as he might seem, the pack could not afford to forget their quirky host was known for being very clever, very cunning, and very dangerous.

Dominic turned his senses to full capacity and his eyes did a fast but thorough sweep of the forest. His vision gained more clarity as the sky darkened. Though its progress was gradual, the pack had already noticed that their strange new world had begun to dim in tiny increments and intervals since Lucius had driven up beside them. Aside from the trees that seemed to glare at them through dark spots in their bark, appearing to throw out stop signals with their hand-like branches, no other living, breathing creature was in sight.

Dominic felt a knot form in his chest. The ability to still experience human fear was the human ability he had wanted to lose but hadn't. Since emotional responses are born in the mind and not in the body, he knew he would remain victim to the same handicaps he'd struggled with pre-transformation unless he surrendered to the darkness. He turned to face his pack with a courageous smile and stance knowing it was his job to keep their nerves calm and to remain alert to any challenges they might encounter.

Dominic was uncomfortable with the strange presence he felt lurking close by but was even more uncomfortable by the disappearance of Stephan and his pack, uncertain why they had hidden themselves. He had almost hoped to see them hanging from their trees one-handed, staring back at him with their dark, mean little eyes. When nothing glared back but the taunting trees and their insulting branch gestures, he turned his attention back to Lucius and almost lost his balance at the glare that awaited his attention.

Pain erupted in his left temple and sliced his thoughts in half. Its intensity caused one of his knees to weaken and threatened to drop him to the ground. Dominic bent down to snap his bone back into place but never took his eyes off Lucius. Penetrating and merciless, the head vampire's glower continued to bore through him, the grip on his irises and attack on his pupils merciless. He had to will his legs not to fail him and forced himself to maintain the eye contact that was causing him such agony. Dominic knew the master was trying to assess his courage and endurance and it was not a test he planned to fail.

He envisioned Raina in his mind and used the power of love to kick-start the magic that Lucius' presence had depleted. Sensing the change in posture among his pack members, Dominic feared his family would make a fatal mistake in the absence of his direction. Though he could feel the weakness of its delivery, Dominic shot a message to the only one he knew could still receive it.

Stay put, Raina, and tell the others to do the same.

I won't let him hurt you, Dom.

He won't. It's just a test.

An invisible hand seemed to squeeze at his neck and its grip tightened by the second. The force resulted in Dominic seeing blurred and shiny stars, rather than maintaining clear vision but still, Dominic refused to break eye contact with the source of his torment. The master stood before him quietly, head tilted to the side, and an odd smile painted above his chin. The ends of his hair seemed to stab at the air and his tongue flickered repeatedly, in and out through his lips like a hungry snake preparing to eat its prey. His hands hung by his sides innocently.

Delirious from lack of oxygen, Dominic wondered if the visual penetration or the strangulation would do him in as the images before him started to blur and his cognitive skills began to shut down one by one. He fell into the stumble that teased his ankles and he felt impotent at his lack of defenses. Both his mind and body weakened under the oppressive pain and he wondered if Lucius could hear his thoughts. Still holding onto the punishing eye contact, he felt his resolve begin to weaken when suddenly, the searing pain in his head and the clutching at his throat stopped simultaneously.

"I'm glad you came," Lucius said flatly.

Dominic steadied himself again and the words he attempted to deliver with courage came out in a raspy whisper.

"Thank you," he managed.

A feeling of carbonation shot back and forth through his hollow veins and he shot a quick prayer up to the Heavens, hoping his role as Bible antagonist didn't preclude a periodic shout-out from the dark side. He had to continuously push away the urge to load his pack into the Porsche and drive away faster than James Dean had on that fateful night. When he started to speak, Lucius cut him off with a sharp and sudden clap of the hands.

"I am so rude!" he said excitedly, startling all of them.

He punctuated the curious apology by leaning into the car and rummaging around the front seat floors as he muttered to himself out loud. The contrast between the pain Lucius had just induced and his sudden playfulness was disorienting. Dominic took the opportunity to shoot a glance at his pack and would have laughed at their expressions if having his heart ripped out weren't a possible consequence.

"Can I interest you in an egg?" he asked, rising from the passenger floor.

Before Dominic could speak, a paper bag was thrust into his arms. It looked to have come from a grocery store and it contained nothing but egg cartons from bottom to top. He didn't understand the obsession and he didn't want to. He wanted to spit out their requests and to find out whether Lucius planned to help them or not. Part of him believed he might, while another part felt that the master was simply toying with them, like a bored child playing with his food.

"All in due time," Lucius answered though he hadn't asked the question out loud. His smile widened as Dominic's disintegrated. "Not used to being the recipient of such a superb power, are you?"

"No," admitted Dominic. "I'm not."

"Don't like it much do you?"

"Not even a little bit," Dominic confessed.

"Don't concern yourself with it. You may find that it helps rather than hinders you."

Without explaining their sudden journey or intended destination, Lucius began to lead Dominic and his pack through the forest. A thick fog settled upon them and when they turned to look behind them, they discovered their past had been concealed by a smoky mass. When they looked ahead again, they realized their future was covered as well, but they continued to follow the master blindly.

Dominic had to quicken his pace to catch up with him. When the master spoke again, it was through telepathy and they were the only two that remained privy to the conversation.

"You have questions," Lucius began and Dominic heard the words echo throughout his mind. "You may ask one now."

Though the pack couldn't hear anything from the two shadows leading the way, they knew that communication hadn't stopped.

"How did you know we were coming?" Dominic asked, feeling the tug of his brain wave as Lucius intercepted his words.

"It wasn't difficult," the echo returned. "There are many of us out there, in all different cities, of all different culture, of all different status... eyes in places you couldn't imagine."

Lucius stopped and the fog began to dissipate, revealing their position before a huge iron gate.

"Besides, you weren't exactly discrete," Lucius continued.

If Dominic could still blush, their host would have seen a red hue sneak into his cheeks. Of course he had known they were coming. Their kills along the way were like Hansel and Gretel's breadcrumbs, marking a clear path for anyone who had been watching. Standing before the massive gate, grocery bag in hand doing nothing to minimize his power, Lucius turned his back to his visitors to recite a chant of some kind.

From the corner of her eye, Raina could see the direct visual line that led down a side pathway and ended in a cemetery. Turning back to look at his house, she stared through the curled designer bars of the iron gate that surrounded it and marveled at the architecture. When Lucius finally opened his gates, he led them to the two-story house.

Passing a black Lincoln Continental that graced the oil ridden concrete drive, they held their remarks and followed him to the front door. After passing through the doorway, the pack was overcome by a darkness so still and so black that it was almost deafening. Delighted to find that their night vision was still intact, each of them paused briefly at the foot of a large winding staircase, its paint sacrificed to the scuffmarks of black leather boots. Once they passed it, their vision shut down and it was in that moment that Dominic began to seriously question their decision to come.

Though unaccustomed to darkness they could not penetrate, they continued to walk forward, instinctively tightening their unit so as to feel the strength of each other's presence, if not their actual bodies. When Lucius stopped abruptly, they crashed into him clumsily from behind. After backing up a few paces, the lights snapped back on and they found themselves standing in what appeared to be a den.

"So what brings my little birds down south for the winter?' Lucius smirked. He made brief eye contact with each of his guests and, before returning his stare to Dominic, fixated on Christoph once again.

They knew his question was solely for his own amusement as his knowledge of their pending arrival was as evident to the master as the marks that made them who they are.

"Ahhh… let me save you from the agony of explanation and get right to my response."

The pack shifted their posture with the anxiety of the possibilities.

"Perhaps the answers you seek and the requests you think you have… lie not with me, but rather, within your group."

Dominic expected such an answer but withheld his comments. Silence filled the room and the sound of footsteps alerted them to company. Lucius turned his back to his guests and shuffled toward a doorway masked by red velvet curtains. Looking back briefly, he swung his arm in dramatic fashion and it sent the left curtain swaying amidst the dead air. Then he disappeared entirely.

A huge movie screen stretched out before them. It ran across the length of the room from one wall to the next, its flat screen designed to titillate onlookers with the promise of a story. The pack looked up at the ominous screen and held their breath as they waited for an unknown projector to bring the stillness to life.

Looking toward one another, the heavy unspoken questions hung between them before a cloud of confusion hovered above their heads, working to drain the pack of their memories and their defenses. Not one of them remembered the road there, their introduction to Lucius, or crossing the power-depleting threshold; yet suddenly, they found themselves sitting in a room of red walls and gold accents.

Red velvet curtains draped over would-be doorways and a breeze from an unknown source blew them into a flowing dance. Leo walked hastily toward one of the doorways and pulled at the soft curtain with unnecessary force. He growled at the brick wall that seemed to smile back at him and then bowed his head in frustrated silence as he made his way back to the pack. The pseudo doorway led nowhere, just as he'd expected.

Christoph carefully picked up one item after another in the hopes that his empathetic powers would explain the story behind each of them. Unable to rely upon his gifts, he pushed aside an egg-shaped ashtray and tried hard to swallow the building frustration.

Golden pedestals with golden-flaked busts began to tell the story of their host, especially the one that boasted a terrifying image of Satan. Beside it sat an intricately handcrafted sculpture of an angel; both carved faces were detailed and similar in nature. The group exchanged glances. When they finally spoke, they did so simultaneously. Out of the mist, Lucius appeared again and his presence broke up any opportunity they may have had to converse.

This time, the headmaster wore striped pajamas and a brown tweed smoking jacket. From his feet, fluffy duck slippers called out for attention and a small bag of M&Ms was gripped in his right hand, a bowl of popcorn clutched in his left. Although his appearance was absurd, Lucius still maintained a stature that commanded respect, as his essence alone brought with it tantalizing mystery and concealed power.

He was taller than they had thought. Neither muscular nor frail, he had taken the permanent form of a middle-aged man and had allowed his hair to turn slightly silver from its jet black foundation. The hair stuck out in different directions and boasted even more thickets than it had before his short disappearance. Their host obviously had no interest in appearing either young, or normal for that matter.

"Have a seat," he commanded his guests with a smile. "I see you've absorbed all you can about who I am in a very short period of time."

Shaking his head back and forth, he continued.

"Still coming up short, I see," he said to Dominic. "Don't fool yourself. Remember, you know nothing yet."

With that, he threw an M&M into the air and held his head back to catch it on his tongue. The candy fell shamelessly to the rug.

"Do you know…," Lucius asked, "that I have never actually gotten one in my mouth? Never, not once."

"Wow," Dominic remarked sincerely. "Really?"

"Really," he answered. "Telepathy, climate control, invisibility… I've got it all but for the life of me, I can't get a damn M&M to land inside my mouth."

Dominic didn't know what to say, so he said nothing.

Chapter XIX

Lucius stared at the movie screen and ignored his guests, as though expecting his movie choice to begin so that he could begin enjoying his selected sweets. The room grew silent and after a prolonged moment of quiet uneasiness from the group, he stood up and exited the room again, through a different door.

"This is bullshit!" shouted Leo, marching toward their host's exit.

"To come all this way and not..."

His words were cut short when he felt Lucius standing behind him.

"Quite the temper you've got there, son," he said.

Refusing to turn and face him, Leo stood in silence.

"And rightfully so Leo... you've experienced great loss. No doubt you are here to gain understanding as to why and perhaps more important, who did this to you?"

Leo turned around slowly and nodded, lacking words for the first time he could ever remember.

"Perhaps... in time... your maker will reveal himself to you," added Lucius, his eyes panning his guests repeatedly and ending on Dominic.

Leo's anger built up again and he found himself losing all ability to maintain the guise of respect to his master, who continued to stare at his leader.

"Why the hell are you looking at him?" Leo asked as he burst out in anger. "He's not gonna do anything to control my response. We're beyond that now. I traveled all this way and I want some answers, dammit!"

"What do you think?" Lucius asked Dominic.

"Still?" Leo yelled, enraged. "I'm the one talking to you! Look at me! And I want to know right now, who did this to me?"

Tilting his head to the side and dropping it slightly, Lucius tried to reiterate his point softly. "Perhaps in time… your maker will reveal himself to you."

"I'm sorry, Leo," Dominic said quickly, the words delivered in a flat, gentle tone.

"What? " Leo asked, partially annoyed.

He was about to tell Dominic to shut up for the first time in their history together. He was getting ready to unleash his rage in a manner that he knew would bring shame to his pack. He had grown tired of the cryptic comments and the waste of time and was preparing to put an end to it in his own vicious, trademark way. But then the words hit him like a ton of bricks and he understood Lucius' comments and Dominic's apology more clearly than he wanted to.

He paused quietly as he looked to the other faces in his pack and he felt the anger rise like bile into his throat. His chest heaved and his fangs were released without inner warning. Seeing nothing but his devoted leader in a sudden hue of glowing red, Leo's mouth curled and he opened it, having no idea what words would come out.

"You?" he croaked out in a raspy whisper.

"You?" he asked again in a tone that had raised several hateful notches. "You son of a bitch!"

He spun in a circle of clouded anger with his fists clenched and the words flowed off his tongue in a rage that circled the room. Dominic knew that nothing he said would matter so he didn't speak at all. Instead, he just stood staring at the man who had once been his brother with a look of remorse that dulled his usually lively features.

"You? You piece of shit! Jesus Christ! I shared a home with you? Son of a bitch! Why, Dom?"

Leo's eyes panned the room rapidly as he paced until a shiny gleam of silver caught them and in one motion, he retrieved the Samurai sword that hung above the fireplace. Pressing the tip against Dominic's neck, he demanded an answer that would never satisfy him.

"Why?"

From the side of the room, Lucius offered the explanation that Dominic couldn't.

"When one of us is nominated to a higher status... there are certain requirements."

"I lost it all so that you could become leader?" he yelled in a voice that threatened to hoarsen with its exertion. "All I lived for, all that ever meant anything to me! You took it all away from me for that?"

As Leo pressed the sword deeper into his flesh, Dominic wanted to speak. Still, he refrained because he knew that no words could describe his sorrow or the guilt he had carried forward from the day of his turning.

"I'm gonna take your damn head!" Leo bellowed as he drew back for the strike.

But right at his point of forward movement, all noise and motion seemed to stand still except for the sound of steel hitting the Italian tile floor. Leo's eyes remained fixated on Dominic, but his anger was gone, the sword lying at his feet. And after a moment, his head slid, severed from its place atop his neck and bounced twice upon the tile, landing face upward before a horrified Dominic. His body soon followed and fell limply to the floor beside his head, revealing a surprisingly calm Raina who stood directly behind him; another sword grasped in her own sweaty hand. Quietly, she held it downward toward the ground, as though it were a cane.

"You missed the second sword," she said in a soft, dull tone.

"Raina! No!" cried Dominic, shaking his head side to side and placing his thumb and index finger to his forehead.

She turned her back to him and faced Lucius.

"My apologies for not asking permission for its use, master," she said, extending the sword handle toward him.

"How very brave of you, Madame," he answered, his words reflecting inspiration rather than disapproval. "Over time, I have learned to not underestimate anyone... and you, my dear... deserve attention for your actions."

Unsure and unconcerned where the conversation was headed, Raina looked down at her hands, expecting to see them shaking and found they weren't. In a situation where the old Raina would have fumbled around for her lipstick, she had surprised herself with calmness and an ability to accept the moment for what it was.

Reaching behind his back, Lucius pulled them back before him and produced a mirror, the same one that she had broken in her room just prior to the onset of their voyage. It was restored in full.

"It's...," she began, confusion showing in every feature. She turned to Dominic briefly and then looked back at Lucius.

"My counterparts in other countries...," Lucius began. "I don't think they would approve but I am not them and they are not me."

Looking into the mirror himself, he continued.

"You see, little lady... when you reach a certain level, you have the ability to do certain things... although most of my kind rarely bother trying."

He appeared to be stalling, as though unsure himself of the gift he would eventually offer her.

"I want you to hold onto this for a little while," he said. "Do not expect anything to come of it just yet as there are certain events that must first unfold."

Raina nodded as red tears began to fall from her eyes. She wouldn't look into the mirror anyway, not yet. She did not want to see her first reflection in twenty years just moments after she had murdered her friend. Instead, she ran from the room and headed for the staircase. Though she had no idea where it would take her, it was where her instincts directed that she go.

Lucius tossed an M&M toward the sky and it landed successfully in his mouth.

"I did it!" he exclaimed before walking out of the room, leaving the pack to their grief.

Dominic turned his attention to Jarek and Christoph, who stood silently by his side.

"This is not how I planned....," he tried to explain, fearful that he had displayed actions unworthy of his pack's trust. 'Had he only kept his cool...'

"We know," Jarek said, offering the necessary words of support his friend.

Christoph extended his hand to Dominic's shoulder and copied the words.

"We know..."

Chapter XX

Raina ran as fast as she could with no real direction in mind. Somewhere at the edges of her awareness, she could hear Dominic calling out to her but she continued to run. Up the winding staircase, she practically flew with an almost maniacal energy. Nothing would come between her and the sudden, desperate need for escape. Memories of Leo's face floated before her open eyes as well as behind her closed lids; no amount of will would banish them. His last gruesome expression, marked by betrayal and duplicity, taunted her mercilessly.

Leo had been miserable and mean and undeniably painful to be around, but he had been a part of her; he had been her family. The overwhelming grief over his loss and the unforgivable guilt for her role in it threatened to drop her to the ground. To prevent herself from falling into the wailing and inconsolable mess that beckoned her, Raina sought an empty spot where silence and solitude might offer respite from the pain. She had to make sense of what had happened and to find a way to come to terms with its harsh reality; Leo was dead and she had killed him.

Eyes closed throughout most of her maddened rush, she squeezed them tightly to prevent fresh tears from falling. She continued to race upwards, wildly, until her weakening equilibrium and the resultant dizziness forced her to an abrupt stop. The only instinct still working was the one that demanded that she numb out every last remnant of human emotion, which threatened despair.

A tear fell from her eye and she stopped to wipe it away with one hand as she tightened her grip on the banister with the other. Leo's emergence in her life had twice turned her into a killer. Through Dominic, she had ended his life as a human and because of Dominic, she had ended his existence altogether. She looked down at her hands and had to strain her eyes through the darkness. She knew her night vision was possible but it took concentration and she was in too dark of a place to focus.

Blood still dripped from her fingers and, as she slowly ascended the staircase, Raina eyed the red line that she had trailed up the banister. Once at the top, she took a right and ducked into a dark bedroom halfway down the hallway, leaving a red handprint on the door casing behind her.

She looked into the huge round antique mirror that hung on the wall. Its frame was made from black wrought iron and there were steel black roses clinging to the ivy that wove itself through it. It seemed to have more purpose than just an offer of a reflection and as she neared it, she felt a magnetic draw that pulled her to its glass and beckoned her to come see herself. The closer she got, the more she felt hope that her image would magically appear and she would be able to look at herself once again.

Raina knew the desire to see herself was perceived by the others as shallow but she knew it wasn't born from vanity. It had been a symbol of humanity that she hadn't realized until she had lost it. Raina wanted to see her face again because she knew if she did, it would mean she'd been restored to the human God had created for her.

Praying that her wish would be granted without further death, Raina finally stopped before the mirror and stood very still. No tear-stained face looked back and no bloody reflection told the secret of her sin. She would never be able to see the pain in her eyes and, without the long self-stare granted to humans, her rage would continue to build because it lacked release; it lacked understanding.

She reached out and ran a finger down the glass, leaving a bloody trail behind. Thoughts of Leo rushed through her brain and her heart lurched at the memories they carried. She had loved him and she had hated him. He had been a miserable man, which was why she had chosen him, but throughout the years Raina had come to recognize the good within the heart of their diminutive train wreck. He had learned to love a day too late and had been turned because of his lack of humanity. Worse, he had never learned to forgive and was now dead for it. Raina felt another wave of tears but she willed them away. She didn't have the luxury of grief and the impending danger she felt had only grown stronger. Leo's death hadn't been the loss she knew was coming; there was more. She just didn't know how to prepare for it and felt suddenly, very alone.

A chair scratched the floor behind her but she did not turn around. Instead, she squinted into the darkness that reflected from the mirror. Not one light illuminated the guest room. If the moon hadn't been full of bright light that shone through the window or if her reflection had blocked the view, she wouldn't have seen that she had a visitor. But the moon was full and her missing reflection did provide her the ability to see what stood beneath the window, still hidden in the shadows not penetrated by the moonlight.

'Who's there?' she asked, working hard to prevent the threatening shake from weaving its way into her tone. Whoever the enemy happened to be, she could not allow him to sense her fear.

There was no answer, yet the silhouette remained in its spot, looming and immobile. There was no telltale bun to suggest a Lucy visit and the shadow was too big to be Joan. Sam wouldn't stay quiet because he would know that the silence would scare her.

Raina felt her powers awaken within but made no conscious effort at their emergence. With the persuasion techniques of a salesman and the manipulation tactics of an addict, she felt her powers sharpen themselves on her inner blades. With carefully chosen words designed to enhance the male ego and eyes that could reflect memories of another's most beautiful moments and most brazen feats, Raina soothed her increasing anxiety and turned away from the mirror to face the shadow.

"Don't wanna talk?" she tried again.

Silence responded again so she took another two steps toward the silhouette. She was only steps from the dark patch where her guest hid and where she would be able to share the darkness and discern his identity.

"What's the matter?" she taunted. "Scared?"

When male laughter erupted, Raina grinned. The male ego was all about attention and the suggestion that a member of the stronger gender might fear her had always worked to flush him out.

"Aahhh, so you do have a voice," she continued, taking one more step toward her uninvited guest.

Raina had known his identity the moment she'd heard his laugh. It was the same laugh that had made her wince in the forest; the realization that she stood alone in a room with Stephan made Raina begin to question her strength and her courage. He would be a powerful adversary and she wasn't sure that she could win in a battle with him.

He stepped out of the shadows and into plain view and Raina had to admit to herself that, despite his off-putting coldness, Stephen was handsome. The deep dimple on his right cheek only enhanced the chiseled nose that brought forth thoughts of a Roman soldier. His jet black hair fell into short, loose waves and she knew somehow that its shine and luster were completely natural. His face could inspire the exposed jugular of many a willing woman but his ingrained manliness and his ability to protect and conquer made him an obvious choice for leader. Raina was of the rare percentage of women who did not fall prey to his charms. Neither his looks nor his appeal nor his power made him a leader she would ever want to obey.

"Can I offer you something?" she asked calmly.

"Ah, good girl," he answered in a smug tone.

"I'm sorry?"

"No, don't be; not yet anyway," he laughed. "Save your apologies for when you break the rules."

"I don't follow your rules, sorry."

"I noticed," he smiled. "You don't seem to follow anyone's rules, do you?"

Raina knew the reason for his resentment. He was of one of the oldest tribes – a league of vampires, which held onto the belief that the female deserved no respect and required male dominance to exist.

"I follow rules," she said, paying careful attention to the confidence in her tone, knowing he would notice the little things.

"Is that right?"

His smile widened and Raina offered one of her own.

"Yes, that's right."

"The way I see it, you have no leader and no rules. You have no boundaries and no structure. How your fledgling little group even got here, I will never understand."

He put a hand to his heart in a dramatic attempt to show his astonishment over their arrival.

"We are a pack," she said, still ensuring that her voice remained unyielding in the shadow of his power. "We take care of each other. We're a family!"

"Well, that's your problem," he shot back snidely. "We're not built to have families. We're built to thrive in the darkness and to survive not on love but on the fruits of temptation."

"Who says?"

"That's how it's always been!" he yelled, shaking his head in disgust. "This is why there should be vampire law that prohibits the inept from being allowed to turn a human! It's worse than human inbreeding when one who cannot absorb the code insists upon becoming a maker!"

"Who are you to say how it should be?" Raina snapped.

An image of Leo shooting a bird raced past her current thought and she staggered backwards from the pain.

Stephan laughed and the sound of it reverberated off all four walls.

"You see?" he asked. "That's why."

"What are you talking about?"

"Your friend, the one back there," he said, pointing at the door she had run in through. "That headless midget who was about to kill your 'respected' leader. He's why you don't develop meaningful relationships."

His voice took on a mocking and sarcastic tone. "That's why you have a leader and you have followers and you follow the code and you kill without remorse!"

Stephan winked at her and shrugged. "You never know when you might have to chop a head off."

Raina ran forward with her hand pulled back in preparation for intense force. Before he had the chance to register her movements, she slapped his face hard.

"Love strengthens us," she insisted weakly.

"Love has done nothing but weaken you, all of you, from the inside out!"

"You don't know anything."

"No?" asked Stephan, raising his eyebrows. "I know quite a lot, in fact."

Raina stared at him but said nothing.

"I know that your leader allowed himself to love you and because of it, lost the powers he was to inherit."

"He has great power!"

"No, Raina," he continued. "Love saps away our intelligence and it dilutes our independence. It's the biggest downfall of the humans and it should never penetrate our species. Your 'leader' could have reached higher rank with an abundance of benefits had he not allowed emotion to get involved."

His head shook slowly but his eyes remained connected to her stare.

"Oh well, at least he figured it out before it was too late and fixed it."

Raina didn't bother to ask how he knew about her and Dominic; any number of abilities could have told him.

"And your other boyfriend?" he asked, shaking his head with disapproval.

She glared at him intensely. She didn't want to even hear him utter the name.

"Jarek, Jarek, Jarek…," he began.

"What about him?"

"You think we're blind? Stupid?" he asked. "That disgusting display in front of Lucius was embarrassing. Loving a woman… sharing a woman…"

His head shaking became more vehement.

"It's an insult to bring your dysfunction and your disrespect here… right into Lucius' home."

"They are all a part of me," Raina demanded. "We care about each other… protect each other."

"You do?" he asked, looking first at her bloody hands and then, glancing around the room skeptically. "Where are they now?"

He walked closer and her heart skipped a couple of beats..

"Where's your loving family in this, your true moment of need?"

Raina backed up a step to alleviate the violation of his closeness.

"They'll be here."

"You think?"

As he advanced another step toward her, she backed up. The shine in his eyes and the upward turn of his lips told Raina he was amusing himself with her.

"You really think they'll give up their time with Lucius to come save you?"

He stepped forward and she stepped back.

"You think Jarek will simply forgo his deepest desire to extricate himself from the rest of us? Or that Christoph will give up the ability to die?"

"Die?" she whispered.

"Or that your fearless leader will ride in on a white horse and trade his greatest desire for you? See? This is why the female shouldn't be allowed free thought," he laughed and the sound seemed to bounce off the walls.

"Anyway, it's your lucky day."

"Oh, yeah?" Raina asked, her eyes darting around quickly but not fast enough to keep up with her brain. "Why is that?"

Stephan's mouth grew and widened as it conformed around his growing teeth. His dark hair fell into longer locks that fell past his ears. His brown eyes turned black and the glow of his skin disappeared as the flesh turned pale white. Transformation never occurred without a bite to follow and Raina was trying to devise the most creative plan she could come up with to escape his intentions.

"Because I'm not going to kill you," he finally answered.

"Thank you," Raina smiled, still trying to find ways to buy time.

"I've decided to keep you instead," he said. "Getting rid of you entirely would be a real waste. I have a feeling you might have a use or two."

He reached for her again and when she slapped him away, his laugh was hearty and real.

"No, thank you," she responded. "I'm happy with what I have."

"Oh yeah? Who are you closest to: the Scarecrow, the Tin Man or the Cowardly Lion?"

His laugh turned to almost a cackle.

"You already killed Toto so it looks like you're down to three."

Stephen reached his hand out to touch her face and she knocked it away forcibly with a laugh of her own.

"You're the only brainless, heartless coward I see here," she bit back.

Without a word, Stephan backhanded her with a blow that knocked her onto the edge of an ancient maple dresser that sat beneath the mirror.

"See how that works? You show disrespect, you get punished. You are the female and your place is at the bottom. You are to listen; to obey; to keep quiet unless spoken to."

Raina touched her throbbing lip and pulled her fingers into her line of vision.

"Don't worry," he went on. "You'll become accustomed quickly enough. A few days of captivity and intense training should have you submissive and silent in no time. I'll be your trainer, and your father, and your husband. I'll be your God."

She pushed his words away and squinted at the fingers she still held before her eyes.

"What are you looking at?" he asked, annoyed. An expression of understanding passed his features and Stephan looked unhappy with his conclusions. "Are you looking for your own blood? We don't bleed until we die, you silly little girl, and if you still imagine that you do, you're even weaker than I had thought!"

He grabbed her wrist and twisted it until she screamed and then he pulled her hand back in front of her eyes roughly.

"You've come to return your gift?" he asked incredulously.

Her anxiety turned to full-fledged fear. If Stephan figured out her reason for coming, no amount of charm or seduction would work. She remained silent.

Stephan's eyes became hard and they narrowed into tight slits. With clenched teeth, he spoke slowly and clearly.

"That makes you an ungrateful bitch. You dare to come here to ask Lucius for your humanity after having been blessed with such a priceless gift?"

She wanted to close her eyes to his presence and open them to his absence. Instead, she turned to race for the door. In the blink of an eye, she was there but just as her hand was about to make contact, Stephan appeared and blocked her exit. He folded his arms and leaned back against the door with a grin.

"Going somewhere?" he asked.

Her nails grew to blades and she sliced at his cheek with an animalistic noise.

Stephan grabbed at his face instinctively and the angry look that spread across his features told Raina to scream and to scream as loud as she could. She opened her mouth but her shriek had only just pierced the air when his strong hand cupped her mouth with a slap.

She continued to exert screams but Stephan caught her pleas in his hand and he pulled her body tightly into his. Pressing his lips to her ear, he whispered his next words.

"What are you gonna do now, huh?" he laughed.

She wiggled and squirmed and tried desperately to pull herself from his grip but he was strong, too strong.

"Ssshhh," he consoled, pulling her face into his neck in an insincere act of comfort. "Listen to my words and listen carefully. You do not belong here. None of you belongs here but you, most of all, do not belong here."

She pushed at him but every attempt she made to free herself only rewarded her with a tighter hug. With his hand at her neck and still forcing a neck nuzzle she did not want, he began caressing her hair as in consolation. Raina cringed every time she felt his hand brush her skin.

"You are a woman and should not be left unattended or allowed free rein to think."

She drew her right leg back and pulled her knee up into his groin with such force she thought her knee might bruise. As Stephan doubled over, she pushed past him and ran through the door into a hallway of darkness.

Knowing he would be right behind her, Raina ran blindly as she tried to block her thoughts. If Stephan could see Leo in her mind's eye, there was no telling what else he could see. A doorway at the end of the hall stood open and she could see French doors facing her from its far wall. Raina used all of her resources and picked up as much speed as she could. With hands hung at her sides and bent slightly forward to guide her way, she ran head-first through the bedroom door and crashed through the second floor French doors. Shards of glass still piercing her flesh, she landed on the Lincoln they had admired before entering and the continued momentum forced her into a painful roll onto the cement.

Refusing to let it slow her down, Raina headed for the forest with no plan in mind.

Chapter XXI

The room Lucius led Jarek into was both massive and intimidating and it seemed to hold no rhyme or reason. He didn't understand anything his gaze fell upon. The gray walls to one side of him were decorated with hundreds of sconces, all intricately carved into the heads of ancient animals. The other side boasted aged paintings of the Old World and previous headmasters. Above one row of antique frames sat a larger frame with the photograph of an egg displayed proudly behind its dark glass.

A hammock swung from one corner, though no wind was present and no rope anchored it to the ceiling. Beside it sat a large cage filled with black rats that climbed over and under one another and made squirming noises that sent a shiver up Jarek's spine.

Walking deeper into the room, he passed a large, four-poster bed to his left that took up the first quarter of the room. It was beautiful and lavish with teak, dark cherry wood, a tall canopy, and it boasted long vines and Indonesian flowers that had been hand carved into the wood. Its ceiling was lined with panels and bars that reached the top of the canopy and wrapped themselves around the bed.

To his right, he passed a bar that carried an old century wine and decanter set on its marble counter. Thinner sconces to each side of it contained long red candles in their candle holders. Further into the room, he stopped at what appeared to be levitation hooks that hung from the ceiling and it produced in his mind visions of a master in training, hanging from hooks that penetrated flesh on the road to enlightenment. The sight made him want to turn back the way he came but a voice from behind changed his plan.

"Welcome," Lucius said in a lower tone than Jarek had heard upon their first meeting.

He turned around to face the headmaster and was stunned to see the dramatic change in his appearance. No longer disheveled or counting in egg measurements, he had become what Jarek envisioned during the road-trip.

The headmaster's previously tousled hair was slicked back and shiny and his red velvet smoking jacket conjured up visions of Hugh Hefner lounging around in his mansion. The thought made Jarek want to laugh but he didn't dare. This was not the quirky Lucius who climbed out of the car with eggs in hand and strange theories in his mind. This was the authoritative and commanding Lucius who would not stand for even a hint of disrespect.

"Thank you," Jarek answered.

"I'm glad you made it," Lucius replied. "I was rooting for you the whole time."

"With all due respect, sir, something tells me that's a fib."

Lucius laughed and used his pointer finger and thumb to pantomime a small increment.

"Maybe a little," he admitted with a warm smile. "I'll admit there were times when I should have had you killed, especially after I heard word of your drive through debauchery," Lucius shook his head and grinned. "But, I refrained. Entertainment value, you know?"

"Yeah, sorry," Jarek said, shaking his head in apology. "Leo."

"Right, Leo," Lucius agreed. "Poor doomed mess of a fellow, he was. Now, what can I do for you, old boy? What have you come to ask of me?"

Thoughts of Leo saddened Jarek more than he had ever expected. Though they had remained adversaries throughout most of their life together, the grief he felt for him filled his heart with dread but he decided to dismiss the thought until later.

"I want to be on my own," he said firmly. "No pack, no League, no leader, no code, no rules... alone."

Lucius spread his hands wide and shrugged his shoulders in question.

"Why would I allow you to have this? There are rules for a reason."

"I'm sure you have your reasons, and I'm sure they're good ones," Jarek continued. "But I wasn't built to live this way and I would rather die than continue like this."

"Ahhh...be careful what you wish for in here," Lucius said, looking around the eerie room. "That last one can be easily accommodated."

When Lucius laughed again, Jarek didn't find the sound as endearing as he had before.

"I will not bother you or your League and my travels will take me far away from here," Jarek continued. "You can tell everyone I was captured or killed or banished."

Lucius appeared thoughtful as he rested his chin on the pointer finger he held beneath it.

"You want this very badly, don't you?"

"Yes sir, I do."

"How badly?" Lucius asked.

Jarek was confused and didn't understand what the master was asking him.

"Badly," he answered.

"What about your lady?" Lucius asked. "Won't she be disappointed to see you leave?"

"I plan to take her with me."

"Does she know of your intentions?"

"She knows some of it," Jarek answered. "I'm not a big sharer."

"I hate to be the bearer of bad news, but your wish and your lady's wish conflict greatly, so whose do you suppose I should grant?"

"What do you mean?"

"Well, if I grant you your wish, you will leave this place with Raina to never be found again, is that right? Live out the life of a lone vampire, ostracized from both the human world and from your new world."

"Yes, sir."

"And if I grant her wish to become a human again, she will be a mortal who is banished from the only world she knows, away from all other humans. This will create a painfully ironic change of life for her, no?"

"It's a compromise we're willing to make," Jarek insisted.

"Are you sure?" Lucius asked.

"Not entirely."

"What makes you think it's the life she would want?" Lucius asked.

'"Because she loves me."

"And do you love her?" Lucius asked gently.

"Of course I do."

"How much?"

"A lot," Jarek admitted.

"Do you love her enough to give up your wish for hers?"

"If I had to, yes."

Lucius remained quiet for a moment as he stared at him. When he finally spoke, his tone sounded gravelly and hoarse.

"I agree to grant you what you ask for because of reasons I don't feel the need to disclose. I will say that you have displayed more courage and skill than most of my League and that I trust you will neither bring us shame nor that you will disclose this opportunity to the world outside," he said.

His tone returned to the low baritone he had entered the room with.

"Wouldn't want everyone else setting out on such an adventure now, would we?"

"No, of course not," Jarek answered hopefully.

Lucius pointed to the sconce closest to his head.

"Look into the eyes of the tiger and say your wish out loud. Remember this, though. Once you begin, you must continue uninterrupted. If you stop for any reason, you will not only lose your wish but also your ability to ever have it granted again. Do you understand?"

"I understand... and I thank you," Jarek answered sincerely.

He looked into the black eyes of the ceramic tiger and had the strong sense that the ceramic figure understood him thoroughly. He began to speak, slowly and carefully.

"I wish to be . . . "

A loud crash sounded from the upstairs bedroom. It sounded like breaking glass and Jarek knew instinctively that it was Raina. His heart told him so before his mind could even begin guessing at its source. He knew also that without his rescue, she would die. Despite the heavy awareness that turning away would cost him his only chance, Jarek closed his eyes and allowed his head to fall forward.

He had considered spitting the wish out quickly but worried he would be rewarded immediately with a new location in a faraway land. Courtesy of the dark humored master, he might find himself suddenly thousands of miles in the distance and unable to help Raina.

Jarek pulled his stare from the tiger and turned it toward Lucius instead. He felt the plea in his heart shoot out from his pupils and penetrate the eyes of the headmaster. Lucius smiled and nodded approval for Jarek to begin again but did not say a word.

Jarek looked back into the eyes of the waiting tiger and began again.

"Help me save her," he wished instead and ran toward the sound of the crash without another look at Lucius.

Chapter XXII

Raina's sprint through the forest started to slow from her exhaustion. Her tired mind began to wander and she thought about Jarek as she pushed her way through unforgiving branches. He and Stephan shared the same brand of sarcasm and the same cool demeanor but that's where their similarities ended.

Jarek had used his penchant for domination to help her but never to harm her. He had pushed her to open herself up and had only broken her down so that he could help to rebuild her. He had insisted that she trust him and then had proven his loyalty in everything he did for her. She had drawn strength and confidence from his insistence that she look into his eyes during the intimacies she had always turned away from and though he had made her fearful at times, it was always followed by tokens of affection and understanding. He had gathered the pieces of her shattered heart and made her whole again despite the fact that she had always been an unsolvable jigsaw no one could ever piece together quite right.

Her heart called out to him as she picked up speed again, running deeper into the forest. Though he didn't have their leader's power of mind speak, she felt that Jarek might be able to hear the desperation inside her heart faster than Dominic would hear the screams for help inside of her mind.

The trees closed in on her as the forest became more dense and Raina had to push away at the branches that tried to block her way. Thorns scratched at her cheeks and the dew from their leaves splashed into her eyes each time she smacked a branch away. When she stopped to regain her bearings, she realized she was completely lost and could no longer tell from which direction she'd been running. Shooting glances in every direction, she utilized all of her senses to their highest capabilities and felt a hot prickly sensation run through the ends of her fingers. Though she heard and saw nothing out of the ordinary, she knew she was not alone.

In sync with her thoughts, she heard something from behind a smaller bush a few feet to her right. Whipping her head toward the sound, she concentrated mainly on her auditory abilities and used them to magnify the sounds around her. The tinny pitch from behind the bush continued but it was difficult to decipher. It sounded like a crying baby or a meowing cat and as she stared at its leaves, her chest shook with the pounding of her heart.

Raina's peripheral vision caught a movement to her left but when she turned her attention to it, a sound from behind made her turn back again. Raina knew someone hid quietly behind the bushes and that she would not be allowed to flee deeper into the forest. When the noise sounded again, she recognized it for what it was. It was laughter and it was the laughter of a woman.

Slowly, a figure began to appear from behind the bush. As it rose carefully, Raina watched it reach its full height of about five feet. A petite woman with the round face of a pixie stared back at her with a shy smile. Her dark hair fell into crimped locks, as though they had just been released from hundreds of tight braids and her eyes were as dark as her skin was light. Her lips were full and pouty and amused all at once and when Raina spoke, she giggled.

"Who are you? What do you want?" Raina asked, breathless.

Though the pixie did not answer, she continued to snicker in a high, tinny voice that Raina found disconcerting. Her seductive appearance was in sharp contrast to her childlike tone and Raina wondered how much of Stephan's training the poor pixie had endured since her turning. More noise from behind demanded her attention and she turned to face it. Nothing was there but when she circled the area slowly, she realized she shared the moment with more than the silly pixie.

Each bush had one of Stephan's underlings hiding behind their strange purplish leaves and as she watched them appear one by one, her last shred of hope diminished. Knowing it was only a matter of time before their leader made his grand entrance, Raina grabbed at the necklace that hung from her neck and gripped tightly at its amber stone.

"Did you really think I wouldn't catch you?" Stephan asked her from behind.

Raina turned quickly but it wasn't fast enough. His swift backhand knocked her to the ground and she lay motionless on a grassy mound, staring up at the faces that began to hover above. The pack closed in around her in a tight circle but did not speak. Raina envisioned them as the munchkins of Oz and prayed that a bright, glowing ball would drift in from the sky to aid her escape.

The two most prominent faces that loomed above her were that of Stephan and that of his pixie. When Raina saw their leader pass his assistant his special cane, she knew that her death would be the pixie's rite of passage into his pack.

"I thought you would appreciate your demise more if it came from one of your own," he said.

"I thought it was my lucky day," Raina tried.

"That was before your devastating disrespect to Lucius' home," he answered. "Now, you deserve death."

The pixie lifted the cane high into the air above her and from Raina's position beneath she realized why it had been so special to Stephan. The cane was really a swordstick that boasted a sterling silver shaft and an intricately designed handle that she could not completely make out from her angle. What she could see clearly was the sharp blade that poked out from the bottom, the one meticulously positioned above her heart.

"Any last words?" Stephan asked.

Raina opened her mouth to speak but her words never found their way into the universe. The only sound that could be heard was the whooshing of a knife in flight as it found its way to the pixie's round, crimped head. The silver blade to her brain sliced through the tiny scamp's thoughts and intentions and she began to fall to the ground with the handle protruding from her temple.

Knowing her hero had arrived, Raina quickly rolled out of the way before the dead pixie fell on top of her. Though the good witch of the north had not traveled to this strange, dark land to offer rescue, Jarek had and this time he most definitely had not come in peace.

Raina tried to stand but Stephan kicked her in the forehead and knocked her back to the ground. He leaned down to the pixie, pulled the knife from her bleeding temple, and flung it directly at Jarek's heart but missed. As Raina lay staring into the pixie's lifeless eyes, she wondered how long it had been since the little woman had spilled blood. Raina felt the darkness tugging her into sweet unconsciousness.

Sounds of a struggle ensuing above her brought Raina back to a reality that she did not want to face but her love for Jarek gave her the strength she needed to stand. Though she wanted nothing more than to intervene in the battle, Stephan's pack would not allow her to break their circle. They made no move to advance toward her but they tightened their unit and held her captive with the implied threat of harm.

Jarek and Stephan circled one another like lions trying to prove who was king of the forest. Armed again with the knife he had purchased at the truck stop, Jarek stared into the eyes of his adversary as Stephan held the bladed cane inches from his heart. Staggering backwards from the weakness of not having fed in several hours and from the injuries that Stephan had inflicted with his blows, Raina fell to the ground and closed her eyes as a new wave of pain exploded inside of her head.

Visions of Jarek lying next to her in bed teased her with their warmth and comfort. Impotent and helpless, she reached out a hand that would never reach him as she remembered the silent hours they had spent staring into each other's eyes. They had seen in one another the souls they had lost and had lived together on a different level than she had ever shared with anyone. Though neither of them had the power of telepathy, they always seemed to know what the other was thinking and feeling without the need for words.

"I love you," Jarek whispered to her from her memories.

"I love you too," she answered, desperation clutching her heart.

Raina opened her eyes and saw that Stephan had advanced on Jarek. With the tip of his cane barely touching Jarek's chest, she knew he was only a stab away from ending her lover's existence. Jarek faced his enemy with hard eyes and a calculated stance. In her weakened state, she could not feel his plan and the words that he had tried to whisper to her heart could not penetrate the pack's circle. The sight of the blade aimed at Jarek's chest filled her with a horror she could not contain and Raina cried out his name.

"Jarek!"

Believing she was in imminent danger, he turned his head toward her and Stephan used that opportunity to drive the blade directly into Jarek's heart. Pulling herself up, Raina wailed in despair at the sight of her lover falling to the wet ground but the finality that quietly draped itself over the forest told her it was too late. Jarek was mortally wounded; she had killed him by calling his name.

He landed in a hard fall but his eyes remained open. Pushing her way through the pack's circle, Raina ran to him and dropped to her knees, grabbing at his face with a feeling of loss she had never known. She cried and pleaded and prayed to the heavens but knew her requests had gone unanswered when she saw the blood trickling from his ears and spurting from the deep gash in his chest.

"Jarek, don't go!" she cried. Her pleas turned to quiet tears and she whispered once more to him. "Please don't leave me."

Tears stinging her eyes, Raina kissed him softly on the lips and put a hand to his gushing wound. She had no plan for how she would escape their circle but she didn't care; she wouldn't leave him behind even if she could. She hadn't realized how much she relied on his guidance until she couldn't ask him what to do or how to proceed. Though his pain was great, Jarek smiled at her and the simple gesture filled her with a resolve to continue to fight, but it was only when his grin fell away for good and the life permanently left his eyes that she turned away from him to look at Stephan.

"Ain't love grand?" he asked proudly.

Raina glared at him but didn't answer. She was too busy fashioning her rage and anguish into a weapon that she could use against him.

"Do you see me mourning the death of this hopeless little idiot?" he asked, kicking at the dead pixie. "No, and do you want to know why? Because I don't care! I don't let love weaken me, like he did."

Stephan pointed half-heartedly toward Jarek's body and she felt a loathing boiling from within.

"I'll kill you," she whispered, teeth clenched and fists balled. "I swear it on my soul, I'll see you dead."

"There you go," he laughed. "That's the spirit! Maybe you can be taught after all!" He began walking toward her and he kicked at Jarek's boots along the way. "Are you ready to begin your new life now?"

"I'll never serve you," she answered in a low, strained voice.

They heard a grunt from a member of his pack and looked in the direction it came from. His tallest and thinnest soldier began to fall forward but how his injury occurred remained a mystery to all of them. Another moan from the opposite side of the circle turned their heads just in time to see another of Stephan's vampires fall to the ground. When Raina saw a silver arrow protruding from his back, she knew what was going on and squinted into the dark forest to find her family.

She saw Christoph sitting high in a tree high, legs dangling over a branch and his homemade silver crossbow aimed toward the circle. He winked at her and made a gesture for her to move. Complying quickly, Raina stepped to the side and allowed the next arrow to take down the vampire closest to her. She turned to the other side of the forest and saw Dominic on the ground, a bow perched on his shoulder as he aimed with precision toward the pack. Camouflaged by a large brush, he placed a finger to his lips that told her to stay quiet.

"What?" Stephan asked, confused, as he backed away from the circle and peered with intensity into the forest.

He shouted commands to his small army as more members of his pack fell forward and landed in heaps around Jarek's body. Raina smiled because it was what Jarek deserved. He had always lived at the center of every battle and it should be so in death as well.

Though Stephan successfully commanded his still living pack members to fight, their confusion as to the source of the attack remained a handicap and it allowed more of them to be shot. With Stephan's attention on his army and his failing tactics, Raina ran through an opening provided by the fallen vampires and raced toward Dominic with weak leaps and an angry heart pulling her along. Christoph continued shooting his homemade daggers until Stephan stood alone with his dead army and dead enemy at his feet.

Raina made it to Dominic and grabbed the bow and an arrow from his hands before turning to run back toward Stephan. Aiming the arrow as she ran, she allowed the pain of her loss to guide every move she made. Avenging Jarek's death wouldn't bring him back but it might allow her to go on living without the guilt of his death dragging her into a bottomless pit. She would kill Stephan and when they had buried him in a manner that would show disrespect to their entire species, she would spit on his grave with glee.

Just before she had the chance to stop and aim, Stephan leapt away from Christoph's last flying bow in perfect timing and he clung to a branch like a trained monkey. Like a trapeze sideshow from Cirque du Soleil, he used short distance leaps to push himself off tree trunks in his escape. Though Stephan appeared to have the skill of flight, Raina knew it was all just technique he had practiced during his long years spent in the forest serving Lucius. As Christoph and Dominic made their way to her, she continued to watch Stephan until he disappeared into the darkness.

Once at her side, they each took one of her arms and pulled them around their necks. Raina was too weak to walk on her own and too grief stricken to speak so they quietly pulled her along, back toward the mansion. Christoph and Dominic caught one another's eye as they turned backwards to steal one last glance at their fallen friend.

Chapter XXIII

The roadtrip had been bittersweet for Christoph and he knew the most difficult part was yet to come. His turn with Lucius had finally arrived, yet he had no idea how he planned to convey his wishes to the headmaster. Having obsessed over his wording throughout every state and having struggled with the potential consequences during every backseat nightmare, he still had no idea how he would reveal his request to die to the great and powerful Lucius.

Christoph was not ungrateful for his existence. On the contrary, he had always maintained a great appreciation for the human species as well as the vampirism he had been forced into. He suffered little regret when looking back on his lives, both mortal and immortal, but had come to accept that he'd simply lived for too long and had already done everything worth doing. He'd grown gravely bored and laboriously tired and just wanted to move onto the next stage where he hoped to finally find a place of serenity and silence.

Christoph tried hard to prevent himself from feeling resentment over his inability to die like the rest of his species. A stroll in the sunlight, though painfully scorching and potentially debilitating for months, would not kill him. A swift stab to the heart by a silver blade would create a deep ache that was emotionally traumatic and physically injurious, but it would not end his life. Only the blessing of the headmaster could free him from the binds that tethered him to an earth he wanted to escape and so the roadtrip had indeed become his last hope.

He walked through the tunnel the pixie girls had led him to and thought about Lucius' obsession with eggs and Stephan's fixation with fairies. He thought about the differences and the similarities between humans and vampires and shook his head slowly at how alike they really were in the end.

Hearing high pitched snickering from behind him, Christoph turned around and noticed the three little pixies still stood at the entrance to the tunnel, waving and smiling. When they started blowing kisses at him, he blew one back and bowed to them in a low and dramatic fashion, causing them to giggle again. Laughing out loud, he turned back toward his destination and headed deeper into the increasingly surreal tunnel.

He couldn't stop thinking about their round little faces or wondering where they had come from. Had Stephan picked them off the Internet? Had he been a frequent visitor on some dating or social networking site and systematically chosen only the ones who could pass as an imp to satisfy some twisted fantasy he still harbored from his human life? Christoph shook his head with disapproval as he imagined Stephan breaking into their safe little homes and attacking them during their sleep. Of course, he didn't know if it was how it really happened but he found it all too easy to envision the sly misogynist as one who would derive great pleasure from attacking women during their most vulnerable moments.

The lights in the tunnel were the same kind Christoph had seen in the forest and, looking around at the care it took to install such an intricate lighting system, he decided Lucius had at least one more obsession. What appeared to be a long runway ahead carried hundreds upon thousands of halogen lamps, all housed in nickel plated brass bodies that stood upon tall posts that had strange markings carved into them. The road ahead illuminated a golden hue from underground and Christoph figured the master had used low pressure sodium bulbs to create such an effect. The street appeared never-ending and he wished Leo were at his side, walking it with him. He may have been a miserable little bastard but he had still deserved his yellow brick road.

Christoph bristled when he realized that a corner was coming up and he hoped deep down that he wasn't destined to run into a lion or tiger or bear when he rounded it. He was too drained to be forced into a battle with one who boasted larger fangs than him but still felt mild shame at his own hesitation. Though he hoped there was no video system detailing his every move, he was pretty certain there was. He knew that Lucius was a leader who would protect his fortress at all costs and a security system with recording capabilities would be mandatory for such protection. He knew the headmaster also had extremely voyeuristic tendencies and would derive great pleasure from watching one take such a dubious walk through the strange tunnel.

Christoph inhaled deeply and held his breath before he forged forward and turned the corner. Once he completed the round, the atmosphere and scenery changed drastically, with the greatest difference being that he was no longer in the tunnel. He was indoors in what appeared to be a long thin room that sported a red carpet, light pink walls, and an obvious fondness for birds. The scent of oranges permeated the air but it wasn't unpleasant. He let go of the breath he'd been holding and inhaled deeply through his nose to gift his olfactory senses with the sweetness.

Bird creatures of all types meandered back and forth in some unidentifiable pattern that he couldn't quite understand. When Christoph narrowed his eyes to get a clearer look, he noticed there was one wingless species among them and that they appeared to be snubbing the winged ones. Crawling gracefully down the middle of the carpet, one of the cats turned around to look at the intruder and its slanted, bright blue eyes shone a strange light into Christoph's eyes, causing him to shiver visibly. Their presence reminded him of folklore he'd heard about Siamese cats who carried the souls of their kings attempting to beat death. Their cats' leader closed one eye and seemed to wink at him and the act made Christoph envision its king inside, living out his next nine lives in complacent joy for having snubbed his nose at destiny. Just as he was about to turn away from its stare, the cat turned its head forward again and continued walking down the long hallway with the rest of his clowder.

An unnerving bird call pulled Christoph's attention to the left just in time and he jumped backwards quickly to prevent himself from getting hit by the huge wing that was opening in his direction. Its dark plumage and the fact that road kill dangled from its beak made Christoph want to back up even more but there was no room. He frowned from anxiety because he'd been around long enough to know that their presence was an omen of death. It worried him because he didn't get the sense that the vultures were there to feast off his own flesh and he imagined the faces of his remaining family members. An unacceptable thought, he shook it out of his head just as quickly and continued on.

It was only when he noticed the ravens ahead that Christoph finally began to see the theme in the room's residents. The cat and the vulture and the raven all shared one thing in common. Known as the harbingers of souls, their presence meant one of two things in Christoph's mind. Either their headmaster had gone completely and utterly mad or Christoph had stumbled upon some inexplicable underground soul system.

It was like an airport where all of the employees were birds working dutifully to ensure that each soul made it to its intended destination. He could almost envision a screen that displayed the names of human souls ready for pick-up and he wondered if the tunnel and the room and the birds were a way for the head pack to hijack them en route.

The raven had been prominent in many myths Christoph had heard through the years but one was more prevalent in his mind than others. Hit with a memory of his time in Puget Sound, he remembered eating Dungeness crab and geoduck clams by the seaside and listening to the tales of the natives who explained how ravens hailed from the land of the spirits. They had told him that the birds had somehow taken part in the creation of humanity and though Christoph wasn't sure how true the story was, he had long before made a rule to never discount any theory entirely.

He decided to walk faster so he could find his way out of the room as fast as possible and as he moved, he glanced around at the rest of the birds, confirming his own suspicions that they were somehow related to the transport of human souls. Small, plump red sparrows flew past him busily and Christoph remembered his mother once telling him a Native American myth about how they carried the souls of the dead from one point to another. He stared at one in particular and cocked his head as he watched its short tail and stubby beak as it ate seeds from the floor. Hearing his mother's voice as she told him how unlucky it was to kill one, he walked faster still.

A crow swooped down close to his ear, making him jump shamelessly. Landing beside him with something clenched in its jaw, it looked up and met Christoph's eyes with a questioning stare. He couldn't help but pay attention to its unnerving bird call as it seemed to be trying to communicate something to him. When he bent down for a closer look, he could see the dead carcass that was clamped mercilessly in its beak and he noticed it was still squirming. Christoph backed away before it decided to make dessert of his nose but just as he straightened himself, a dark brown vulture with a bald neck and head whizzed by. He could feel its plumage as it brushed his face and its hard gaze seemed to look right through him. He found it somewhat intimidating with its powerfully hooked beak and wrinkled pink skin and clearly remembered seeing one just as close on a battlefield hundreds of years before as it feasted on the decaying flesh of someone very close to him. Dubbed the guardians of the wisdom of life and death, humans were right to regard them with fear. It had been said that two giant vultures stood guard at the gates of hell and he knew their presence was a bad sign.

Fortunately, Christoph saw a door at the end of the hallway and he sped up as he made his way toward it. As he touched the handle, a dove with downy wings of white, like those of an angel, perched itself on top of his hand. It looked up at him with a knowingness that he seemed to understand and on a level he couldn't quite reach. Though he knew its presence was also associated with death, he also knew the peaceful bird was said to be the messenger of departed souls and was somehow related to life, luck, and love. Just as the vulture brought forth thoughts of dying flesh and bad omens, the dove was pure and wise and above reproach and he felt that their connection at the end of the room was somehow special. When they made eye contact, he saw love emanating from its eyes and it filled him with the strength and courage he needed to continue the rest of his journey. Christoph petted it softly with his other hand and smiled for the first time since entering the bizarre room. The dove fluttered its wings and hovered for a moment before flying off again. He opened the door and stepped into the next room, knowing instinctively it would be the last one he would enter.

The room was dark but Christoph's night vision allowed for him to see what the human eye would not be able to. The large canopied bed at the far end told him that it was a bedroom and instinct told him it belonged to Lucius himself; he knew the headmaster was probably watching him from one of the dark corners, if not from some hidden beam in the ceiling. Of all the intriguing items he could focus his vision on, there was one wall in particular that called out to him and Christoph found himself gravitating toward it before he had even made the conscious decision to do so.

He made his way to the far wall, drawn by the many artifacts that adorned it. His solemn thoughts treaded down the road of his memories as he studied the various items and he realized that each piece reflected different periods in history. Deep within the annals of Christoph's mind, he smiled a knowing smile because he knew the stories behind most of them.

Crossing the distance from the door to the wall, he finally stopped before it and his roving gaze stopped on a cutlass that brought forth visions of a pirate in a stance of pending attack. Christoph remembered how the weapon had been perfect for the close man-to-man fighting necessary on a ship and he grinned at the memory. When his gaze shifted to a long sword alongside a mace, he envisioned an armored knight on horse, striking at his enemies with devastating effect. Beside it was a short stabbing spear, a battle axe, a long bow, and a cavalry saber.

The entire wall was a history of man's killing prowess and Christoph felt the same fill of pride looking at them as he knew Lucius must have felt hanging them.

The next wall displayed the shields that he himself had utilized as a soldier, protecting the brothers to his left as he wreaked bloody havoc on anyone who dared come at him. Though the recollections were jarring, nothing shook him like the Roman soldier's battle dress, which his eyes stopped on abruptly. A bronze, leather helmet, a bright red crest, and a leather tunic with an interwoven breast threw his memory into overtime and Christoph reached out to feel the scales that overlapped the fabric. Running a finger down the iron breast plate that had been necessary to prevent a killing thrust to the torso, he remembered details about the old battles that he thought were long forgotten. He reached out to reverently caress a scabbarded Gladius and his thoughts ran away from him; a thousand miles and three thousand years away from the spot he stood in.

"Ever the sentimental soldier, huh Christoph?"

The feeling that Lucius' voice instilled within him was indescribable. A mixture of warmth, joy, respect, and fear overcame him and filled him with the same awe that it always had. It had been over fifty years since he had heard it until earlier in the forest when he had pulled up to them in a Spyder and started spewing ridiculous theories about egg measurements. When he found his own voice, Christoph responded.

"Ever the strategist, huh, Lucius?" he replied as he turned to face his maker.

Lucius walked toward him with the easy style of old world grace and confidence that belonged to the immortal. He stopped before him and stared intensely with his dark eyes. Though the lights were off, they could see each other clearly through a different kind of vision that he had never known as a human.

"It's been a long time since we last met," Christoph continued. "You're looking well."

Lucius' eyes continued to hold his stare but slowly, a smile began to spread across his face.

"Long only to a mortal who measures his life by mere heartbeats," the master finally responded.

He reached out and took Christoph's arm in the Legionnaire grip, with hands clasped to each other's forearms. He then pulled him close for a long and sincere embrace before speaking again.

"Come," Lucius said, his own voice warm and friendly. "We've much to catch up on including how you've come into association with this motley crew you're traveling with."

Lucius strode purposefully from the chamber and toward the shadows from which he had emerged and as Christoph followed him into the darkness, he thought about the Roman uniform proudly displayed on the wall behind them. It had belonged to him and had been the same one he had worn on the fateful day so long before when he had first met his maker on the same day of his rebirth. Memories of his last day as a human swarmed his heart and his mind and Christoph fell into a reverie that he could not control.

Bleeding beside his tent after an ambush that had taken down his entire unit, he remembered lying immobile as he stared out at the campfires, as numerous as the stars in the sky, and he recalled feeling the enemy's hatred like a palpable entity. They had been hardened, grim-eyed men with superior armor and weapons along with the most disciplined training in the world and their sudden attack had been his final one; until Lucius had come along baring incisors, he had heard rumor of but never seen. Christoph remembered how he had stifled a gasp at the sight, even as he lay on the ground, broken and dying.

Though filled with terror, he had reached his hand out to Lucius weakly and had tried to speak. The vampire, having fallen to his knees, had pulled him into his arms and cradled him to his chest all the while staring deeply into his dying eyes. With all of his strength, Christoph had whispered to him with his last breath and in a voice no louder than a butterfly's wings.

"I don't want this."

Without explanation for why he had chosen Christoph, Lucius spoke in a calm voice that contradicted his monstrous appearance.

"You will come to accept this one day, Christoph."

He had remembered wondering how the vampire even knew his name but had been too weak to ask. He could only listen and absorb the words that would never, no matter how many years he had lived, escape his memory.

"I don't…want, , , this."

"You will grow to love your new existence and to see me as your family. I will do this with or without your permission but I prefer to have your blessing. Give it to me now, before it's too late."

"No… don't…"

He remembered how the master's eyes shone with determination as his fangs lengthened and gleamed in the night.

"I'm sorry," Lucius had said. "I apologize not for taking you because you are a great and noble man but I apologize a million times over that you did not ask me for it."

And with that, he had lowered his mouth to Christoph's neck.

"I remember that night as clearly as you do," Lucius said, reading his thoughts. His tone was gentle but his presence remained as powerful as it always had.

"Yes," Christoph answered. "I'm sure you do."

"Please sit, sit," Lucius insisted, gesturing a hand toward an uncomfortable looking wicker chair that had already begun rocking by itself. "Make yourself comfortable."

"Thank you."

Christoph sat on black satin pillow as he scanned the room with his peripheral vision.

"You've had a rough night."

"I've had better," Christoph admitted.

'The loss of a friend is never easy," Lucius replied with meaning he understood all too well. "Why have you stayed away for so long? Do you not miss the great times we shared? The wars, the plague, the hunting… the satisfaction of feasting off the humans after we'd worked so hard to secure them for ourselves? You've been gone for fifty years!"

"I know," Christoph replied wistfully. "And I must admit that I do miss our camaraderie but. . . . I told you long ago that I did not want this for myself. I simply don't enjoy human pain and suffering as you do and I never will."

"Such the softie!" laughed Lucius. "I had believed that our years together would have cured you of such... 'sensitivity' toward the humans."

"Is that why you cursed me with this... this empathy? This affliction to feel their pain and their fear every moment of my existence?"

"Well," the master answered, "that and the inability to die; but why do you see it a curse?" the master asked. "You spurned my gifts and my offerings for their sake so I thought it only right to give you what you wanted. Complete and total dedication to their ridiculous thoughts and their pointless feelings! Do you now regret having chosen their species over your own? Over me?"

"I have the utmost respect for you, Lucius. Not to mention a bond of brotherhood. I did not choose them over you. I chose good over evil and that has not changed. It never will."

Lucius shook his head and appeared vulnerable to Christoph for the first time in their history together. Dropping himself into the seat beside his charge, the master dropped his sarcasm before speaking again.

"Ah... that old insolence of yours... the same reason I chose you to begin with," Lucius explained, not for the first time. "As well as your dedication, your strength, your nobility, your courage in the face of terror... I knew you would be the perfect partner for eternity and I do not regret my decision, not a day of it. Until now, that is."

"Why now?"

"Is it not your wish to leave me forever?" Lucius asked accusingly. "And not just for a spell or a generation to gather your thoughts…?"

"It is indeed my wish," Christoph answered. "I am finished here. I have been for a long time."

"Even if I remove your empathic powers?" the master tried in vain. "You will not reconsider then?"

"No," he replied sadly. "I will not reconsider and for every moment that you keep me here against my will, I will despise you that much more. It is not fair to force me to continue with an existence I do not want just because you are lonely for a friend!"

"Do not disrespect me!"

His angry tone halted the movement of the strange tanked creatures and disgusting rats at once. Christoph noticed how his master's chest rose and fell and he watched as his fangs grew and sharpened without warning. But when Lucius spoke again, his voice was calm and his tone had softened.

"You are my brother, Christoph," he said. "You are my son and yes… you are my friend," the master returned with pain evident in his black eyes. "Have you forgotten everything that I once meant to you?"

"Of course not! I will never forget but I beg of you… don't keep me here one day longer."

"But what of your new family?" Lucius asked. "Don't they need you? Don't they… love you?"

Christoph smiled.

"That's the first time you've ever admitted that we are still capable of such emotion," he said to the headmaster. "Thank you for such acknowledgement."

"You're in great pain, Christoph," he answered. "Though I do not have your powers of empathy, I can still feel it and I do not wish for it to continue."

Christoph felt a surge of hope at the master's words. He knew in that moment that his maker would allow him to die and the respect and affection he had once felt for him came flooding back without restraint.

"You have brought me a gift, have you not?" asked Lucius. He had given all the permission that he was going to and the change of subject told Christoph that his beautiful end was finally near.

"You mean Dominic?" he asked the master. "How did you know?"

"I've had Stephan follow you since you left your little hut in New York City," he answered. "But even if I hadn't, I have a telepathic link to you greater than any I've ever known with anyone else. Why, may I ask, do you believe that your new 'leader' would be of any interest to me?"

"In all of my travels, I have never met another of his kind. He reminds me of… of me, and of you. He understands the humans and the vampires alike. He is steadfast in his beliefs and he is more courageous than anyone I've known throughout all of my years. You would be lucky to have him in your counsel."

"Aaahh… but you don't know my plans, Christoph. Perhaps that is not what I am looking for any longer."

"Don't harm him, Lucius," he warned. "Neither he nor Raina."

"Would you sacrifice your own request to spare them my wrath?"

"I would," answered Christoph. "Though I am hoping that our history together will not require such a decision on my part."

"I told you," Lucius said. "I will not keep you here any longer. And I will allow Dominic to create his own path, just as I did with your other friends. He will be given a choice and I will trust your judgment, just as I've always trusted you. That is all you need to know."

"And Raina?" Christoph asked. "You will give her the same, even though she is a female?"

"Yes," Lucius smiled. "And Raina too. Though I do believe that their decisions might somehow become intertwined. For the life of me, I will never understand how you have all managed to hold onto your humanity without the presence of a soul, but the fact that you all have tells me all I need to know."

"I do warn you," Christoph added. "Dominic is righteous and noble. While he is capable of the brand of viciousness you covet, he holds tight to such qualities and will fight you to the death over his beliefs. He will take down the unworthy in ways that would make even you blush but he will not pursue the innocent, just as I wouldn't."

"That's why you brought him to me, I am sure," the headmaster grinned. "You know how I love a challenge."

Christoph did not answer. He simply took hold of his maker's hands and thanked him with his eyes.

"Will you allow me to make my wish now?" he asked softly.

"I know your wish already. You need not say it aloud. It will only hurt me more."

"I don't wish to be insensitive, Lucius. I do appreciate the life you have given me and the gifts you have offered to me. I know that our time together was truly my destiny, as is this moment, and this decision right now."

The master nodded and then bowed his head. After a moment of silence, he raised his eyes to Christoph's and spoke to him one more time.

"My forest is beautiful, is it not?"

"It is quite beautiful."

"Though I've never been able to enjoy it in the sunlight, I hear it's quite remarkable in the daytime."

Knowing where his maker was headed, Christoph's excitement felt close to bursting and he was more ready than he had ever been to watch the sun rise, just one more time.

"Take the tunnel," Lucius said. "Your way back will not be hindered by the birds or the pixies or anything else. It is just a long peaceful walk that will end in the heart of the forest. There's a tree that I especially like to sit beneath… perhaps you will find it and enjoy it as I always have."

Christoph jumped up from the chair and saluted his maker excitedly.

"I will find your tree and I will never regret a moment of my time here," he said, feeling both elated and sad at once. "And as the sun rises, I will focus my thoughts on our time together before I transport my mind back to the battlefield where I should have died. I cannot thank you enough… for everything, for all of it."

"Enough of this sentiment!" Lucius said. "I have business to tend to."

Standing before his charge one last time, he pointed toward the door Christoph had entered before speaking to him one last time.

"Goodbye, Christoph," he said. "I do hope you find the peace that you deserve."

Christoph headed to the door as elation filled him with every step. Unable to shake his smile, he reached for the doorknob and turned backwards for one final look at his maker and he spoke his last words to the vampire who had turned him so many years before.

"Take care of my friends."

Lucius answered with a nod and a wave as he watched Christoph walk out the door for the very last time.

Chapter XXIV

When they entered the bedroom, Raina and Dominic immediately sensed Jarek's presence. It felt heavy, as though he was still there somehow and Raina played with the idea of curling up in a corner and never leaving. Rats screeched at them from the corner and meat hooks swung from the ceiling, hinting at the possibility of a torturous experience. After a few moments, Raina found the courage to let go of Dominic's hand and walk through the room unassisted.

"Don't go far," he warned.

"Does it really matter at this point, Dom?" she asked sadly as she turned back to face him.

"Of course it does."

He moved forward to meet her at her chosen spot in the middle of the room and called out to the walls as though checking out a theory.

"Hello!" (Hello, Hello!)

They listened to his voice echo off the walls and bounce back at them but neither of them acknowledged it out loud. They just continued to circle the room and hoped their growing anxieties wouldn't blossom into pure terror.

"We're still here, aren't we?" he asked her softly.

"Yeah, but why?" she asked, distracted by a tiger head that was mounted on the far wall.

"What do you mean?"

"I mean, why are we still alive?"

Dominic knew that her curiosity was increasing when she started shifting her weight from one foot to the other and twisting thick clumps of hair through her nervous fingers. His stomach lurched and his hands began to sweat because he knew that once sparked, Raina's interest would not wane until she'd found whatever answer she was seeking, no matter how detrimental it might be to the both of them.

"I don't care how lucky or skilled we are, Dom. If they wanted us dead, it would have happened already." Her vocal chords stopped working when visions of her fallen pack marched by one by one. "Like them," she added.

She diverted her own attention from the unwanted images by staring at the canopied bed by the door they had entered. Wondering if Lucius were watching them, she felt a chill rush down her spine and she shivered visibly. Stephan entered her thoughts and she felt herself become more alive and energized by vivid fantasies of spearing him through the heart. She grinned at the thought of his blood dripping from her hands and looked forward to waving goodbye to his wicked soul as it floated past her on its way to hell.

Stephan's face morphed into Leo's and she began to understand his desperate need for retribution. Though her rage continued to grow, she was glad for it. Anger trumped sadness and it was a trade she was more than happy to make.

As she paced the floor, it didn't escape her attention that Dominic never strayed more than three steps behind her no matter how fast or slow she went. Raina heard the ding of an invisible timer and knew the time had come to face some important truths.

"Dom?" she asked hesitantly.

"Yes?"

"Can I ask you a question that you have to be completely honest answering?"

Dominic glanced back toward the door hoping that someone would interrupt but it remained closed and the question still hung heavy in the air. Settling his eyes back on Raina, he accepted that the time had come to have the conversation.

"Shoot," he answered after a long pause.

"Why did you choose the pack over me?" she finally braved.

He stepped forward to close the small gap between them and caressed her cheek with his hand.

"I chose the pack for you, Raina," he answered in a tone that insinuated he had spoken the words many times.

Her eyebrows lifted slowly and she raised her own hand to touch the one on her cheek.

"What do you mean?"

"Think about it," he explained. "What would happen to you if you had another leader?"

Without considering the question, she jumped at the only answer she had ever allowed to enter her heart and mind.

"We would have been able to stay together, that's what would have happened!" she answered furiously.

"No," he said as he shook his head vehemently and backed up. "We wouldn't. You would have belonged to him and would have lost all opportunity for freedom and purpose, like one of Stephan's pixies! They would have forced you into the darkness and there wouldn't have been anything you could do about it. When they started moving in closer and demanding our status, it was the only decision there was to make; why can't you just understand that?"

Dominic's head fall back and he stared at the ceiling, exasperated.

She stared at him blankly as she processed his words. He had tried to explain before but she hadn't wanted to hear it. Betrayal and resentment had taken on lives of their own the moment he had ended their relationship and she had allowed the anger to block the truth from herself. A sick sensation of shame began to swim through her bloodstream and crawl under her skin. She had turned on him after he had kept them together and saved her life. Raina bowed her head and spoke softly.

"I'm sorry."

"I know but I don't want your remorse," he said. "I just want your understanding."

She reached toward his ear to curl a stray piece of hair around it and thought about how hard it must have been for him to see her with Jarek. Feeling a rush of gratitude for his sacrifices, she spoke to him from the heart.

"You are a true leader, you know that?" she asked.

Just as his smile began to widen, the door creaked open and Lucius walked in. His slicked back hairstyle and burgundy smoking jacket were a sharp contrast to his earlier appearance but neither of them was shocked. It was only appropriate for him to appear as powerful as he really was and Raina appreciated that he had taken his mask off.

"Good evening," his voice rumbled.

The greeting sounded smooth and comforting as he guided them toward a black sofa that sat caddy corner from the hooks.

"Please, sit down with me," he said. "Take a load off."

Raina glanced at Dominic nervously but didn't wait for his permission to speak. He knew that her time had come and that the internal silence meant he was giving her permission to make her own decisions.

"Where's Christoph?" she asked, turning back to Lucius.

"Christoph is off to find greener pastures," he answered softly, and there was sadness about the headmaster that surprised them both.

"Will we see him again?" Raina asked in held breath.

"Not in this lifetime, beautiful lady," he answered as he bowed his head.

She felt a shock of pain shoot through her heart that the world no longer contained her friend and recoiled slightly when the master's head came back up suddenly. Regaining his zest as quickly as he had lost it, Lucius slapped his hands together and moved closer toward her.

"Raina," Lucius began slowly. "What do you remember about your turning? I want you to really try to remember. Come now, close your eyes and think."

Raina complied without argument or words. She squeezed her eyes tightly and pictured herself as she'd been on her last night as a human. The memories that had always eluded her flew from her mind faster than she could process them. She slowed down the images and tried to look at each one in order so that it would tell her the story she'd forgotten.

She remembered the apartment where she had lived alone and where she had wished every single night for something different. On the lonelier nights, she would talk to herself in the mirror because she had withdrawn from her friends and her family and anyone who might end up caring about her. The trials and tribulations of her humanity had pained her on so many levels that she had secretly wished to become someone else.

One night she closed her eyes to a cold and empty apartment and had reopened them to discover she was not alone. The sound of movement had awakened her and, when she sat up straight and alert, she saw a silhouette swaying in the shadows. Raina had called out to the figure but there had been no answer and when it flew at her from across the room, she had raised both arms too late to block the attack. The intruder had pulled them apart without effort and had plunged his teeth into her neck with ferocity.

Raina remembered lying on her bed half naked and with nothing but her own blood to keep her warm. She had experienced a fever higher than she'd ever known and had continued to fall in and out of consciousness for hours. At times, she would open her eyes to find the silhouette running a finger down the length of her body and though she had tried to push him away, his sickly presence stayed to drain her of herself even more. It had been the most horrifying part of her strangely evolving reality and had been enough to convince her that the only way of survival was to run and hide.

It had been difficult because recovery was a slow process but during one of her maker's infrequent absences, Raina had gathered enough lucidity and strength to take advantage of the moment. Though teased by her new abilities with small bursts of intense energy, her escape had been weak but she had made it out of view before his next arrival. Fleeing as far as she could go, Raina found herself alone and confused in a nightclub in Lansing, Michigan.

Drawn to the stage, she had pushed her way through the inebriated crowd and hadn't stopped until she was directly in front of Dominic. Watching him hypnotize the fans with his voice and mesmerize them with his music was the first moment of comfort she had experienced since her turning. After the show, she had caught him backstage and offered him a deal that he did not refuse and together, they built a family. Had Raina foreseen that he would one day be forced to leave her in order to save her, she wasn't sure she would have made the same choice. She opened her eyes and looked at Lucius without expression.

"You can't turn me back, can you?" she asked solemnly.

He shook his head gently.

"No, dear lady, I can't. I'm sorry. That is a job that only God can do."

Raina stood up, sturdy, accepting and filled with a new awareness.

"The silhouette… in my room," she said to Lucius.

He hadn't yet moved away from her because he knew she wasn't finished. There was one more piece of business for her to tend to and he knew it was necessary for her to move on.

"Yes?" he asked her.

"It was Stephan, wasn't it?"

He nodded.

"It was."

Raina felt a sense of absolution and of closure but also of a new beginning. She had hated Stephan in the forest and had despised him even more in the upstairs bedroom. She had loathed every fiber of his being in the forest but nothing compared to the ire she experienced at the knowledge that it had been him that turned her. Raina understood Leo in that moment more than she ever had

"Where's the mirror I gave you?" Lucius asked, his tone upbeat and excited. "Do you still have it?"

"Yes," she answered quickly and slipped it out from the inner pocket of her long cape. She had held onto it throughout her escape from Stephan, despite her falls to the ground and pondered its purpose during her trek back to the mansion, knowing it would come into play somehow. Raina held it out to Lucius but he held up a hand to say that he did not want it for himself.

"What do mirrors reflect, Raina?" he asked.

"Our faces?" she asked.

"Is that all?"

She glanced over at Dominic but he turned away from her to let her know that he would not intervene in her moment, even if she wanted him to. He leaned his back against the wall and looked around the room knowing that if he made eye contact, she would draw him in and make him part of something that had been meant for just her. He didn't turn back to her until he saw with his peripheral vision that she returned her attention to Lucius.

"We see ourselves," she tried again. "Our eyes, our lips, our hair, our skin..."

"Is that what you miss about yourself so much?" Lucius asked as he pulled the mirror gently from her hand after all. "Your skin and your eyes and your hair?"

"No," she answered quietly.

"Then what is it you miss the most about looking in a mirror?"

She was quiet for a moment as she thought about her answer. Visualizing her own eyes as she remembered them, she could still see the blue hue that more often than not changed to green or gray, depending on her mood. When she would look at them in the mirror, they would remind her she was unique. Through them, she could see her smile and share in the happy moment with herself. When sad, she could look upon herself in consolation and watch her own tears as they fell from her eyes and when she was angry, she could use her own enchanting stare to calm herself down. But when the tiny lines began to form the road map of her life upon her face, Raina hadn't been prepared to watch them deepen and she had always felt that because she hadn't fought off her maker with more vigor, she had taken part in the destruction of her soul. It wasn't until she could no longer look at her own face that she realized it wasn't just the features that she missed reflecting back from the glass but also her spirit and her mortality. The sight of her own image had been the biggest piece of proof that she was a human and that had been the greatest gift of all. She just hadn't known it until it was gone.

Raina reached for the mirror that Lucius held out to her and looked directly into it.

"The truth," she finally answered. "I miss seeing the truth of who I am."

"Are you ready to see the truth now, my dear girl?"

Raina's heart pounded with the possibility of seeing herself again. Curling her fingers around the handle, she looked into Lucius' eyes with appreciation and then she held the mirror out before her. Though her face didn't appear immediately, she could see that an image was trying to form itself from somewhere beyond the glass and though it alarmed her, she did not turn away. As it melded slowly together, the morphing image took on a face with clearer features and Raina experienced a rush of familiarity and affection. It was not her red hair or her pale skin or her penetrating eyes that stared back; it was Sam. She squinted to look deeper into the face of her beloved entity and then relaxed her eyes again as his features transformed themselves into another person entirely. First, he changed into Lucille Ball and then just as quickly Joan Crawford stared back at her with a warm and empathetic smile.

Finally tearing her attention from the images, she looked back into Lucius' eyes.

"I don't understand," she said.

"What's not to understand?" he chuckled. "They're you. They always have been."

"What do you mean?" she asked as nervousness and excitement collided inside of her.

Awareness settled in with his words and Raina understood what he was telling her. The spirit she had been visited and comforted by had been real but it hadn't been who she thought it was. The humor she had always relied upon to pull her through her most difficult moments had manifested itself into the image of Lucille Ball. The part that protected her, the one that she had always counted on to manipulate and convince and enchant, had transformed into the image of Joan Crawford. As a child, Raina had absorbed her mother's admiration for Sam Elliot and the warmth she had felt toward him had never left her. The knowledge that she had never been separated from her soul forced Raina's priorities to quickly reorganize themselves and the sensation was jarring. She closed her lids and tried to remind her heart to beat. When she reopened her eyes, she found herself looking back into those very eyes for the first time in almost twenty years.

They shone with the happiness of one who had just been reunited with an old friend after a long and unwanted separation. Raina's gaze fell to her lips and she watched them tug at both sides as they formed into a grin. It traveled to her nose and to her cheeks and to her hair and to her chin as she tried to drink herself in before her reflection faded away forever. A laugh escaped without her knowledge and when she looked down, she almost expected to find her feet nestled into ruby slippers. Raina clicked her heels, just in case.

"Does this mean?"

"What, my dear?"

"Am I... human?"

Lucius pulled her hands into his and gave her a sympathetic smile. Glancing over at Dominic, he sent him the message to intervene just enough to offer her the support she might need. He complied without hesitation and walked over to stand closer to her.

Grabbing Lucius by the hand, she spoke her words carefully.

"Do I still get a wish?"

"By all means," he answered. "But you must be careful."

"Of what?" she asked.

"Of what you wish for."

"With all due respect," she said firmly. "I haven't been this sure about anything in a very long time."

He guided her toward the tiger and Raina could see Jarek reflected in its eyes, so she allowed herself to absorb his essence.

"Look into the eyes, Raina. Don't interrupt yourself and don't turn away until you're finished or you will lose your chance."

"He did this too, didn't he?" she asked Lucius without turning from the tiger.

"He did."

"He gave up his wish for me, didn't he?"

Lucius didn't answer but he didn't need to. She knew exactly what had happened and she looked over to Dominic for support. He winked at her and she turned her attention back to the tiger.

Inside of its eyes, she saw the faces of her fallen pack as they had been on the roadtrip. Leo, with his face pressed to the car window as he looked for something to be angry with. Christoph eyeing every highway sign in search of a McDonald's and Jarek running his fingers through her hair as she napped on his lap. She knew that she hadn't lost her humanity because she hadn't lost her ability to love and hadn't lost herself in the darkness.

Raina lowered herself to meet the tiger's glare on an even level and she spoke her wish clearly and without interruption before walking to stand beside Dominic. She pulled his hand into hers and looked up at him with newfound motivation and purpose.

"Your turn," she whispered.

Chapter XXV

Lucius saw the apprehensive expression on Dominic's face.

"What troubles your heart, my boy?" he asked gently.

"Many things, sir," Dominic answered. "At the moment, getting Raina and me out of here safely seems to be sitting at the top of the list."

"Of course," Lucius replied as he patted Dominic on the back. "You felt the same protection for the others, I gather?"

"Yes, sir," he answered against a shock of pain and guilt. He was trying hard to not allow the grief to overwhelm him before they made it out safely. "I came on this trip prepared to give my life for all of them if necessary."

"And you?" Lucius inquired with curiosity that may have been real or may have been feigned as the headmaster seemed to know a great deal more than he should already. "What did you want for yourself from this great venture?"

Dominic's eyes darted toward Raina but he glanced away just as quickly. Standing finally in the spot he had waited so long to stand in, he found that he was still uncertain of the answer himself.

"I don't know," he began. "I guess I wanted to make sure my pack made it to you safely and away from you alive."

"Ah… just the noble kind of answer I had expected," Lucius replied. "But tell me… what bothers you the most about your own life, about your own turning… about this new existence that you've found yourself living?"

Dominic considered the question carefully so that he could give both the master and himself a truthful answer.

"I worry that because of my immortality, I will I never know my true purpose."

"And you believe that your human life would have answered this for you?"

Shaking his head back and forth to signify his ambivalence, Dominic answered the best he could.

"Maybe? Yes? I don't know…."

"Well," Lucius pushed gently. "Did you know your purpose when you were a human?"

Dominic envisioned himself on stage, looking out at the excited crowd as they screamed his own lyrics at him.

"I thought I did," he answered.

"Yet upon your turning, you did not abandon what was in your heart, did you? You found a way to bring it with you. You allowed it to breathe life into you and to simulate the soul you had lost. This is very rare, Dominic," he commended before switching back to the interrogation again. "What have you found to be your greatest loss because of your turning?"

"Knowing that no answer will be provided at the end," Dominic answered. "The humans are gifted with all of the answers upon their death. As much as they fear an end to the only life they know, they are still rewarded with that place and that time when their purpose is disclosed to them."

"Do you know that for certain?" Lucius asked, somewhat amused.

"We both know He's there," Dominic said, gesturing his eyes upward. "They get their own Supreme Being who will take them under His wing when they're finished here… all that clarity and all that comfort, denied to us simply for the sin of our existence. Maybe I feel cheated that I will never have that for myself now."

Lucius laughed softly.

"Are you sure that's how it happens? That He doesn't simply toss them back onto the earth in a new body to start all over again?" he asked. "Repeatedly perhaps, until they come to determine their own purpose?"

Dominic answered honestly.

"I'm not sure of anything anymore."

"Your immortality gives you the chance to determine the purpose of your life while you're still living it, while you can still do something to change it," Lucius explained. "It gives you protection from God's wrath and His vengeance and His cruel sentencing guidelines."

Dominic wasn't sure what to say or think but he felt a frown furrow its way into his eyebrow.

"But this life makes us slaves to him," Dominic answered firmly as his eyes gestured downwards in reference to hell and its king.

"Would you rather be his slave here on earth… where you are given the ability and the freedom to enjoy his offerings? Or down there, on his turf, living out only the consequences of your temptations and none of the pleasures?"

"But partnering up with Satan feels… wrong!"

"Why?"

"Because… I was always taught he was the enemy."

"My point precisely, Dominic," he answered, pleased to find an opening in the conversation where his explanation might finally make sense. "Ever hear the saying, 'Keep your friends close and your enemies closer'?"

With that, Lucius stood up and walked over to a modest mahogany dresser that seemed almost lost beside the massive bed. Several photographs lined the sides and corners of the oval mirror attached to it and he just stood staring at them for a long moment. Reaching for one of the photographs, he held it close to his eyes and then pulled it into his chest lovingly. The gesture inspired his guests to move slowly to the right so that they could see his profile but they still gave him the respect of silence, understanding his need to make a connection with the old black and white photo of himself.

Lucius stuck the picture neatly back into its designated spot on the mirror and walked over to the bare gray wall beside it. With a small pump of the fist, the wall slid open and they realized it was actually a door. They also noticed it held a large aquarium behind it and they looked on curiously as bubbles shot out from the small rocks lining the bottom. Unfortunately, it did nothing to block the face of the creature that stared back at them from inside. Though by all accounts it appeared to be a long black, coiled snake, its face was more human than reptile and the combination of its long scaly tail with the expression of understanding in its eyes was unsettling on too many levels to count.

Black coral took up a corner of the watery underworld and a 'no fishing' sign sat right beside it. Larger rocks that had been carefully spread throughout the tank welcomed the eerie creature to swim throughout their deep holes. As though the human serpent wasn't troubling enough, there sat in the far corner on a small, homemade pedestal one lone egg. Lucius lowered himself to peer into the aquarium more closely and when he tapped the glass lightly seemed to connect telepathically with the disturbing creature. It half floated, half slithered to the glass where it pressed its face against it and met the master's gaze with affection in its eyes.

"Humpty Dumpty didn't really sit on a wall, you know," he announced randomly, hands clasped together behind his back.

"I'm sorry, sir?" asked Dominic, slightly worried that the egg obsession had reared its bizarre head again during such an important conversation.

"It was a river," he continued, unaffected by the visible concern of his visitors.

Turning around to face them, he noticed the worried looks on their faces and chuckled before turning back to continue his strange tale.

"In the seventeenth century, during the reign of King Charles I, the king wanted a new weapon," he began, running a finger gently across the glass. "He was solicited by an inventor of war machines who convinced him to experiment with one that had been used on the Romans. Knowing that the River Severn would have to be crossed so that his army could breach the city walls, the inventor realized they would need a wheeled contraption that could roll downhill and gather enough momentum to make it to the other side."

Lucius tapped again on the glass and the simple act sent a message that the snake seemed to understand. As though assisting his master with the narration of the story, it slithered through the water toward the egg and then hovered beside it, as though awaiting further instruction.

"The machine had to be laden with troops for the attack to succeed and news of the plan traveled to the spies," he continued. "By the time the Royalists were ready to launch their new weapon, the enemy had widened the river and when 'Humpty,' as it had been dubbed, was propelled forward, it collapsed mid-stream, drowning many of the king's men."

Raina and Dominic watched in awe as the snake knocked the egg off its pedestal with a swift brush of its long slick tail and a pained expression marking each bizarre feature on its tiny face. The white shell floated for a moment before landing softly on its side upon the aggregate. When satisfied he had fulfilled his master's wish, the snake drifted back to the front of the tank and stared at Lucius longingly through the glass.

Finding he could no longer resist the morbid curiosity, Dominic blurted out the question without first forming the words in his head.

"With all due respect, sir, may I ask… what's with the eggs?"

Lucius laughed heartily and turned to face them while he spoke.

"For any mind to continue its existence without cracking, pardon the pun, it must find ways to find focus beyond what it can see with just its eyes."

Though their expressions belied comprehension of his words, he continued with confidence and ease.

"During childbirth, a woman is encouraged to find a focal point so that she may suffer the pains of labor without concentrating her attentions on the ripping and tearing and stretching of her body. She must find for her mind another plain of existence so the agony does not become too overwhelming."

They nodded their heads in understanding as he painted the picture more clearly.

"Long ago, I realized that such a focal point works also when serving an eternity," he continued. "We all need something to divert our attention away from the suffering and the conflict and the internal demons that threaten our very core."

Dominic thought about music and realized he had done the same thing for himself without knowing it. Raina grabbed the amber at her neck and squeezed it tightly.

"But why eggs?" they asked in unison.

"The egg symbolizes life. Why do you think the church adopted it as a representation of Easter, of the resurrection of their leader?"

He turned back to the waiting snake and tapped again on the tank. The creature's small mouth opened just enough to shoot its tongue out in apparent answer to his silent question. Long and forked, it licked the glass perversely and then swam back to the fallen egg. Using its tail repeatedly and with concentrated rhythm, it worked hard to nudge it back out of the rocks and to right it into its spot on the pedestal. When Lucius began to recite a chant, they kept their eyes on the snake.

"Of Darkness an egg, from the whirlwind conceived,
Was laid by the sable plumed Night.
And out of that egg, as the seasons revolved,
Sprang Love, the entrancing, the bright."

On his last word, the snake successfully pushed the egg back onto its spot and then floated back and forth in front of it, protectively. When Lucius tapped again, it swam to the front and peered through the glass at him with question in its large, round eyes and a sad pucker on its mouth. It appeared expectant, still awaiting further direction.

"The egg represents rebirth in both Pagan and Christian beliefs," he said. "It's one of the only things the two groups have ever agreed upon. Do you know of another, by chance?"

Dominic didn't need to think too hard.

"Music," he grinned.

"That's right," Lucius said proudly. "Though their tastes may differ in regards to lyrics and genre, both groups perceive music as an honorable tribute to their beliefs."

He strode quietly to the other side of the room, removed a screeching rat from its cage, and then walked back to retake his previous position at the tank. Staring at the egg with affection, he continued his explanation.

"The shell is the earth, the membrane the air, the white the water and the yolk, the fire," he said. "All the elements, you see?"

Understanding the master's convoluted words, Raina and Dominic moved forward to stand before the tank with him. They watched as he dropped the squealing rat inside and couldn't remove their eyes, much as they wanted to, when Lucius' reptilian friend stuck its tongue out to ingest the rodent in one bite.

"This is Basilisk," he said by way of an introduction. He is a strange and dangerous beast half serpent and half cockerel. Hatched from the egg of a toad, he is thought by some to be the offspring of the Devil himself and has the reputation to kill by simply breathing upon its prey. But he still has the capacity for love, kind of like you two."

Dominic realized that Lucius was trying to make a point in his comparisons so he cleared his mind of everything to let the moral of the story find its rightful home.

"That egg in the corner," he stated, pointing at it as though his guests didn't already have their eyes glued to it. "She was Basilisk's mate until they were cursed by your loving God and he's waited for her rebirth longer than you have been alive."

The serpent looked up with eyes filled with respect and love. Though it was his long-awaited mate sitting atop the pedestal, he had proven his devotion to his master by knocking her from the safety of her perch to the ground and it spoke volumes of his service and sacrifice. With one more tap of Lucius' pointer finger, it swam back and forth in front of the egg and then wrapped its long body around it protectively.

"One of the most difficult things in our existence is to adapt to the situations forced upon us," Lucius explained. "It was the reason behind Leo's inability to accept his fate and Jarek's inability to conform to the laws devised to guide him."

He glanced over at Raina with a sympathetic look and she bowed her head to stare at the floor instead of him.

"Unfortunately for all of us, it was also the reason that Christoph could not find a way to continue despite the abundance of pleasures that life still had to offer him."

He slid the door closed and it looked like just a bare, gray wall again. Dominic glanced quickly at the other walls and wondered what oddities Lucius hid behind them and then, without knowing it, positioned himself between Raina and the headmaster.

"You have adapted well, Dominic," he complimented. "You not only accepted your fate but you embraced it and looked for ways to continue your new existence without losing your passion or your compassion. You took on the role of leader but not with the same intentions as the others."

Stephan's face jumped into Raina's mind and she pulled her head back up, high and confident.

"You chose to lead for unselfish reasons and you found a way for you and your pack to exist uninterrupted by either the humans or by our kind," Lucius finished, sounding sincerely impressed. "A very difficult task, indeed."

"Thank you," Dominic answered, wondering how Lucius knew all that he knew and surprised at being commended for the same things he thought would bring wrath upon them.

"You did not lose your love for life just because you found yourself looking at it through different eyes. You brought your music into your new world with you and you made it the focal point that would keep you sane and nourished. Those are the qualities of a born leader and because of it I ensured the safety of your journey."

Dominic looked at Raina with raised brows. They had believed that Lucius meant to thwart their success and the revelation that he had actually guided them was more jarring than the headmaster's horrifying pets. It wasn't difficult to believe because it made sense. Lucius could easily have arranged their deaths at the snap of his fingers but instead had given all of them the opportunity to carve out their own destinies.

Lucius walked to stand directly before Dominic and it caused a shiver to run down his spine. He knew that his time had come and he experienced a rush of anxiety. Having waited so long for his own moment of truth, he felt surprised by the sudden urgency of his flight response that begged him to run or crawl or leap away, whichever mode would provide the fastest escape. His fear of the impending moment made him want to catapult himself through the window at a very high speed.

Lucius held out both hands, palms up, in an implied invitation for Dominic to place his own hands upon them. Complying quietly, he flattened his hands upon the master's and did not resist when he felt Lucius hooking him into his own penetrating stare. The headmaster's face became a liquid blur as flashes of a different reality rushed through Dominic's awareness. Snippets of memories, images and visions flew at him and Dominic felt the compulsion to cover his eyes to prevent collision. Suddenly, everything went black and the atmosphere changed drastically. No longer feeling the master's hands beneath his, he let his arms fall down to his sides and stepped back to assess the darkness.

"Hello?" he called out softly.

A dim light clicked on in response and Lucius stood before him smiling, illuminated by the golden light that filled the tunnel in which they were standing. Dominic's eyes darted from left to right and from front to back as he marveled at the hundreds of halogen lamps lining the amber-hued runway. Birds of all types walked or flew in packs of their own and they all appeared to be tending to specific tasks as they moved with efficiency and purpose. Noticing a long, sleek leopard lying against the right side of the tunnel a few feet ahead, Dominic stopped abruptly.

"The Aztecs believed that the leopard was the messenger of forest spirits in eternal struggle with the solar eagle," Lucius informed him. "It's okay; he won't harm you."

Though the leopard continued to lie very still, breathing deeply in apparent slumber, the wild animal's eyes remained open and they stared at Dominic with intensity.

"What is this?" Dominic whispered. "Where are we?"

"Think of this as a very sacred storage facility."

"You're storing animals?" Dominic asked, confused. "Why?"

"Not exactly," Lucius laughed. "Not animals, Dominic, souls. The birds are the pilots, the wardens and the gatekeepers."

"I don't understand," Dominic said as he turned around slowly to take it all in. "Whose souls?"

As they neared the leopard, Dominic switched places with Lucius so that the master would have to walk between him and the animal when they passed. It was the only time in his existence where he hadn't taken the protective stance, but it was because he knew Lucius would not need protection from the beast. He just wasn't so sure about himself.

"Our souls," Lucius answered. "Where do you think they go upon their turning? You didn't think they just disappeared, did you?"

The news jarred him even more because they had reached the leopard and something about the animal made Dominic incredibly nervous. Its untamed eyes bore through him with familiarity that was so potent he knew deep down that it wasn't their first meeting.

"Our souls?" he asked, lacking any real understanding. "They come here? Why?"

"They're waiting," Lucius answered. "Waiting for the day when they will reunite with their bodies."

"You're… imprisoning souls?"

"No, Dominic, not imprisoning," he answered, almost defensively. "Protecting. Souls are extremely valuable and once no longer contained inside the mortal, become very vulnerable to predators."

"Predators?"

"You don't truly believe we're the only ones who covet the spirit?" Lucius whispered.

It was difficult information to process and the news was made no easier by the presence of the leopard that had just risen from his sleep and had begun glaring at his oncoming visitors. The knowledge that Lucius had been storing and protecting souls made Dominic feel new warmth toward him and when the master ended their stroll directly in front of the giant cat, Dominic began to understand that it was meant to become a part of their moment for some reason. The animal gazed up at Dominic and tilted his head as he sized him up.

"Our species relies on the decisions and the protection of our masters; there have been many who do not understand the sanctity of the soul, a fatal flaw that jeopardizes vampires and humans alike," Lucius explained as he shook his head with heavy concern. "We cannot afford to be careless or greedy with such precious cargo. He who guards the souls must remain unwavering in his character and his conviction."

Dominic visualized a horned and homely creature selling off lost souls to an Underworld of abusive masters and he wondered again why Lucius was sharing so much information with him.

"It comforts me to know that such an important job is in your hands then, sir."

"Call me Lucius."

Dominic was shocked. Being asked to address the headmaster by name was an honor and a courtesy he knew was not extended to most; he found it difficult to not obsess over the reasons behind it.

"Thank you," Dominic smiled, "Lucius."

He tried to ignore the leopard that stood upon all fours and continued to stare at him from the other side of Lucius, but he wasn't doing a very good job at it. The cat seemed to be waiting for instruction, just as the human serpent had, and Dominic wondered how the master had come to demand the subservience of so many different species. He diverted himself from the leopard's intimidating presence by maintaining eye contact with Lucius.

"Why… even your soul is here, Dominic," he said in a pensive tone. "It's been here for a long time. How do you think I know so much about you?"

There were no words in Dominic's vocabulary to form an appropriate reply so he stared at the headmaster blankly. As the creeping awareness began to sink in, he started to understand why they had stopped beside the leopard.

Dominic slowly turned his head to face the beast he'd been avoiding and when he met its eyes saw the answer with clarity he couldn't dispute. There emanated love and understanding and intimacy from the animal's stare and when he reached out to touch its silky fur, the leopard nuzzled his hand gently.

"Oh my God," Dominic finally said.

"Interesting choice of words," Lucius smiled. "I've known you for awhile now, Dominic. You came to my attention through your music. Every note… every lyric… every strum of your guitar could be heard and felt right here."

Lucius placed a hand on the leopard's head, beside the one Dominic still used to caress it.

"And right here," the headmaster added, flattening his hand upon its soft chest. "I've never seen it before, this continued connection between a soul and a body. Your music affected him just as it affected you and I knew that you had somehow bridged the gap between the two worlds in a way that I had never been able to do myself. When I sought you out and found that Christoph had somehow become a part of your pack, it was when I knew…."

"Knew what?" asked Dominic, still mesmerized by the eyes of the leopard, of himself.

"Let's keep walking for awhile," Lucius suggested as he bowed his head slightly and continued forward. Dominic followed but he kept his hand on the leopard's head until the increasing distance no longer allowed it. They reached the end of the tunnel and when the ground changed from runway to road, Dominic became dizzy from the lack of mental preparation. Looking around, he realized they were on the street he had grown up on and he ran excitedly to the small, familiar house on the left.

Changing his mind at the front door, he jogged back down the small stoop and raced to the window instead. When he peeked through a small opening in the curtains, he watched a tow-headed boy of about five years as he played on the living room floor with miniature cars and Star Wars action figures. Switching back and forth excitedly from one game to the next, Dominic knew what the boy was thinking. Choosing one toy would force him to ignore the other and it was a prospect that was unacceptable to him. Even as a child, he had wanted it all and had gone to great pains finding ways to make it work for himself.

Seeing himself so small and so human made Dominic's stomach drop. There was a part of him that longed to run into the house so that he could play with the cars and the action figures and the boy who would one day grow to become a vampire. Turning away from the window, he looked out at Lucius who stood in wait at the sidewalk.

"Why are we here?" he asked him.

"You need to remember all of it before making your decision."

"What decision?" Dominic asked, mildly annoyed with the cryptic suggestion.

"Come now," advised Lucius, guiding him to the end of the short street and turning the corner to another world entirely.

There were no more houses or yards or busy boys to occupy his attention. They had stumbled into a club in a world twenty years from the last one and they were squashed uncomfortably among a crowd of singing and screaming fans. He didn't have to look up to know that it was Eight Ball Grifter rocking out the eerie melodies and that it was his own voice screaming the haunting lyrics into the mic. His buddies backed up his every word with thunderous drums and guitar and he tried to whisper to their minds how proud he truly was of them. Smiles on their sweating faces and confidence in their movements, his boys played together, combining their talents into music that would remain forever branded into the hearts of their fans.

Dominic felt the same magnetic draw that he always experienced in the face of his greatest passion. He wanted to stay there for as long as possible but Lucius was already tugging at him to leave and he knew that his only choice was to follow. Pushing their way through the crowd, an annoyed fan threw a dirty look their way for blocking his view and Dominic wanted to scream at him.

"That's me!" he heard inside of his own mind. "That's me you're worshipping!"

He experienced the same pang of envy that he had so many times in the past. It had been the worst kind of envy because it was envy of himself – for the god that he was onstage before the regular man that he would be forced to transform back into after the songs and the party ended. Dominic had wanted to keep that feeling forever and it had remained his greatest inspiration for the trip. Knowing that his journey with Lucius had not ended though, he knew he would have to push that feeling aside for another time. Dominic inhaled deeply and walked quickly out the side exit door with Lucius in tow. When he turned back for one last look, he noticed the back of a woman standing at the front of the crowd. As she stared up at him, Dominic felt a rush of warmth to see her familiar movements and the telltale bounce of her long red hair because he knew that he was looking at Raina and himself on the night of his turning.

Once outside again, a new world appeared to them; another street… but this one much more recent. The house that beckoned him was his own New York home where he had left for a roadtrip with his pack of misfits only days before. Dominic's first impulse was to race through the front door to share his adventures with his family and the reminder of their losses made his heart lurch from grief. It only intensified when the door opened and his pack walked outside, dragging luggage behind them and carrying totes on their backs. They walked in the same fashion they had in their real lives: Jarek at the front, Christoph in the middle, and Leo at the back. He knew that he and Raina were not with them because this was not a memory as the others had been.

As they packed the car, each of them sent him a message… a goodbye. Christoph threw him a wide smile and a small wave before opening the passenger door and disappearing inside. The last Dominic saw of him was the hand that reached out to pull the door shut. Jarek gave him a knowing wink and yelled something to a trailing Leo before jumping inside and taking the wheel. After an entertaining and angry stride to the trunk, Leo carelessly tossed the last of their bags in and then slammed the trunk shut with the loud bang he had always enjoyed. His small friend turned around with a pointed salute before crawling into the backseat to travel with his fallen brothers to places unknown. Though he knew it was another roadtrip they were destined to take, he didn't want to watch them leave.

Dominic took the lead as they walked to the end of the street and Lucius followed closely behind. Though they didn't speak, he knew instinctively that the next turn was to be their last and he became panicked at the possibilities. Feeling the change in atmosphere as soon as they made the next turn, Dominic could sense immediately that their new world was to be darker than the last few. Dusk had fallen and the sky was dim but the whole world was made blacker by the sin and temptation that permeated the air. Dominic suddenly felt ravenous.

Though he tried to stave off the increasing need, he discovered that it was too powerful to diffuse. His incisors, nails and hair began to grow despite all attempts to stop the process. Fresh and innocent blood wafted toward him from someplace close by and it caused the need to squeeze him in its sickening grip and demand for immediate gratification.

Standing beneath a flickering streetlight, adjacent to the worn edges of the sidewalk, a girl in her mid-twenties stood shivering, undoubtedly paralyzed by Lucius' power. The rapid changes to his physical existence and the timely placement of the innocent before him told Dominic that this would be his test – or at least part of it.

His hand reached out for her but the will that still fought from within stopped it before he touched her face. Dominic backed away two steps and the simple act of retreat caused his stomach to feel as though an ice pick had penetrated his abdomen. As the pain grew stronger, his hunger became an afterthought. Dominic had to physically and mentally pull his hand back to his side. Instinct was forcing him to reach out again and he worked hard to think innocent thoughts so as not to give more power to the situation within his mind.

The darker part that lived within him waged a battle inside. His dark passenger wanted for him to allow the still yet unachieved process to take over. Dominic, the man, might have won if not for the familiar aroma that defied invisibility through its potency as it floated mercilessly toward his face. He smelled her vanilla perfume and lotion. The scent was no stranger to him, reminding him of strip clubs of years past.

In his mind, Dominic could hear the voice of Lucius.

"Take her! You are the chosen leader to replace me! You have no choice of life or death. No option for alternatives."

Pain. His eyes started to blur and he did not know how much more he could endure. Dominic could not have foreseen this process and to the physical strain it would take on him. In a grasp of desperation, Dominic turned his attention from the girl to the neon sign flickering above the Victorian stone building, located across the street. It read, 'Jesus saves.'

He knew that not even Jesus would save him or the girl who stood trembling before him. She was a girl Dominic had ultimately saved years ago, by ridding her life of her abusive father, but in doing so eliminated the family income and eventually, the young girl was forced into employment as a dancer so that she could help her mother put food on the table. If he did as Lucius demanded, the poison would enter her body until her soul could take no more. Perhaps she welcomed an end to her struggles. Still, he did not want to take precious minutes, days, weeks, months, or years away from her.

"The time is now, Dominic!" Lucius insisted, appearing from behind the shadows. "You have made your journey and now you must choose your fate. I do not need you to tell me what your wish is. I am making the decision simple for you. Take her and you commit to serving in my place. My time is done and it is you who must lead the world of darkness."

Dominic cracked his neck from side to side in an attempt to alleviate the stress and muscle tension that had built up inside.

"What if I choose to remain as I am and lead the double life of experiencing both the vampire world and the world of music?"

"What makes you so sure that you even have that as an option?" replied Lucius. "If you choose not to take her soul, I shall give you another option. He will present himself momentarily. Take his soul in place of hers and you become my replacement, an honor that no one would deny. Either way, Dominic, you must choose the soul of one of the two in order to take my place. Choose…"

From the depths of nowhere, others had arrived – mortals who did not intervene but stood in wonder at the sight before them. A working class man with nerves of steel approached Dominic. A man who worked days and nights to ensure his family was well cared for. A man who never asked for a thing in return, but gave to others unselfishly his entire life. Dominic knew instinctively that this man represented both the immediate and the extended family who had raised and who had loved him. Dominic had let him down, if nothing else, by not being there. He would not take this man's soul.

Amidst the small gathering crowd, a young man with a guitar slung over his shoulder held in place by its strap walked slowly forward. Aware that this was a last minute adjustment on the part of Lucius, Dominic glanced up and smiled, knowing the true test was finally at hand.

It was time for him to decide whether or not to sacrifice the man he was, the man he had missed for so long… or to fully embrace a life of darkness for all eternity.

Dominic's attention swayed back and forth to the various icons surrounding him.

"Choose!" demanded Lucius.

An overwhelming gust of wind accompanied the statement, filling Dominic's ears and mind with a painful and powerful whistle, as all surroundings turned completely black. All those standing before him had disappeared, leaving Dominic to stand alone.

As the wind died down, the darkness remained. Dominic shifted his stance in preparation for battle and moved to speak.

"I need more time!" he shouted into the darkness, knowing that his potential mentor was still there, despite the fact that he had made himself unseen.

A voice that resembled Lucius' but lower in tone stressed the seriousness of what was at hand.

"You must make a decision, Dominic."

The words seemed to float above his head and then faded off into the darkened sky.

"I did. My decision is that I need more time to consider the options," Dominic replied with conviction, knowing that his assertiveness would not fall lightly upon his superior's ears. From the darkness behind him, Stephan snatched Dominic's arms, held them forcefully behind his back, and lowered Dominic to his knees. He struggled to regain his footing, but to no avail. From the side, Raina appeared but kept her distance from the struggle. In a cloudy mist, Lucius appeared in front of him.

"I offer you the chance of all eternity, the opportunity to replace me in this world. Your remarks are cowardly and disrespectful. I offer you all of this and you spit in my face?"

Trying not to tremble from fear or rage, Dominic replied.

"I spit not, Lucius, but ask for your consideration. This was highly unexpected…"

In a swift movement, Stephan shoved Dominic to the side, spitting in his face as he landed. Dominic sprang to his feet immediately, facing Stephan within inches of his face in an effort to show Stephan that he would not back down from him.

"Stephan is eager to replace me," called Lucius. "Perhaps he is my obvious choice?"

Dominic responded with the confidence he had always known.

"If that were so, you would not be placing so much effort into me and my decision."

Inside, Dominic struggled to not allow Lucius to sense the fear that existed inside of him. Yet, he knew that with every word, he was walking the fine line of ensuring his own existence and that of leading himself to the perpetual noose and sheer destruction at the hand of his leader.

"I need more time in order to know that I've made the right decision," he repeated.

Thoughts swirled through Dominic's brain. It was a moment he had anticipated, but did not plan for. It was a moment where his decision would be etched into all eternity. If he chose to accept leadership of the vampire world, he would be sacrificing any connection to all things dear to his heart. Yet, he knew that if he chose to accept this role, he would be awarded with an opportunity to reform the vampire society, its rules, and its norms. If he opted to embrace the chance to rejoin his band mates and the music scene, he would again know the life he once led, but would lose an opportunity to facilitate a positive change in the world of darkness. His thoughts expanded further.

He wondered how each of the decisions would affect Raina and of what would become of her, if his decision would alter her fate on the spot. Transporting himself at a speed too fast for him, Lucius aggressively collided with Dominic and began yelling in his face.

"Why shouldn't I just kill you?" he shouted.

"Because when you selected me, you knew this would be a difficult decision. You knew from day one how all of this would play out," Dominic said.

Lucius raised an eyebrow in curiosity. Brushing the dust from his clothes, Dominic added, "With all due respect, Lucius, Raina and I are going to walk out of here and in thirty days to the minute, I will meet with you again, right in this spot if you wish, to discuss our plans… whatever they may be."

Dominic grasped Raina by the arm and began to walk, guiding her past Stephan, beyond Lucius, bowing respectfully as they passed.

"DOMINIC!" Lucius' voice boomed with anger, the ground below them shaking in response.

Turning back slowly, Dominic caught the eye of his superior, fearing an untimely demise as the result of his actions. The world around grew silent. A cold yet gentle wind flowed through the street, sending a chill down Dominic's spine as he awaited a response. Lucius shifted his weight to his right foot and slowly reached into the left inside breast pocket of his jacket with his right hand, gradually producing a set of keys. A smirk emerged from the side of his mouth, as Lucius threw the keys into the air, landing perfectly into Dominic's hand.

"Take the Lincoln."

Wade Lijewski was born and raised in Manistee, MI. Wade draws inspiration for his writing from his many years touring the country in the underground music scene, which can also be gritty and humorous at times. He currently resides in Lakeland, Florida with his wife and three children.

Doreen Serrano was born in Massachusetts but moved to Florida at the age of twelve and has resided there ever since. She has been an avid lover of literature and music for as long as she can remember and she published her first novel, *11:11,* in November of 2008. Doreen continues to write stories that are inspired by both personal experience as well as her vivid imagination. She currently resides in Valrico, Florida with her two sons.

JimSam Inc.

Please visit our website at
www.JimSamInc.com
to order additional copies.

JimSam Inc. Publishing
P.O. Box 265
Lobelville, TN 37097
813.748.9523

CPSIA information can be obtained at www.ICGtesting.com
231472LV00001B/5/P

9 780984 107469